Shark Week

An Ocean Anthology

Edited by Ian Madison Keller

Shark Week
First Publication 2021

Edited by Ian Madison Keller

Cover by Beleoci
Copyright © 2021

Published by Rainbow Dog Books

Table of Contents

The Ballad of Lobster Island

By Louis Evans

"Near to [Lobster Island] was [Whelk] Island... which looks entirely similar to [Lobster] Island from the surface. The seabed, however, told... a very different story."
— *"When Snails Attack"*, Christie Wilcox, *Discover*

Lobster Chorus: We are the lobsters who live in the sea

        Lordly and mighty and armored are we

        Ruling from reef to surf and scree

        In this our island home

        Kings in our island home

Whelk Solo: I am a whelk in the lobster's land

No mighty pincers can I command

No aged frame growing free and grand

And what's more: I am alone

Solo and on my own

Lobster Solo: I am a lobster; my hunger's great

My barren land yields a barren plate

Such appetite will the whelk flesh sate

Smash I my claws through the whelk's thin pate

Strip I the flesh from the bone

Suck I the flesh from the bone

Lobster Chorus: One of a pair lobster island is

One of two twins in the blue abyss

Only on one do we lobsters live

To the other we never roam

Never to there do we roam

Marine Biologist: I am the human who watches the sea

Lobsters live here; whelks nearby grow free

No explanation occurs to me

No answer that I have known

No, nothing that I have known

Questions have answers that all can see

This is the faith that enlivens me

In experiment the true answer be

Thus has the book of truth grown

Been tended and carefully grown

Lobster Solo: I am a lobster, seafloor-bound

Suddenly soaring away from the ground

This bipedal god brings me 'cross the sound

Far from the lands I have known

To an island where I walk alone

Whelk Chorus: We are the whelks of the other isle

We have been living here all the while

3

On our lush seafloor we abound sessile

Happy and free in our domicile

Flourishing where we have grown

O, predators we've never known

Hark! Comes the lobster; that mighty foe

Arise we as one and to battle we go

Covering him in a ceaseless flow

Like snowbanks aborning windblown

Like numberless seeds being sown

Mighty his armor but joints are sprung

Questing and scraping comes each whelk's tongue

Through his defenses our war is brung

Strip we the flesh from the bone

Suck we the flesh from the bone

Always in armies do we aggress

Digesting the foeman despite his distress

Once more our island is lobsterless

Defended have we what we've known

Dead is the threat to our home

Stripped we its flesh from the bone

Marine Biologist: From this brief tale many lessons flow

Applicable here as in sea below

Fools wander in where the wise dare not go

Wander or find themselves blown

As I brought that lobster alone

One who is weak may yet become strong

By joining their purpose with mighty throng

Learn you this pearl from my song

Add it to what you have known

Hoarding the wisdom you've grown

One final moral is last of all:

No single fate must surely befall

The invincible may yet rise or fall

It's all in the future we've sown

Our choices and outcomes they've grown

The whelks and the lobsters remain in the sea

The songs and the stories shall stay here with me

The fate of the future remains up to thee

To thee and to all of thine own

We choose it, but never alone

From seafloor to stars, not alone

This poem relates the results of a real experiment performed on the seafloor surrounding Marcus Island in Saldanha Bay, South Africa, in 1983. The resulting paper, published in Science in 1988, was an important contribution to the academic debate on "alternative stable states", an ecological theory that posits that individual ecosystems can exist under multiple distinct equilibria. The account in this poem is lightly fictionalized (actually, the experiment was performed on many lobsters), but represents the author's best efforts to capture the real significance of the discovery.

Bibliography:

Barkai, Amos, and Christopher McQuaid. "Predator-Prey Role

Reversal in a Marine Benthic Ecosystem." Science 242, no.

4875 (1988): 62-64. www.jstor.org/stable/1702493.

Wilcox, Christine. "When Snails Attack: The Epic Discovery Of An

Ecological Phenomenon." Discovery, Aug 27, 2018.

www.discovermagazine.com/planet-earth/when-snails-

attack-the-epic-discovery-of-an-ecological-phenomenon.

The Bedazzling Dragon of Vanderlyst

By Allison Thai

*This story is dedicated to the captain and crew of
Jamunda: the Norwegian oil barge that rescued my
mother and grandmother from dying overseas during
the Vietnam War.*

I sped through my English essay like a mako shark, and when I
thought it looked good enough to squeeze by with a C grade, I put
it aside and swam for the surface. I'd promised Faye that I'd show
up for her water polo game and cheer her on.

On the way up, I passed by a pair of manatees, a mom and her
kid. The kid wore a shirt that said "Tampa Bay Buccaneers" under a
pirate's skull on a red flag.

He pointed a round flipper at me. "Mom, who is that?"

She ushered him along. "That's a dragon, dear. An Asian dragon. Don't point and stare, that's rude."

They didn't have to open their mouths for me to know that they definitely weren't from around here, that they were tourists far from home. Probably from Florida, if the shirt was any hint. The locals were used to the sight of me, though it wasn't too long ago when I had stirred up the same curiosity and excitement. Not that I remembered any of that myself — Mom and Dad had told me. There had never been dragons in Norway before, let alone Asian dragons. I had moved here with Mom and Dad just days after I had hatched. As far as I was concerned, I was Norwegian through and through.

The game wouldn't start for another hour, but I wanted to be there early for a good viewing spot. I didn't want to show up so early, though, that Faye's dad could easily spot me. He couldn't do anything to chase me out, but I could really do without the dirty looks he'd throw my way.

At the surface, the playing teams and their families had already shown up. My school's team would play against the one from upcoast — green caps versus red caps. I decided to wedge myself behind the orca parents of Faye's teammate. The floating couple left enough of a gap for me to peek through, but also provided enough cover from Finley's stink-eye.

Faye was the goalie today. One of just two dolphins in her team, and the only bottlenose dolphin, she bravely held her own against the bigger whales and orcas in the field. You wouldn't think she'd be a good goalie, but she made up for her small size with lightning speed. Sometimes I thought she had a rostrum and chest of steel, too, which she'd use to bounce off the ball if it came in too fast for the swat of her flippers.

I clapped my paws and whistled through the whole game. The spectators floating around me sent up heaving waves and big splashes with their own gusto.

Faye and her team fought hard, churning up enough water to turn almost the whole field white and frothy. But by sundown, at the end of the game, they lost 6-7. I swam up to Faye as she pulled off her green cap and hung her smooth gray head. At the sight of me, her dark eyes lit up and a smile tugged at the corners of her lips.

"Hey, Long, glad you could make it out here."

"Good game, Faye. You were so close!"

"Yeah, but 'close' isn't going to take us to junior nationals."

Finley swam up to join her side and rest a consoling flipper on her back. "It's not too late to think about joining the troupe, you know."

Faye groaned. "Dad, I've told you a million times, I'm not going to quit water polo."

"Don't you get tired of losing after a while? When you're in the circus, there's no winning or losing, just fun."

"I can find plenty of fun out on the playing field, thank you very much." I knew how hard she fought back rolling her eyes by seeing how tight her jaw clenched up. "Winning or losing, it doesn't matter. Not really, anyway. I'd rather punt a ball with my team to score points than jump and spin around for show." She threw me an apologetic look. "No offense."

"None taken," I said.

Finley squinted at me. "Shouldn't you be at rehearsal? It's starting earlier than usual tonight."

"I didn't forget. Mom gave me enough reminders."

"Swim along, then. I'm sure she's looking for her favorite boot to spit and shine."

Faye frowned. "Dad..."

I just laughed it off. "He's right." Mom would polish my scales up so much that when she could see her own reflection on me, she knew she did a good job.

I dove back down several hundred feet to the seabed where Vanderlyst made camp. Schools of fish veered past me, but I wasn't interested in snapping them up now. Not a good idea to stuff myself before rehearsal. Dinner always came *after*.

Even with the sun setting, when the sea would turn almost pitch black, the troupe's colorful, glowing lights weren't hard to miss. It was also very hard to miss Tahu blasting Queen songs from his radio. I could feel the rocks vibrate to each beat. As usual, the long-finned pilot whale fixed his game face to the mirror, and only when he finished dotting his dark, bulbous forehead in white waterproof body paint did he put his all into mouthing the lyrics of "We Will Rock You." He waved a long, skinny flipper at me as I streaked in and out of his mirror's reflection.

My mom, Kari, hunched over the seabed, leafing through waterproof sheets of paper. My dad, Bjorn, peered over her

11

shoulder, double-checking the troupe's income and expenses for her. He was the first to catch sight of me, and he spread his black flippers.

"There's our boy," he said.

"Our birthday boy," Mom said next, and she dropped the papers to pull me into a big hug.

Dad ruffled the hair down my long neck. "How does it feel to be fourteen?"

"The same as when I was thirteen yesterday," I said.

Mom pulled back from me and clicked out laughter. "Oh, you'll feel the difference tomorrow, I'm sure of it."

Excitement sent a shiver down my spine. Now that I turned the minimum age to work in Norway, I could start being a proper part of Vanderlyst as a performer. I may have turned fourteen today, but I've been preparing for my first performance ever since I was five, when I learned how to bend and twist my long, scaly body for all sorts of tricks.

Anita swam over and tossed up a bundle of string lights — the aquatic equivalent of throwing up glitter in the air. "Happy birthday, Long!"

I beamed back at her. "Thanks, Anita."

Being a right whale, Anita looked like she had a perpetual frown on her face, but she was a ray of sunshine even without all the LED tags and suits the troupe would wear for show. In two years, she'd be old enough for me to really call her my vodka aunt.

I gave her a wide, toothy grin. "Do that thing with the lights."

"The thing I do every year? Much obliged." She sang the happy birthday song while wrapping the string lights around me from neck to waist, like stringing lights on a pole. Then she pulled hard at the end of it, drawing out the last "you" in the song, and like a top, I spun free. I shut my eyes and laughed.

I spun into a pair of long, sturdy flippers, which caught and steadied me. "Whoa there, kid, hold your seahorses. You keep doing that, you're going to steal the title of Spinning Champion from me."

Eli peered down with a joking grin along his knobby snout.

I shook my head. "I can't ever take that title from you. You're the best breacher in all the seven seas."

A deep, throaty chuckle got trapped behind his lips. "I'm not even going to pretend being modest. That, my boy, is the correct answer, and your parents taught you well to say such."

Breaching already came as a natural gift to humpback whales, but even by humpback whale standards, Eli made breaching an art. He could squeeze in the most spins in a single breach, which was a big deal down here as much it was up there for a figure skater to pull off a triple-axel. He's been in this circus business, wowing people with his stunts, for twice as long as I've been alive. I've always admired Eli's confidence and experience. I felt a surge of pride to be in the same troupe as him, to finally be his fellow performer.

I was proud to be in the same troupe as the rest of this pod of dolphins and whales, really. Everyone here, even the crabby, grumbly, stink-eyed Finley, was a circus star in his or her own right. To anyone else with passing knowledge, Vanderlyst was an open-sea circus troupe from Norway. To me, Vanderlyst was family.

"Long? Is that you I hear?" a voice came thundering from the nearby gorge. "Congratulations for completing another revolution around the sun."

We all winced from the ensuing echo, then I had to smile. That had always been Rune's way of saying "happy birthday."

"Rune, you're late," Dad called.

The grizzled sperm whale poked his oblong head from the gorge, peering at us through squinted, baggy eyes. "How am I late for an early rehearsal? I believe that I'm here on time."

It was Dad's turn to bite back a smile. "Get over here, you old rascal, and remember to keep your voice down, or you'll blow out all our eardrums."

Rune cruised away from the gorge and toward us with the pondering majesty of the Hindenburg. A half-eaten giant squid trailed limply in the grip of one flipper. In his glory days — like, decades before I was born — he'd been a big breacher like Eli, but recently he retired from performing to manage choreography. When he wasn't managing choreography, though, he'd be away on squid-hunting dives. On occasion, like today, he'd lose track of the time.

Mom beckoned to me and patted the seabed. She didn't have to say anything; I already knew the routine. I sat down and held still to let her comb my hair and polish my scales. I could reach most parts of my body and polish myself, but Mom was best for covering my back.

"We want you to really shine for your debut," she murmured

into my ear. "Tomorrow, everyone will come from far and wide to see the Bedazzling Dragon of Vanderlyst."

At the sound of my stage name, I curled up my tail with pleasure. I'd been breaching, porpoising, tumbling and twisting since I was little, but tomorrow would be the first time I perform in front of a live audience. I wanted to make my troupe, my family, proud by putting on a stunning show.

My eyelids drooped and I slumped forward. Mom would rub my scales in a way that felt like a massage at a spa. It made me drowsy. She liked me to be squeaky clean, free of barnacles and algae and other gunk in the sea. As a dragon, I was covered from head to toe in glittering scales that flashed all the colors of a rainbow when I moved. The word for that in English was "iridescent," which I had learned in class just last week, and that became my favorite word to say.

As I sat still, I tried to keep from tapping my tail on the seabed. Across from me, Rune replayed videos of past performances, probing for holes in flow, aesthetic, and execution to fix for next time, all while finishing off the rest of his squid snack with slow, deliberate chews. It was that old sperm whale who had found me in the first place, wedged in some trench in the South China Sea, about fifty miles off the coast of south Vietnam. He'd been hunting for squid as usual when the many-colored gleam of my egg caught his eye. Usually he'd resurface with squid scars to show off, but that day he had brought me up with him.

Rune may have found me, but it had been the gentle, warm wrap of Mom's flippers over my egg that made me hatch. Dragons only hatched when they were bathed in warmth, ideally their own mother's warmth. When I had hatched, I should have first seen the scaly face of my mother, her curved deer-like horns, long fish whiskers, and golden snake's eyes. Instead I had first seen the round black and white face of an orca, the face that I'd come to associate with the thought of Mom, no matter how hard I squeezed my eyes shut and tried to picture someone else.

Dragons were wiped out by the end of the Vietnam War twenty years ago. Or so everyone had thought, until Rune brought up my egg from the bottom of the sea. My mom, my real mom, must have been one of the boat people fleeing from the country, arms full with a clutch of eggs. A storm must have tossed me and my siblings overboard. If it had been pirates, Rune once said, they would've seized me and sold me for a high price at the black market. So I had sunk to the bottom like a rock, and sat there for a few years, until Vanderlyst came along for their first tour in Asia.

My hatching was a worldwide sensation, shaking the world like a tsunami. As I had learned in geography, a tsunami didn't come in just one wave, but many. The next big wave that shook the world was the troupe's decision to adopt me. My hatching had brought back my species from extinction, but hope didn't last long with the sole survivor of genocide. After a century or two, after I kicked the bucket, Asian dragons would be extinct again. Soon I'd join the European dragons, who had died out way before me, during the Black Death. Soon I'd be a page in a history book, something to be forgotten if proof of me wasn't written down. When I was little, I had always hoped that Rune would fish up another egg from his dives. I used to hope that he'd bring up another miracle, and prove to the world that I wasn't alone after all.

By now I squashed out that wishful thinking. I was the only living Asian dragon in the world, with orcas for parents and all kinds of dolphins and whales for aunts, uncles, a sister, and a grandfather. That made life more colorful and exciting. I wanted to share that color and excitement to the world with my debut tomorrow night.

Mom swam back from me and nodded with satisfaction. "There, all tidied up. Let's run through your routine."

On the next night, we swam out to meet our audience offshore. We performed for a Norwegian Cruise parked twenty miles from the city of Stavanger — not far out enough to be on international waters, but still far out enough from city lights to command the undivided attention of the audience with our spectacle. In other words, typical clientele over home turf, but Mom and Dad wanted me to start off performing in familiar waters before I could go on international tours.

Mom, Dad, Finley, Tahu, Anita, Eli, and all the rest were decked out in LED wetsuits in psychedelic colors, which would light up the water and, for a few moments, the air. As for me, with my natural iridescent sheen, I had the least amount of LED on. I wore lighted cuffs at my wrists and ankles, and one around my torso like a tube top, just enough to bring out the shine in my scales without overwhelming them.

Finley began the show with his cohort of fellow dolphins,

tumbling and spinning through buoyed hurdles. Anita was next to steal the spotlight with her contortions and breakdancing on a giant floating mat. Tahu, originally from New Zealand, brought a dash of Maori flavor to the show with dances that sent up big splashes with stamps of his tail and rhythmic shouts in between. Eli, a long-time crowd favorite, pulled off his tried-and-true routine of spinning breaches. Mom and Dad accompanied him with somersaults that vaulted them clean out of the water. Then I was next, saved for last.

"Ladies and gentlemen, boys and girls," Rune boomed in the way only sperm whales do. "Come one, come all, to behold the new star of our show, the only Asian dragon in all the seven continents and the seven seas: the Bedazzling Dragon of Vanderlyst!"

Even with my head submerged, the roar and cheers of the audience gathered behind the cruise rails filled my ears. I shot loose like an arrow from a bow for the surface, then bunched up my long body into coils to break the waves with my own style of porpoising. I tried to pull off the resemblance of a small pod of dolphins or porpoises running in a row. My body dipped in and out of the water in rollicking, gleaming sections. The oohing and aahing from the crowd was reassuring. I made two rounds of porpoising before I dove back into the depths. I burst straight out of the water, soaring into the air high above the cruise, but only for a few breathless moments, because Asian dragons couldn't truly fly. Instead of real wings, I had skin flaps at the crooks of my arms and hips for gliding. My flaps pillowed out to make my descent a slow, snaking, fluttering one. On the way down, I twisted, spun, and coiled like a ribbon in the wind to flash my scales against the night sky.

Doing that also got me the best view of the awed crowd. All eyes were on me, and none of them held the pity they'd have for me otherwise, the pity that came with being the last living Asian dragon on Earth, a dragon living in Norway when he was supposed to live in Vietnam. Here in the show, all they could think of was how I dazzled them. I spotted Faye among the aquatic spectators, all bright and glowing from lights she had borrowed from her dad. "You always come cheer for me at my games, even when Dad hates it, so the least I can do is come support your debut," she had told me.

I couldn't resist waving back at my biggest cheerleader before I hit the water. I wished that I could dazzle the crowd all day and night, but like all good things, the show had to end.

Faye was the first to swim up to me after the show. "Long, that was amazing! You came up with those tricks? Your mom had told me earlier, but I just couldn't believe it!"

Warmth rushed from my face to the tips of my whiskers, and I tried not to puff out my chest. "Yeah, I came up with them all by myself." Being the only dragon in a pod of dolphins and whales, I looked and moved differently from the rest. I was longer, skinnier, more flexible. Rune had encouraged me to come up with some of my own choreography. I had to stretch my imagination as much as I had to stretch my body, but the hard work had paid off.

Mom was beside herself with joy for the next few days after counting up the money Vanderlyst had made with my debut. "It's a record-breaking high," she exclaimed. "And we've never had this many reserved tickets for the next show before." She planted a big fat kiss on my forehead. "You did such a fabulous job, my little star."

I basked on the emotional high, enjoying while it lasted before people would look at me with pity again. The worst kind of look was disdain from Finley.

"He should be back in Vietnam, among his own kind," he'd grumble. "Even the English he's learning in school is better than his Vietnamese. What good are we doing keeping him away from home? We're confusing the poor boy."

That made my jaw clench and my whiskers quiver. I'd never snap back at Finley, because that'd mean hanging out with Faye was off-limits. Fortunately for me, Mom and Dad always spoke up on my behalf.

Mom would retort with "Long's already home," and Dad would say, "The 'poor boy' is quite sure of where he wants to be, thank you very much." But this reply from Mom was the trump card: "He lost his mother and I lost my calves, so we were meant to find each other." And that would shut Finley up. He could never sneak in more argument past that.

Faye had once told me that her mom had died from a great white shark attack before I had hatched. She mentioned it once and told me to act like I had never heard it. Mom bringing up her dead calves would remind Finley of his dead wife, and that would "put him in a place deeper than the abyss," as Faye would put it.

Mom showered me with more congratulatory hugs and kisses that anyone else my age would have pulled back from with teen embarrassment, but I didn't mind. Before I came into her life, she had lost three calves, all within weeks or months of being born. They had died in their sleep, never to reach the first year of their lives. Mom and Dad had lost the third one a month before Rune had found me. They didn't think twice about taking me into the pod, and almost no one had dared to argue against it. So I let Mom give me all the hugs and kisses she wanted, like I tried to take in all the hugs and kisses her calves could never get.

With my debut a resounding success, I was slated for another appearance on my first international tour. I would be performing next in the Gulf of Thailand, 120 kilometers from the closest coastal town. Vanderlyst would swim over there at the start of winter holidays. I was so excited that I could barely concentrate in class before school was out.

The winter chill would make the waters in Southeast Asia more tolerable to swim in, but it would still be like a hot spring for our Norway-based troupe, so we made sure to pack a lot of coolers. Faye had no water polo games to play over the holidays, so she would tag along with her dad and the troupe.

"You excited to see home again?" she asked, pushing around a polo ball with her tail.

"Home's already here," I said, and I flicked my own tail at the troupe members who were clearing the seabed of our belongings.

"I meant the other kind of home, where you hatched."

I shrugged. I was more excited about performing there than actually seeing it. I wanted to bathe in the wide-eyed adoration of an audience, not take in the sights the way a bumbling tourist would.

We set off for Vietnam a week in advance, taking the currents to dip down Africa and across the Indian Ocean. I buried my nose in a book while riding the currents, trying to brush up on Vietnamese. I felt no real connection to the letters and words I should have grown up with. It was just like English, something else to study and likely not use again. I'd hate to embarrass myself if I met any locals, though, so I had to be ready. I adapted to the warmer waters better than the rest of the troupe. Everyone else had strapped on puffy cooler tubes over their chests and tails.

Dad kept me close to his side all the while, especially when we swam through the Sunda and Karimata Straits: shortcuts through Indonesia. "You won't go wandering off again, will you?" he asked me.

I shook my head and shuddered. Dad's question was laced with a warning he didn't have to give. Never ever would I go on another solo deep-dive on a huge gamble to find the rest of my family. This upcoming show wouldn't be my first time revisiting Vietnam. I'd been back before when I was ten, before I was old enough to perform. At that age, I was just about to outgrow wishful thinking, but I teetered at the most dangerous point, right over the edge of a cliff and into a pit of reckless, last-resort initiative. I had it in my head to go on a quest and find any of my brothers and sisters who might have survived the war. If Rune couldn't find them, then I would find them myself.

I had read that dragons could dive into waters as deep as the abyss, where all the scary bloated anglerfish live. I had snuck away from the troupe while they were in a show. I had trusted my anatomy and dove deeper than I ever had in my life, plunging into the gorge where Rune had found me. On the way down I had batted away anglerfish, gulper eels, and oarfish that had tried to take a bite out of me, but my scales were tough as they were shiny. I had hoped to unearth dormant treasures in the crevices, braving the dark, high-pressure waters to reunite with my family. Dragon eggs always came in a clutch. I couldn't have been the only egg laid, so there had to be more just waiting to be found.

But as much as I had looked and hard as I had tried, I found nothing. Not even bones or broken egg shells. I hadn't realized how long I'd been searching until Rune's voice came booming down. Even more amazing was Dad swimming alongside him, his cries of my name turning from panic to relief when he spotted me.

Orcas weren't deep divers. Swimming down that much had almost crushed Dad to a bloody pulp. How he went out of his way to find me, even if it could've killed him, brought on a crushing guilt inside me. Although I hadn't felt the crush from diving, I'd felt it from the guilt after.

Dad brought me back up to shallower waters with Rune without asking me what the hell I was doing down there. He had seen the twisted pain on my face and already knew. I had learned then that my family wasn't down there — if they really had been down there — but with the troupe. After that, I didn't go looking or wishing for more dragons like me.

My next performance was off the coast of Phu Quoc, an island at the southwestern tip of Vietnam. A menagerie of locals and tourists alike gathered at the rocky outcrop overlooking the waters, necks craned forward for a better look at Vanderlyst floating below. We used the waning afternoon to put up our floating stages and props. Loitering on the rocks farther down, where ocean waves slapped and broke into spray, otters and sea lions from another troupe peered at us with scrutiny, waiting to see what tricks we had up our sleeve.

Tahu squinted back at them and whispered to me, "Seaside circus troupes are popular here. They're our biggest rivals and want to run us open-sea troupes out of the circus scene. So we've got to give it our all and show these folks what we can do." He patted my back with his long flipper. "No pressure."

I cracked a grin. "Don't worry, I won't crack."

"That's the spirit," Anita said beside me.

We always performed after sundown for maximum dazzling effect. For this show, I decided to use Vietnamese pop for the audible backdrop of my show. I didn't understand a lot of the words, but it seemed to get the crowd raving, which was exactly what I wanted. Taking Tahu's words to heart, I used the open sea to my full advantage. The depth of deeper waters gave me the springboard to leap as high from the sea as I could, to give the illusion of soaring with the stars. I ran and sped my long, glimmering body across the entirety of an arena that spanned five times larger than the one a seaside troupe would use. The bigger, the better, they say, and that was especially true for an open-sea circus troupe. You just wouldn't get much of a wowed response with a much smaller stage. The show ended with my head reeling and ears ringing from the beat of the music and the roars of the crowd.

"Another rousing success, my boy," Eli cried. "You've won the hearts of your people."

"They look to you as a symbol of hope," Mom said with a fond smoothing of my hair. "You're a welcoming sight for a country that was torn apart by war."

My cheeks warmed. "I couldn't be that important." And I wasn't that selfless. I didn't come here to be some shining beacon after a war I couldn't possibly fix. I just wanted people to see me in any other light besides pity. I just wanted to put on a good show.

To celebrate, some of the pod broke away to get drinks on the coastline. Faye stayed behind with me, staring after Finley's retreating dorsal fin.

"He's probably going to grab beer with his seaside friends again," she muttered with a roll of her eyes.

Finley was tight with members of the Sastry Brothers, the top seaside circus troupe based in southern India. They had been Vanderlyst's rival for as long as I could remember, going back to when Eli was young and knew the brothers' father. We'd run into them on many a coast, vying for the money and attention of the same audience. With me now in the picture, I bet that the Sastry Brothers would work even harder to bring the flow of money to themselves instead of us. Usually Finley would turn up his nose at our seaside competitors, but lately he found common ground with the Sastry Brothers in complaining about me.

I knew this because I had eavesdropped them on the coast of Sicily a few years ago. I was *still* too young for bars, and back then I was *definitely* way too young for them, but my scales let me blend in with the moonlight flickering on the waves, and I got to listen in on all the juicy gossip surrounding me.

Booze loosened up tongues, and the four otter brothers would gripe with Finley over how I was being paraded by the troupe as a prop, as the token dragon, and that I was only kept to get attention and easy money.

They couldn't be more wrong. I might've been taken in and adopted by circus performers, but I was given the choice to take another path if I wanted. Mom and Dad put me in the same school as Faye and made sure I was learning about everything the world had to offer. The troupe only taught me tricks because I asked them to and they agreed. I didn't start earning money for the troupe until this year. No one forced me into anything. Circus performing was my choice as much as it was my destiny.

"Long? Hey, Long!"

"Huh, what?" I snapped out of my thoughts to blink at Faye waving her gray flipper in my face.

"I said that I want to check out more of the area. You want to come? I heard there's a river market nearby, and it's really aquatic-friendly." Faye glanced down at my paws. "Not that it makes a difference for you, but it'll be so convenient for the rest of us."

To my surprise, Mom said, "I think you should go, Long. Your dad and I feel bad that we didn't put in enough effort to reconnect you to your culture, so you should go explore."

I raised my eyebrows. "All by myself?"

"Oh no, you're coming with the rest of us to get dinner."

That sounded more like Mom. She didn't like to let me out of her sight since my deep-diving stunt four years ago. I had planned on just catching yellowfin tuna out here, but everyone else seemed to want grub on shore, so I had no choice but to tag along with Mom, Dad, Faye, and Anita.

We swam past Phu Quoc for the mainland, to a town called Rach Gia. True to Faye's word, water chutes sloped down from the docks and shore, bridging the gap between land and sea. Having paws let me walk as well as I could swim, but I was so used to swimming with my family that I slid along the chutes on my belly, just like them.

Water chutes were built to provide access to the likes of dolphins and whales, who couldn't otherwise stay safely on land without getting dehydrated and stranded. Whoever came up with water chutes took inspiration from water slides at theme parks, so the chutes were made of the same PVC or nylon and vinyl, cut in half from whole tubes, and water from the sea was pumped into the chutes to keep them wet and partly filled. Towns right by the sea adapted to these slides, propping up their markets and venues to widen accessibility. Cities farther inland were less accommodating of water chutes — for those from the sea, anyway — so it wasn't like we could slip and slide anywhere. The farthest we could go was ten miles in. Freshwater chutes that were more common in cities were also much smaller, so they'd break under the weight of dolphins and whales.

Here in Vietnam the system of water chutes was very friendly, as Faye said. Chutes snaked white or blue coils through the town, and only a few parts were sectioned off from us. We had as much ease as the land-dwellers to visit almost any restaurant or part of the market we wanted.

I had set foot on the coasts of Norway before, but not in Vietnam. Bits and snatches of unfamiliar language swirled all around me. The humid air pressed on my body like a thick invisible blanket. Being used to the crisp, drier climate in Norway, I felt smothered by that blanket of humidity, but the locals in their loose clothes and cone hats didn't seem to mind. A light shower sprinkled down, and I thought it'd make people keep their heads bowed and eyes to the ground, but they fixed stares on me. I was not performing, or being at my bedazzling best, so there was no awe and wonder in their eyes, only the pity that I hated so much.

I wanted to slink back into the sea on an empty stomach. But the rest of my family slid themselves down the chute farther inland, and I forced myself to follow. We settled for the largest noodle house in town, one with counters big enough for even Anita to lean on without breaking.

A furry binturong waiter took the order, and naturally he looked to me for it. I fumbled for words under his piercing brown stare. I managed to get hot, steaming bowls of pho for the five of us. Because what would a trip to Vietnam be without pho?

We were served bowls tapered at one end, like a beaker, so we could tip the soup into our mouths. Dolphins and whales didn't have the dexterity for chopsticks, so no one in the troupe knew how to use them, so I was saved the embarrassment of not knowing how to use them either. The noodles were long, thin, and white, like my whiskers, so it looked like I was slurping down dragon whiskers.

I set down my finished bowl when drumbeats and cymbal clangs drifted into my ears.

Anita tipped her large dark head away from the counter. "You hear that?"

"Yeah, what is it?" Faye asked.

"Oh, I almost forgot," Mom said. "The local Christmas festival starts today."

I frowned. "But Christmas isn't for another week."

"I read that Tet can go on here for a whole month," Dad said with a laugh. "So I'm not surprised that the Vietnamese party early as much as they party long."

"Sounds like there's a dance going on," Anita said. "And it sounds like a little rain isn't enough to ruin their parade."

I couldn't help tapping my footpaw to the rhythm of the music. I didn't watch dances for fun but as a learning opportunity. I'd use some of them as inspiration for my own choreography and future shows.

"Go check it out, Long," Mom said. "I know how much you like dances."

That took me aback. "It's off-chute. I'd have to take the regular roads to get there."

"It can be just for a few minutes, and you won't be too far." She reached over to pat my paw. "You're fourteen, old enough to work now. I can't baby you forever, much as I'd like to. You should spread your wings sometime."

I pecked her on the cheek. "Thanks, Mom."

I looked over to Dad, who was hunched over the counter and not meeting my eyes. "You okay, Dad?"

He managed a tight-lipped smile at me. "The food isn't sitting right in my stomach. Probably put in too much sriracha sauce." He made a little wave of his flipper. "Your mom's right. Go have fun."

"We'll hang around the market next door and wait for you," Faye said.

I left the counter and climbed out of the chute. I perched on the edge of it and looked over my shoulder. My family smiled and waved at me. I waved back and hopped off the chute to land on the wooden dock. I trotted on all fours toward the sounds of music, dancing, and cheering.

When I got closer, my heart sunk. A large crowd had already gathered to watch the dragon dance ahead — not a real dragon, but one made of fabric and propped up by poles. The frilly head bucked over the tall, hulking elephants, water buffalos and tigers in the crowd, flashing festive green, white, and red. That was about all I could see. I hunched my shoulders and frowned. I was still a juvenile dragon, not grown up enough to stand taller than the elephants, water buffalos and tigers, even if I stretched out on two feet.

I tried to politely squeeze my way through the crowd, hoping to move up to the front, but they pressed in on me and even threw back dirty looks. My whiskers quivered with indignation. They'd gape at a dragon made of cloth and poles, but wouldn't be nice to a real one? A real dragon like me could put on a better show than the fake.

Someone tapped on my shoulder. "Hey, you want to get a better view?"

I turned to the Malayan tapir standing next to me. He was about my age but half my height, with white spots dotted all over his black hide. Not old enough to be totally black from head to chest, and totally white on the rest.

"Wow, your English is so good," I blurted out, then I wanted to slap a paw over my face. "Sorry, you probably get that a lot."

The tapir grinned from ear to ear. "No, I love it when people tell me that." He stretched out a paw. "I'm Tien. Who are you?"

I took his paw and shook it. "I'm Long."

"Oh, Long," he said, saying it differently from everyone I knew, including myself. I said it like the English word "long," but he said it in the same sound and motion of opening your mouth and closing it to make air puff out your cheeks. Must be the Vietnamese way, the right way. "A dragon named 'dragon,' huh?"

Embarrassment squeezed a weak chuckle out of me. "Yeah, my parents wanted a Vietnamese name that's easy to pronounce."

"Anyway, I'm even shorter than you," Tien said, "but I've lived here my whole life and I know a good place where we could sit high." He beckoned with a curl of his fingers. "Come with me and I'll show you."

I blinked. "Uh, sure, thanks."

He led the way, pointing to a nearby roof. "We have to crawl through an alley to get up there."

I followed Tien into a street that narrowed and darkened from the rooftops overhead. He started climbing up a winding staircase, where a couple of clotheslines stretched out to connect with another building.

I looked up with a frown. "Doesn't someone live there?"

Tien raised a finger to his lips. "They won't know if you're quiet about it."

I paused for another moment before jumping up after him. That took the street below out of view, and all I saw were walls and more stairs. I tried to make out Tien's white spots in the shadows. Then a funny-smelling cloth was pressed over my face. My eyes rolled back, and the last thing I felt was my legs giving way like jelly.

Lukewarm saltwater splashed onto my face. Some of it went down my nose and throat. The burn made me cough and gasp. I blinked my eyes open, feeling like I'd been body-slammed by a sperm whale. I lay on my back on something hard and flat, and I felt water rushing by, framing my face and tugging at my hair.

Fuzzy gray filled my vision with the first few blinks. I blinked longer and harder, and the fuzzy gray sharpened into Finley's face hovering over me. With his flipper he splashed some more water in my direction.

"Long, can you hear me? Are you with me? Say something if you are."

I let out a groan. "What happened?" My question came out in a heavy slur.

Someone wrapped their flippers around me. "Long, you're okay! I was so scared!"

I looked down at Faye wrapping a big, tight hug around my chest. I reached up a shaky paw to pat her back. I couldn't see past the walls of the chute, but the commotion and clamor on the other side filled my ears.

"What happened?" I asked again.

Finley leaned away from me to rest his belly back on the chute. He closed his eyes, and pressed a flipper to his face. "Where should I even start?" he said in a low voice. He sighed and met my eyes. "Well, first things first: you're safe now. You were saved."

"I was? By who?"

Four smooth-coated otters poked their heads over the side of the chute, and with graceful leaps they slid down it to join Finley. One had a swollen eye, and the other pressed a towel over his bloodied mouth, but otherwise they peered down at me with jaunty grins.

"Well, look who's had his beauty sleep."

"Looks like the chloroform's wearing off."

I sat up, biting back a wince as muscles screamed in protest. An Indian accent tinged their English. "You... you're the Sastry Brothers."

"They're the ones who saved you," Finley said.

"We sure did," one of the brothers said, the one sounding muffled around the bloody towel. "We clobbered the dealer scum who tried to make away with you. We dragged you out of the alley and back to the chutes, so you got knocked around a bit, in case you haven't felt that already."

"Sorry in advance for random bruises that'll pop up later," a different otter brother said.

My head spun like a disco ball, and the back of my eyes hurt. "Wait, hold up. You're telling me that I almost got kidnapped?"

One of the uninjured brothers spat over the wall of the chute. "Yeah, that tapir brat was doing a real good job with throwing out the bait, and you snapped it up, hook, line, and sinker."

"Too bad that dhole and pangolin trying to stuff you in a rice bag weren't as good with their job. Not against these guns." The other uninjured brother flexed his arm and curled his sharp claws.

The brother with the swollen eye flashed his teeth. "The sneaky bastards could knock out a helpless dragon kid from behind, but they don't know how to put up a real fight. We caught them in the alley Finley said you'd be at and ganged up on them, so they had nowhere to do what they do best — run."

"That tapir knew how to run, though," another brother grumbled. "Little bugger slipped away while we had our paws full with the other two."

I pressed a paw to my numb face. I felt so stupid. I should've known that Tien wasn't trying to be my friend. Tien probably wasn't even his real name.

I looked up at Finley. "I thought that you were all getting drinks on the other side of town. How did you know where to find me?" My hairs stood on end. "Did you set me up to get kidnapped?"

Finley's cheeks puffed out. "What? Hell no!" He looked like he'd spew out steam from his blowhole. "You may get on my nerves, kid, but I'm not that callous."

"Then how did you know? You told the brothers I'd be there."

"Yeah, that's because..." Finley dragged a flipper down his face again and sighed. His eye peeked from the top of his flipper at the otters, who just stayed quiet with their arms crossed.

I couldn't take the silence anymore. "Well? What is it?"

Finley actually flinched at my snap and couldn't meet my eyes. "I got a call from Bjorn about where you'd be, and what would happen."

My blood ran cold. Bjorn was my dad's name.

"It was Kari who had made the arrangements with the dealers. Bjorn was in on it too, but at the last minute he ratted her out and called me."

Kari was my mom's name. I could barely feel Faye squeezing my paw between her flippers.

"So I sent the Sastry brothers after you, and what they enjoy more than a good drink is a good fight. They jumped into the off-chute streets and came just in time before you got whisked away to the black market."

Despite all the water running below and around us, my mouth went dry. "No way. You're lying."

For the first time since I'd known Finley, sympathy glimmered in his dark eyes. "I wish I was lying, but I'm not."

I couldn't bear to meet his gaze. I tried but failed to get on my feet. "Where's Mom and Dad? Why aren't they here?"

This time it was Faye who spoke up. "Your dad called mine a few minutes after you left to watch the dance. Your mom reached over to try stopping the call..." Her voice, already softened, started to shake. "He tackled her like a football player. They went over the counter and the side of the chute, onto the street. He held her there so she wouldn't be able to move and get away. She bit and slapped him, but he wouldn't budge." She shook her head. "Anita and I were so shocked, and so confused. We just froze up in the noodle house and didn't know what to do."

I squeezed my eyes shut. I almost couldn't hear over the blood pounding against my eardrums.

Faye went on. "The police came for your mom and dad at the same time the Sastry brothers dragged you and the dealers out of the alley."

"We just got out of handing over the dealer scum to the cops," the brother whose mouth finally stopped bleeding said.

"Our part's done, I guess." The brother who still had the swollen eye winked at me with his good one. "You owe us drink money next time we see you, eh?"

Finley admonished him through narrowed eyes and the corners of his lips pulled back. "Hit up the bar and pay for the drinks yourself." As the otters streaked down the chute past us, he looked back down at me with more sympathy than I thought possible for him. "Your shiny, flashy scales would have sold for millions at the black market. Apparently they're at peak brightness when dragons are in their mid-teens. With you being the last Asian dragon, those scales are worth triple the usual amount. They would have sold for more than if you had spent another ten or even twenty years performing for Vanderlyst. Turns out Kari had been running the numbers for a while, right under our noses."

My stomach churned. I felt like throwing up my dinner. Finley and the Sastry brothers had saved my hide. Literally. I swallowed down bile collecting in the back of my throat. "Where's Anita?"

"Went off to tell the others what happened," Finley replied.

"What's going to happen to me now?"

He took a lot longer than usual to reply. Then he said quietly, "I don't know yet. Right now Bjorn and Kari have been taken into custody along with the dealers. They've committed a crime here, in a foreign country, for attempted child trafficking. The whole troupe's roped into this mess, because we don't know who else might be in on it, so we'll have to stay here longer than we had planned to get this all sorted out."

What happened next was not so much things getting sorted out, but things tangling up in a bigger, messier web than any of us had imagined. It took up the rest of our winter holiday. The Norwegian authorities got involved, and together with Vietnamese law enforcement, they had us held at the local seaside police station for questioning. Rune, Eli, Tahu, Anita, Finley, even Faye... they all swore of having no prior knowledge of my mom and dad's plan to sell me off to the black market.

The web grew bigger and messier when Mom and Dad themselves were interrogated. They confessed to being in touch with black market dealers all over the world online. Dragon scales picked off of the war's dead fetched a high price, and after my hatching, my scales were even more desirable. At first Mom and Dad had wanted to sell me as a hatchling, but since that wouldn't be as profitable they decided to keep me. They had waited another fourteen years to maximize profit. Mom did most of the legwork to arrange handing me off to the dealers in Vietnam, where she and Dad would earn the most share of the sum. Vanderlyst's southeast Asia tour and first stop in Vietnam was just a cover for that.

In line with what Finley had told me, Dad confessed to knowing about Mom's plan to make money off of me since the day I hatched. But in the fourteen years that had passed, he had come to genuinely love me as his own son. I thought of how he had plunged into the abyss looking for me... that look of crushing guilt I mistook for indigestion at the noodle house... and of course, how he had caved in to calling off the kidnapping and calling Finley for help. I could believe that he really cared. If he hadn't, I'd have my scales stripped off by now.

As for Mom, all I could think of was her constant, daily reminders to keep myself neat and clean, which I had assumed for the longest time was out of love, but now I knew better. She wanted me looking my best so my scales could sell for the highest price. To top it off, in the event of "losing" me to kidnappers in Vietnam, she would have collected boatloads of financial support.

She knew this because she had done it before, with her three calves she had smothered and drowned. All those years of getting away with killing them caught up to her now. Dad didn't know about the calves. He really thought they had died in their sleep, so he was shocked as the rest of us to learn the truth. All the blood was on Mom's flippers. My blood could have been on there, too. The last time I saw Mom at the police station, she was slumped against the wall, staring down at her tail. She looked sorry, but sorry that she got caught.

Needless to say, I wasn't in Mom and Dad's care anymore. They were sent to prison off of Sognefjord, Norway's largest and deepest fjord. Vanderlyst petitioned the court for guardianship over me. The legal dust may have settled, but once I swam with the troupe back to Norway, I couldn't bring myself to attend rehearsals. My school was nice enough to give me some days off, but I was going to need a lot more than a few days to get over how gutted I felt. Gutted was the right word, because my chest and belly hurt like they'd been stabbed, and I was left feeling empty.

I barely ate anything. I lost appetite for even my favorite fish: haddock and Atlantic cod. Neglecting my self-care routine made me lose my luminous sheen. My scales became dull and dirty. My hair became matted, tangled, and too long. Rune and Eli tried to make me eat more. Tahu and Anita took turns helping me clean spots I couldn't reach, but they weren't as thorough as Mom had been. During that week I had no school, I'd curl up on the seabed, blending in with the rocks. I didn't want to show my face to anyone.

Memories of being floored on the water chute by the truth made me want to curl up into a tighter ball. I've been used to living my life like the star of an act and having my part roll out the way I want to, with all the pizazz that came with being a star. I was used to pulling off the dazzling stunts with cool soundtrack blaring in the background. I liked calling the shots. What really happened — being saved from goons by guys who didn't like me when I wasn't even conscious. I had missed out on the action. I didn't even get to see Mom, Dad, and the dealers getting cuffed. Instead I woke up to getting filled in on the worst plot twist possible by Finley and his drinking buddies, of all people. I didn't know anything else that could be so wrong, so humiliating.

I put my paws over my muzzle, as if to cement it further into the seabed. Finley's voice floated from above as he swam down to me. "Hey, school's starting tomorrow, in case you forgot."

I didn't say anything.

"I'm going with Faye to get her new supplies. I bet you need some, too. Come on."

I still didn't say anything. I heard a bubbling sigh through his blowhole. He swam around, settled his belly on the seabed, and propped his chin on his flippers to be eye level with me.

"Look, Long. Life just dealt you a real shitty hand, and that sucks, I know. You probably don't believe me, but please try to when I say how sorry I am for you."

I glared down at a little crevice off to the side.

"I was against having you adopted, but you probably heard that from someone else already. I believed you were better off with people from your own culture, so you didn't have to grow up being uprooted and cut off from where you belong. Of course Kari brought up her calves, and I thought she'd been really grieving for those poor babies, that she was looking at you as something to fill the hole they had left in her. So how could I say no after that?"

I closed my eyes, hoping he'd swim away when I opened them again.

Instead he went on. "To be honest, I had always thought she treated you like a shiny new toy, prettying you and propping you up to be adored by the masses." He grunted in disgust. "I didn't think in a million years that I'd be right. I didn't *want* to be right. I really didn't. You didn't deserve to be used like that, kid."

Tears pooled behind my shut eyelids. I liked being under the sea because if tears leaked out, no one could tell from all the saltwater around.

Then Finley said, "It's okay to cry, you know."

I couldn't help looking up at him with surprise.

A corner of his lip tugged up. "You didn't think I'd know crying when I see it? It's okay to cry... that's what I always tell myself whenever I miss Faye's mom. Faye was too young to remember her mom, so she'd cry more over losing in water polo. I tell her it's okay to cry over that, too."

If I was on land, tears would be streaming down my cheeks. "I don't think I can ever get over this, Finley," I croaked. "I lost a mom and a dad. You know what it's like to lose someone. How do you get over it?"

Faye's dad didn't say anything for a few moments, then he let out a dry "hah" and said, "I don't, and I don't think I ever will, so

31

we're in the same boat. I just know to keep on swimming."

I frowned. "Aren't those two the same?"

"No, not really. Stuff like losing someone stays forever, for as long as you live. It's not something you can 'get over.' But you can keep swimming and keep your eyes forward." Finley lifted his gaze to the distant surface, where I could make out the rippling clouds and sunlight. "I keep looking at Faye, for example. I always got my sights on what's best for my daughter. Or what I *think* is best for her, anyway. I tried to nudge her into the circus business, but that was just what I wanted. I've come around to letting her do what makes her happy."

"Does she know that?"

"Not yet. I'm going to surprise her with a new polo ball — you know, for the new season. But don't tell her."

I cracked a smile for the first time in days. "I won't." My smile faded as I stared down at my paws. "I'll go back to school, but I don't know if I want to go back to performing yet."

"Whether you want to or not is your choice, and yours alone. No one in the troupe, including me, should make that choice for you. Rune, Eli, Tahu, Anita, and I... we all decided to be your guardians not because we expect you to perform with us, but because you're family. That doesn't change whether you choose to be on the stage with us or not."

I nodded, which was about as much as I could manage with the gratitude that overwhelmed me beyond words. I planted my paws on the seabed to lift myself from it.

Finley drifted up along with me. "Remember what I said: keep on swimming. You don't have to swim fast or a lot, just as long as you keep moving forward."

"I do need new school supplies."

"So you're coming with me?"

"Yeah." That was a start. A small one, not much, but still a start. I followed after Finley, and each ripple of my long, snake-like body felt like a big step forward.

I didn't know when I would return to be the Bedazzling Dragon of Vanderlyst, if ever. For now I was just a dragon of Vanderlyst, and that was perfectly fine with me.

Source and Sedition

By Koji A. Dae

Each morning the summer my sister was born, I followed the rest of the girls from my village to the beach and watched the breaking waves explode into hisses of foam. I collected seashells and traded stories my aunts had told me. But I no longer believed an octopus would come on our shore and snatch me to the source of the ocean. They try to get people when they're young. Compact. Easy to transport. Twelve was the cusp of never. I was shooting up in height, growing breasts, and putting a layer of fat on my childish hips — too old to believe that an octopus would lure me to the deep.

"Your hair's too short, Kayla," Bonnie told me. She was a neighbor girl, barely four years old. "Octopuses like braided hair. My aunt said so."

"Oh, if your aunt said so." I held up my palms as if to ask what she would have me do about my boyish haircut.

She was too young to understand sarcasm. Her wide, brown eyes believed everything her aunts told her. "I'll braid it for you."

I sat on a rock as her fingers, still sticky with baby sweat, stumbled through a couple of tiny braids. As she tugged, I daydreamed about summers on the mainland: empty boarding houses, except for the other kids who couldn't afford to go home, no one to talk of octopuses or braid my hair.

Bonnie kissed my cheek and I touched the lumpy, uneven braids.

"Thanks, babe. Let's go find you an octopus." I stood up, took her hand, and spent the rest of the afternoon splashing in the shallows with her.

When she went home for supper, I stayed in the warm water and swam out to the depths, where there was nothing but salt, seaweed and me. I dove deep, opening my eyes to a world of blue-green. Not an octopus in sight.

Tempers grew short in the dry heat of summer, and come September everyone was irritated by someone. I was irritated by my aunts for lying about octopuses, my baby sister for crying through the heat of the day, and my mom for having my baby sister.

When Angela was seven days old, my mom constructed a tight wall of sheets around the porch and put her bassinet outside.

"You can't be serious," I said. "You're not going to leave her out all night."

"It's tradition. I did it with you, too. That's why you will carry the wisdom of the ocean, even when you leave this island."

"It's a stupid superstition."

Two aunts came over to keep my mom from going out to Angela as she cried for comfort. Between her screams and the frantic pacing of my mom's bare feet, I couldn't sleep.

By morning my irritation reached a boiling point, and I stomped off to the beach without breakfast or a goodbye kiss.

I let the waves lick my feet, but I didn't submerge myself.

"Come in with me!" Bonnie pulled at my arm, nearly yanking it out of the socket.

I dug my feet into the sand. "Go in yourself."

"But what if an octopus is waiting for you?" The girl always spoke in screeches and exclamations. It had never bothered me before, but that day I wished she would speak like a normal person.

34

"There's no octopus waiting for me." I jerked my hand away from her. "Or you. It's a made up story. You'll see when they send you to the mainland."

Her smooth face wrinkled with pain and confusion. "I'm going to get one. Mama had a dream."

The brown sand tickled beneath my fingernails as I traced swirls in it. I grunted, hoping to leave it at that, but curiosity got the best of me. "A normal dream or a water dream?"

Normal dreams could be ignored. They were the fantasies of mothers or fever from the sun. But water dreams — a murky future seen by a submerged dreamer — were worth listening to.

She jutted her chin forward and looked me square in the eyes. "Water dream."

I threw a pebble into the waves. "Even water dreams can be wrong."

She stuck her tongue out at me before trudging off on her own.

Someone had to dash her hopes, or she'd grow into a fanatic, raving about magical octopuses. That would do her no good when she was sent to study with the mainlanders. She'd spend her last summer stripping away the silliness pounded in during her childhood, like me.

I continued throwing pebbles until Bonnie's high-pitched shriek sounded from far down the beach. The other girls, all dark from the sun and in various states of undress, looked at the sound, but no one moved. I groaned and pushed myself up to run through the wet sand to the rocks where the beach curved around the cape.

"Bonnie, what's wrong?" My words fell between huffs of short breath.

Her eyes were even wider than usual. She pointed with a trembling finger. "Kayla. Is that a...?"

In a large tide pool lay a pile of rust-red limbs with purple undersides. They floated like jelly, as if the octopus might be dead.

I leaned close to the surface of the pool. "I think it's hurt."

"But is it one? Really one?" Bonnie whispered, her voice finally tempered by awe.

The legs were too tangled to count, but I was certain there were eight. "Yeah, it's an octopus."

It wasn't just an octopus though, it was a huge one. Like the ones from the stories. It could easily carry Bonnie, maybe even me.

I looked from the tide pool to the ocean. "I think it's stuck here.

Maybe we should move it into the open water."

Bonnie didn't move, so I stepped forward and reached my hand into the shallow pool. The octopus oozed towards me. My fingers brushed over its rippled skin, and it shuddered, like a happy dog. I moved my other hand beneath it and a sharp pinch made me draw back.

Drops of blood fell from the back of my hand. "That thing bit me."

My mind clouded over, as if I was deep under water. Bonnie's words were impossible to make out. But other words came to me. *Let me take you.*

"Stand back." I sheltered Bonnie behind me—half to protect her from the violent creature, half to have it all to myself — and reached into the water again.

The creature jumped out of the pool. The webbing between its tentacles stretched taut as it skittered towards me. I pushed Bonnie away and two powerful tentacles, thick as my arm, wrapped around my waist and knocked me over. The beast dragged me over the hot sand and plunged into the water.

I gasped and floundered as its webbing compressed my chest and pulsated, forcing water into my lungs. The creature darted forward, and I hung limp, like an extra set of arms dangling from its head.

The sun stopped illuminating the water. My blood turned to icy slush, no warmer than my captor's suction cups. It twisted and swirled, and we spiraled down to the depths where cold and darkness put me to sleep.

When I came to, the sun was shining on my shivering body and I was on a different beach, with white sands instead of brown.

Sputtering, I sat up and pushed my hair from my eyes.

"Greetings, sister Bonnie."

"Bonnie? I'm—"

"It's been a long journey. I trust Phearidus kept you from harm."

"Phearidus?"

The speaker had long black hair and dark skin. She looked to be about seven or eight. Her eyes were muted green instead of brown, but she could have been from my island.

"It's confusing when you first come here. I'm Shauna. I'll help you."

Shauna guided me through a cool pine forest to a small village filled with girls dressed in long-sleeves and pants going about their daily chores.

I rubbed my hands briskly over my arms, trying to warm up.

Shauna guided me to a fire and motioned to one of the girls nearby. The girl looked down at a bundle of clothes in her hands then scurried off.

"We thought you'd be younger," Shauna said.

The fire thawed me. "I've never been so cold."

"The source of the ocean is further north than most people think, but you'll get used to it. You've been chosen to be Phearidus' rider."

Bonnie was chosen. I just happened to be protecting the little girl at the right time. I should have said something, but my teeth chattered from the cold and that was my only answer.

The girl returned with pants and a long-sleeved shirt. They were dull brown, not the colorful rainbow outfits I'd imagined for the girls who bore the secrets of the sea, but they were warm and comfortable.

After a bowl of soup, Shauna took me to a hut. Inside, a spring bubbled up from between flat rocks. The water pooled about a foot deep and ran back down the rocks around the edges. The scent of rotting eggs made me hesitate, but Shauna waved me next to her. Around the walls of the hut hung several empty vials tied with braided ropes of seaweed.

"This is the source of the ocean. It contains the secrets of coexisting with the ocean. Once you build your water-suit, you'll carry these secrets to babies born on our islands."

Like Angela, crying all night last night. I thought forcing a baby to spend the night alone, wailing in the dark, was cruel faith. But it was true. Octopus riders weren't some stupid myth. I was one. Or Bonnie was.

Somehow I kept not telling Shauna what my name was. When she introduced me as Bonnie, I didn't correct her. I learned to turn quickly when someone called me Bonnie. As I wove seaweed, colored by the spring of secrets, I became Bonnie.

My suit crafted itself, my fingers numbly twisting until the green threads turned purple and red. Not my favorite colors, but they sparkled and shone, creating delicate webbing throughout the fabric of the suit. I tried to remember what Bonnie's favorite colors had been. This suit was meant to be hers. But it slipped over my body and held me close, warm and snug like a hug.

It took all winter — a season I had never known — to finish my suit. By spring, when the snow on the island melted and the days warmed to an echo of my life as a child, I was ready for my first ride.

Shauna presented me with a vial to carry the water, and I filled it from the hot spring, carefully corking its secrets.

"Phearidus will take you to your first child," Shauna told me, standing on tiptoe to kiss my forehead.

I waited on the beach alone until the heavy red and purple octopus washed ashore, dashed to me, and carried me into the current.

You're not Bonnie, it thought to me as it dove deeper, spinning in a slow spiral.

No, I admitted. *Are you going to tell them?*

It swam faster, until I grew dizzy. *It was my mistake.*

When Phearidus surfaced, the sun was dipping down over my own island. I gasped as several boys and girls boarded a boat at the pier. One of them, with a jutting jaw and dull eyes, shared the same flat nose and pouty mouth as Bonnie. But this girl was twelve, heading to school on the mainland.

It's not possible. Bonnie is just a little girl.

Octopuses don't just travel the depths of the oceans, but the depths of time as well. When you ride with me, I will take you to the future and the past. Wherever and whenever you are needed, Phearidus explained.

She unwrapped her tentacles from me and I floundered in the water, reaching for the safety of her embrace until she pushed me into the shallows. I waited for the boat to leave and the sun to set before going ashore.

Once on land, my feet knew where to go. The wailing of the newborn guided me to a rickety porch. I climbed through the sheets and found in a bassinet a baby with a full head of black hair and dark, curious eyes.

He stopped crying when I approached. I smiled down at him and opened my vial. I poured three drops over his head—one to understand the creatures in the ocean, one to understand the waves in the water, and one to understand the history of his people. Then I kissed his forehead and left. He was crying again before I reached the shore.

Phearidus took me from island to island to anoint the babies. I didn't know what year it was, or even the season. Most islands I didn't recognize, but Phearidus took me to my island a few times. I always stayed a few extra minutes on the beach, my toes in the familiar sand. Eventually she would crawl out of the ocean and bring me back to her magical world without mentioning my homesickness.

When my vial was empty, Phearidus returned me to the source where Shauna and the rest of the riders waited for me.

I took off my suit and it disintegrated.

"You had some long rides, Bonnie," Shauna noted.

"Huh?" I was slow turning around. I'd gotten used to Phearidus thinking of me as Kayla.

"You'll need to weave a new suit."

I shivered at the thought of staying on the tiny pine forest island for months. But at least it was summer, and I wouldn't freeze through another winter. I'd have to ask if Phearidus could always drop me off at the beginning of summer.

As if reading my mind, Shauna shook her head. "We're like the octopuses, pulled out of time."

I wanted her to explain more but, though she knew everything the source could tell us, she didn't understand how the octopuses' magic worked. Not even the octopuses did.

I spent the strange out-of-time summer on the beach, weaving a new water-suit. This one was also purple and red, but threads of dark blue like the sky before a storm began to show up towards the end of summer.

My favorite color, I told Phearidus, who had taken to splashing around the shallows while she waited for me.

My next ride felt longer, though it was impossible to tell for sure. But Phearidus seemed to keep us underwater longer, selecting our targets more carefully.

Is something wrong Phearidus?

The octopus hugged me tighter and spun with precision. *I'm getting old. I got you too late.*

Got me too late or got me too old? With the real Bonnie would she have had more seasons? She didn't answer.

When she took me to my island, I stayed outside the window of the house where I anointed the baby. The mother was pacing inside, talking to two other women.

"She's crying. It isn't safe out there. Let me go to her."

"It's okay Sabina. She'll be fine. You went through this, too. All babies go through this."

"Not on the mainland. It's a stupid superstition."

The third woman cleared her throat. "At least you still have this superstition. Bonnie will have her baby next month. A baby that will never learn of the ocean, that will never know where it comes from. Better to leave your baby to cry for the night than to forsake your home."

The mother quieted. As if understanding what was going on, the baby on the porch stopped crying, too. I was the only one left crying, silent tears streaming down my face.

Can you take me to Bonnie's baby?

Bonnie's baby? Phearidus released me, and I almost fell out of her arms. *No. Bonnie never has a baby.*

Yes she does. Next month. I just overheard.

Phearidus rippled her suction cups — her equivalent of a shrug. *A baby born on the mainland isn't one of ours.*

But Bonnie's from the islands. If I hadn't taken her place, she wouldn't have a mainlander baby. Of course, she would have been a four-year-old forever and never had a baby, but I don't think about that. Only that I stole something from Bonnie, and finally I could give something back to her. *Take me to her.*

Phearidus took me to a shallow, stinking bay filled with ships and bustling with cars. It made me shudder, and Phearidus was slow to let me go. *Don't do this, Kayla.*

I pushed her arms off me and swam to shore. People pointed as I got out of the water in my dripping, skin-tight suit. I ignored them and asked my feet to carry me to Bonnie.

They took me further away from the ocean than I ever imagined an island kid could go. I walked through the city, through the wilderness, and into the next city. I was exhausted when I found Bonnie's small apartment building, which took me three tries to scale.

The baby wasn't laid out for me, of course. I had to ease the window open. Bonnie was sleeping in the living room with her baby next to her. I crept on tiptoes to them, trying not to wake her.

But Bonnie shifted and stirred, letting out a high scream.

I covered her mouth and recognition dawned in her eyes. "Kayla? Impossible."

"I've come to bless your baby." I held up my vial and uncorked it, but Bonnie snatched her baby close.

"You died. Got carried out to sea by an octopus."

I shook my head. "I didn't die. I became a rider. You always believed in us. What happened?"

Her tense biceps relaxed enough for her to lower her baby to her lap. "The mainland. It's hard to keep believing in all the backwards island ways when faced with everyday reminders that they can't be true."

"But they are true. And your baby will know them." I measured out three drops of stinking water onto the baby's forehead and bent down to kiss it. "But it's your job to keep them alive, too. Tell them to your child. Help them grow in her."

Bonnie, wide-eyed as ever, nodded.

After that, I demanded Phearidus only take me to the mainland babies — the ones who came from the islands but would never know their roots. She argued with me, dragged me to the clean shores of islands. But I refused to go to the babies until she gave up and carried me to the polluted shores of the mainland.

We spent the rest of our season spreading memories of the islands to babies born out of place. I touched some of the mothers, too, reminded them to keep the stories in their hearts and on their lips, begged them to take their babies, just once, to see their birthright islands.

When Phearidus returned me to the source island, she was weak. She no longer zipped through the water, and she was a pale yellow instead of her usual vibrant red.

"I think Phearidus is sick," I told Shauna.

"She's dying," Shauna said. "It's her time. You'll get a new octopus after she passes. She'll send one to you."

"Let me take her on one more ride."

Shauna said she was too weak, but I filled my vial and insisted.

Phearidus. Take me to my baby sister. Angela.

Phearidus pushed off from the rocks and floated to the depths of the ocean, letting my weight sink us rather than propelling us forward herself. She barely had enough energy to surface, and I had to kick to help us reach the beach.

I went to Angela, kissed her head, and blessed her. My heart pounded as I heard my own mother pacing the small living room. I could go to her now, see her and tell her I would be alright. But I didn't.

I waited on the cape while the sun rose. Phearidus was too weak and tired to force me into the water. She floated next to me, and I stroked her rough head.

There Phearidus. A group of girls scattered along the shore. *There's Bonnie. You could take her now. She's younger. Has more life to give you.*

But you... Phearidus faded to white at the tips of her arms. *I can't leave you.*

You were never supposed to take me. It was always supposed to be Bonnie.

Phearidus pushed an image into my mind. It was me, going to the mainland for the first time. *You were the only one who would insist. Keep insisting.*

I clung to the image, but her thoughts faded from my mind and her body floated limp next to me. I bit my trembling lip and released her body, letting the current take it, and a piece of my heart, back to the depths.

Before my sorrow could blossom, another octopus rushed up to me. It wrapped too hard around my waist and pulled me to the depths without pause. It bit my neck and blood spilled out behind us as we went on to the next baby.

You do Phearidus no honor by struggling.

I relaxed into a sulk. The new octopus was right, Phearidus wouldn't understand why a human would need time to grieve. *I only work with mainland babies.*

I know, Bonnie.

I didn't tell her my name was Kayla. That was Phearidus' secret.

Namug

By Gustavo Bondoni

The ever-present weight dragged on her arms. Every movement, every keystroke seemed to require ten times the effort that Ruth was willing to supply. Epsilon Eridani II simply wasn't meant for human habitation; even those humans genetically modified for high-gravity environments found three times Earth-mass a bit of a stretch.

Living on this planet was torture — not the torture of agonizing pain, but the torture of continuous slight discomfort during every moment, waking or sleeping.

Colonel Ruth Khazak knew that the gravity wouldn't hurt her, and that it wouldn't hurt any of the other genetically modified colonists, but the pressure to find a solution was mounting: even people who volunteered to move to the most inhospitable regions in the galaxy needed some comfort. And it was her job to find the way, which wasn't helping her sleep any easier at night.

"Damn," she said, and turned to her lab assistant, whose flat, broad features and squat high-gee build had grown on her to the

45

point in which their relationship had gone well past what was proper. She couldn't care less — no one among the colonists would complain, and none of those fragile one-gravity idiots from Earth could stand on the surface of the planet without more discomfort than they'd care to endure. "Any luck?"

It was a rhetorical question. She knew what he was working on and, though it might be a promising avenue, they wouldn't know whether it was actually viable for a few days at least. But Kinney still thought about it before answering. "About the same as yesterday. We can graft heek legs to human nervous systems with no problems, but the arms are useless unless I can get human hands to work at the end of them–and the muscles just aren't there." The heeks were large, feathered primates, slow moving and strong, perfectly adapted to life on the surface–but which had never developed opposable thumbs.

Ruth was working on trying to make the second colony on the planet a viable one. Her specific assignment was to find a way to adapt the human body to the environment without having to use prohibitively expensive imported bionics.

The first set of colonists had, logically enough, been aquatic. It was much easier to modify a human to breathe through gills than it was to make them comfortable in high gravity, and life in the sea was an immediate solution to gravity; natural buoyancy helped offset part of the extra weight from Newton's law.

Unfortunately, humans, who tended to ignore any kind of carbon-based unintelligent life, had overlooked the enormous squid-like creatures which prowled the depths of the oceans that covered ninety percent of the surface. They'd paid for this oversight with their lives when a huge phalanx of the creatures had come out of the depths and, despite high-tech resistance from the colonists, destroyed every structure in the colony. The colonists themselves, deprived of their metal walls, had quickly been picked off and, as far as anyone could tell, eaten.

Of course, the first thing Ruth's wave of colonists had done was to capture one of the creatures and test it for intelligence. The only thing that even remotely resembled a brain, a structure in the central trunk of the squid-like being, was the size of an apple. No intelligence there. The attack had been written off as an instinctive reaction to the intrusion, not a coordinated action at all.

Namug felt the cool, caressing flow of the water on his surface. He could dimly sense the ripples that his neighbor was making nearby. Dwuugag could probably feel Namug's own happiness in the secretions he'd been leaving all this way. It was a good thing that his neighbor was a nice sort, or this open display of emotion would have been a cause for strife.

Even so, it would have been pointless for Namug to try to hide his emotion. He recognized this part of the sea by the temperature and the taste of the water. The colony was nearing the migration point where they always met Yunnin's colony. Sweet-scented Yunnin of the strong embrace. It would not be long until they were together again.

Namug was content.

Ruth's eyes opened suddenly. *That's it*, she thought. And then she agonized a little. She'd promised Kinney that, whenever a sudden inspiration struck at–she checked the glowing face of the status display–four fifteen in the morning, she would jot it down on a pad that he'd given her for precisely that purpose and go back to sleep. He argued that she was having these midnight flashes of brilliance often enough that her sleep cycles were shot to hell.

She smiled, glanced at the unused pad beside the display and got up carefully. It wasn't actually necessary to be silent, since Kinney was the type who could sleep through a meteor strike, but old habits died hard.

Five minutes later, she was in the lab, seated at one of the mainframe workstations. This wasn't the place where she preferred to work–the Stylus tablets were much more comfortable for lab work–but in this particular instance, she wanted to use the forty-inch screen on the workstation.

It took her less than a minute to find the recordings she needed, and she was soon watching the feed from one of the recorders salvaged from the wreckage of the original Epsilon Eridani settlement. The feed was 2-D and a bit cloudy, but that couldn't be helped: all they'd been able to recover were a pair of recordings from security cameras that had been hastily converted to underwater use.

The resolution, such as it was, should be more than enough to show her what she wanted to see. The creatures, after all, were huge.

She sat back, coffee mug in hand, and studied the attack on the old colony. Despite what she herself had concluded after dissecting a number of the things, the attack definitely did look coordinated by some kind of intelligent agency. She watched as they first demolished the power cables and then systematically went about removing all the remaining heavy weaponry. The people, dressed in body armor and armed with various harpoon and projectile weapons, they left for last. They represented the smallest threat. Long before she could see what had happened to them, the camera was pushed away, facing into the depths of the ocean.

The second recording showed the flooded interior of one of the habitation spheres. A single tentacle entered the camera's sight through an aperture in the wall, attempting to capture one of the colonists, armed with a harpoon gun, who was huddled next to a wall. The amazing thing was that the tentacle wrapped itself around the gun, tore it out of the helpless colonist's grasp and, with a mighty wrench, tore it in two. Then it withdrew leaving her alive.

After forcing herself to watch the destruction of the underwater habitat a few times, she watched more footage of the monsters, taken with better quality equipment, filmed after the arrival of the land colonists. For some reason, the creatures didn't see the submersible film cameras as a threat—probably too small—and never attacked one.

Although they referred to the animals as squids, there were some significant differences with their earthly analogues. In the first place, these creatures were organized radially, like giant starfish, and the central hub was just a small, flattish dome in the center as opposed to an elongated cone. This layout precluded quick movement, but, when not attacking large stationary targets, these starfish seemed to enjoy lolling horizontally about on the currents, submerged at immense depths like gigantic floating plates. There were air bladders on the tentacles so that they could be maintained at the same altitude as the rest of the body.

The tentacles themselves were the second major difference. Long and slim, they held no suction cups, being instead covered in long, strong cilia. They seemed much too thin to have caused the damage she'd seen on the tapes, but one had to remember that on this high-gravity world, the pressure in the ocean depths was unbelievable. The tentacles had to be extremely strong just to be able to move effectively.

Once she'd re-familiarized herself in how the starfish looked, she activated the final set of recordings. These were the ones she was most interested in.

Namug had changed states. Before, he'd been content, now he was ecstatic. Yunnin had agreed to disengage, to join his colony. That she'd agreed to undergo such pain to be with him was a dream come true. The fact that he'd have to wait until the next migratory round for her excision to be complete was torture. But the torture went well with the ecstasy—he'd have something to dream about as the colony drifted along the great circle it had established since times immemorial.

He could await the currents, could await the time. Fulfillment would be his, very, very soon.

Kinney entered the lab to find Ruth's head resting on one of the consoles. She was sound asleep. Rolling his eyes, he almost left the lab in order to avoid disturbing her. Heaven knew she needed to rest.

But he'd left a correlation program running last night, and was anxious to see what results, if any, it had delivered. He was a scientist, too, after all. Maybe not as mad Ruth was, but mad enough to volunteer for the terraforming of an extremely uncomfortable place in the galaxy, a place which had killed off the first group of people to try it. He might be able to resist his nature better than she could, but ignoring it altogether was out of the question.

He initiated the active mode on his Stylus tablet, and heard the soft humming of the memory core as everything came back on line.

Ruth stirred, moved slightly, and finally displaced a light pen which rolled off the table and clacked onto the floor. She woke immediately and sat up with a start, looking around as if surprised to find herself in the lab. When her gaze settled on Kinney, she shrugged and gave him a sheepish smile. "I know, I know," she said. "I should get my sleep. But I think I've found a way to solve our little gravity problem."

Kinney tried to glare at her, but his heart just wasn't in it. Why bother? He knew that she'd never change, especially when dealing with a challenge. Anyhow, her hangdog expression was so completely inappropriate to such a forceful woman that it would have been impossible to stay mad at her. "Tell me," he said with a slight smile.

"We need to go aquatic again," she said, all business once more.

"What? That certainly wasn't what I expected. I assume you have a plan for dealing with the squid-things."

"I shouldn't even dignify that with an answer. Of course I have a plan. You should know me well enough by now not to ask such silly questions."

That was more like the Ruth he knew. He grinned. "Well, are you going to enlighten me or do I have to figure it out for myself?"

"No, I'll tell you. If we wait for you to figure it out by yourself, we'll be here until the end of time." Her smile belied the words. "Look here."

Ruth punched the replay command and the mainframe's screen lit up. It showed an underwater scene, which, though slightly murky, had to have been computer-enhanced; the light under the ocean was too slight to get the contrasts that they were seeing. And the scene must have been filmed at a considerable depth, since it showed not one, but two of the giant tentacled monsters. Kinney knew they never came together near the surface.

"The mating tape," he said. "I've seen it."

"Yes, you've seen it. But did you notice that the central section of the bodies never come together?" She pointed at the screen, in which the two creatures had fused into what looked like a bowl of spaghetti. How they managed to interact without becoming hopelessly tangled was a mystery.

Kinney immediately realized that she was right. Some of the tentacles wrapped around a tentacle from the other creature. They were perfectly paired up, always one from each creature in a group, and the distribution seemed to be random, as opposed to having adjacent tentacles pair off. Still other tentacles floated free, seemingly uninterested in the proceedings. But the central sections, where both the nervous system and the reproductive organs were presumed to be located, never came into contact with one another.

"I see it," he said. "But I still don't understand how it's going to solve our problems."

"Even with clues..." Ruth said in mock exasperation. She was in a great mood, which boded well for the success of the Colony. Colonel Ruth Khazak was very seldom wrong–if her gut told her she had the solution, Kinney would be willing to wager that she did. "Look at the evidence. We know the squids will attack anything large that invades their territory, but don't attack each other. The only contact between them is tentacle to tentacle, right?"

"Yes."

"And we haven't seen eyes, right?"

"Nothing we can identify, anyway."

"Oh come on!" she exclaimed, as if lecturing a particularly slow student. "You know as well as I do that there's absolutely no reason for a species living in that lightless water to have developed eyes."

He held up his hands, palms out. "All right, all right! No eyes."

"So if they can't see each other, they must identify each other either through sound–and we haven't found much on them that would indicate a vibratory membrane of the type you'd use to project sound underwater–or through some kind of chemical fingerprinting."

"They taste each other?"

"The tentacles taste each other. The hairs–cilia–must have specialized taste organs. They must be able to sense the presence of one of their kind in the water around them. And I'm also willing to bet that the tentacles themselves secrete the telltales."

"So how does this help us?"

She rolled her eyes. "If we graft one of the tentacles onto a gilled human, we should be able to fool the squids into thinking that one of us is one of them."

"That's ridiculous! Those tentacles must be fifty feet long. They weigh two tons each!"

"So? They'll be in the water, remember? Buoyancy will help, and they've got their bladders for flotation – all we really have to work out is how to graft them to a human nervous system, and how to keep them secreting the right kind of chemicals."

Kinney had his reservations, but held his peace. Ruth had done this kind of thing often enough that he preferred to keep his mouth shut. It wasn't fun to be proven wrong.

Namug writhed in agony in the lukewarm water — impure, bathed in chemicals he couldn't identify. He tried to break free of the pain. But to no avail — he was being held immobile by giant metallic structures clamped painfully to his body.

The nightmare had started on the day the colony had first been taken. A huge artificial structure had enclosed them, so strong that the combined efforts of the entire colony had been unable to make even the smallest of dents in the flat, dull surface.

And the pain. It was unbearable, as if some unknown agency was attempting an excision. But didn't they know that separation was the work of many days, that it should be an act of love, never an act of violence? He felt another wave of agony as his body shredded before the onslaught of something sharp. And then he felt a severance, a loss.

As he drifted into unconsciousness, he wondered if sweet Yunnin would ever learn what had become of him.

The water in the tank had just subsided following her victory lap when Kinney walked up the steps to the causeway that circled the enclosure.

Ruth looked up at him, nearly exhausted, but not unhappy. She could see all the lab equipment arrayed around her: scanners, readouts, and even film equipment. Everything seemed to agree that things were getting better and better, that the discomfort of the operations and the hard work of the bio-integration had been worth it after all. "Watch this," she said.

She dived under the surface and pushed herself along with the tentacle. It was the latest in a series of movements she'd mastered and it wasn't yet second nature. She could still feel the skin of her back, just above her buttocks — where the tentacle had been attached, grafted onto her spinal chord — stretch with the movement. She also noted that breathing no longer presented any problems — her body had finally accepted the gills.

On resurfacing, Ruth found Kinney watching her with a slightly amused expression.

"What?" she demanded.

"You look like a giant tadpole," he said, chuckling.

She swung the tentacle — it was so tempting to call it a tail — around and showered him with water. "I've just managed the first successful melding of alien and human bodies in which the extraterrestrial component outweighs the terrestrial by such a large factor and all you can say is that I look like a tadpole? I ought to have you expelled from the colony for contempt of science."

"At least I wasn't the one who decided that all this equipment would work better wet than dry," he replied, shaking the water out of his hair. "Anyhow, how's it coming?"

How could she possibly describe the feeling of relief that came with no longer being subjected to the eternal crushing of the planet's gravity? But he knew how it felt. He'd spent a few nights in the tank with her. But the tentacle, now that she was finally mastering it, gave her a speed of movement she hadn't known since coming to Epsilon Eridani. "Better now," she said. "At least I don't feel like the damned thing is fighting me anymore. I'm the one controlling the motion."

"Well, I suppose you weren't expecting it to be easy."

"No, but I wasn't expecting it to be this tiring. It isn't fun trying to get two tons of alien muscle to bow to your will, let me tell you."

"I still can't believe it worked."

"You realize that this might be useful on other worlds as well–a great bit of defensive biology for aquatic colonists on high-gee planets?"

"And another promotion for the great Ruth Khazak?"

She swished her tail–tentacle–contemplatively, coquettishly, she thought. "Probably not. You need to have commanded combat troops for them to make you a general."

"Pity. I can just imagine the name of the army: 'Khazak's Tadpoles.'" This earned him another sluice of water from the tank.

"Stop clowning and listen. I think I've got enough control over this thing so that I won't get pulled to the bottom of the ocean. Now we've got to get out there and test it, to make sure that it works as a way of communicating with the squids."

"I've been thinking about that. You've shown that it can be done. Why don't you let someone else do the testing. We've got a full complement of colony marines that were specifically assigned to us to take the risky jobs. Why can't you graft a tentacle on to one of them and let them test it?"

She shuddered inwardly. There was no way she was going to return to the hellish gravity of the surface, and if someone else was testing the squid's reaction, she'd have no excuse to keep the tentacle. "It would take too long. Think about it, a marine would take the same amount of time to get used to it as I have—those are weeks we simple don't have to spare. And I just need a few more day's practice. No. I have to be the one to do it." She paused, making certain that he wouldn't voice any further protests. "Now get in this tank before I use this tentacle to pull you in. I feel like celebrating."

The next two weeks were a blur. Everything had to be coordinated. Her tank had to be transported to the ocean's edge, she had to undergo a period of acclimatization to the ocean's temperature and salinity. And there was another unexpected snag: as soon as the tentacle hit the ocean, it seemed to regain part of the independence that had characterized it in the days immediately following the graft. A frustrating few days were spent in the shallows getting her full command back.

But, soon enough, she was ready for the final test. Ready to go out into the open ocean to find one of these behemoths, to confront it and see whether her experiment would insure the continued survival of the colony.

Kinney made some noises about accompanying her with a squadron of helicopters—massive things that flew with difficulty in the high gravity. Knowing they would certainly frighten the squids into acting violently, she just smiled. Right after sunrise the following morning, set out without telling him. She'd make it up to him later.

She swam straight to the point where the continental shelf suddenly ended and dived. She wanted to find one of the squids *right now*. And, somehow, she felt that her own eagerness was complemented by a sense of elation actually coming from the tentacle itself.

This stopped her cold. If her tail acted up now, the weight would drag her to the bottom of the ocean. And she'd be crushed long before getting there.

But there didn't seem to be any problem, other than the feeling of well-being coming from the tail. She briefly wondered what it was. Feedback from some instinctive reaction to temperature and salinity parameters? Something else? She quickly dismissed it and got back to the matter at hand, namely finding and... befriending?...

one of the giant aquatic monsters. Her tail pushed her on, further and further from the shore, deeper and deeper into the dark water until a shadow, large and tentacular, appeared in the distance.

She was nearly there.

Namug felt the cool water caressing his surface, something he thought was lost to him forever. He was back where he belonged, in the timeless expanse of the deep ocean. But this, he knew, was merely the illusion of freedom. He had no control over his own movements: no matter how hard he struggled against it, his body would not react to his commands. He was anchored to something unspeakably alien, sundered forever from the joyous interaction with his colony – were they even still alive? – and unable, even in the glorious deep water, to move freely.

He remembered the happiness that accompanied the endless wandering of the colony. He longed for just one more chance to meet one of his people, to feel once more the caress of another surface on his. He didn't even ask for Yunnin; that would be too much. But he would give what remained of his life to be in the presence of any of his people once more.

And his wish, suddenly, unexpectedly, was granted. He sensed a that there was a colony in the water with them – he could taste it on the current. And the monstrosity he was attached to, instead of denying him this one last wish, swam straight towards the thickest concentration of colony-taste.

Soon, incredibly soon, his body was being ordered to extend towards the outstretched body of one of the colony's members. The approach, under alien control, was a clumsy thing, and it was a familiar approach inappropriate for greeting a stranger. But in the end, the stranger accepted it, and they intertwined in the accepted fashion.

"Greetings," the other said by moving the hairs on her surface. "I am Guniod of the Carinaa colony."

"Greetings. I am Namug of the Woogen."

"You are alone. Are you the only member of the Woogen?"

"No. The Woogen are many."

"They are not here. Your hub has only one individual. How can this be?"

"My root is not a hub. It is a sentient creature, like one of us. But it is evil. It has taken my colony and excised me forcefully. It has damaged me beyond repair, and it controls my movements."

"But not your words."

"Not my words."

Guniod *was still for a few moments. "Can you be transplanted to another colony?"*

"No. I have been maimed."

"Do you wish to continue with your new hub?"

"No."

"What do you wish?"

"You are a strong colony. Destroy this atrocity."

"You will die."

"I am already gone. Do it quickly."

She signaled assent. *"We will do it. Your name will echo in the ocean,* Namug."

"May knowledge of this come to Yunnin of the Raugee."

"It shall. Goodbye."

"Thank you. Please do it quickly."

The entire colony wrapped around the monstrous creature that had planted his base on its skin. Each individual applied his or her strength to the alien, crushing it and tearing it into tiny globules of flesh and droplets of blood.

And, as he sank to the bottom of the dark, murky ocean, Namug was at peace.

On the Surface

By James L. Steele

The stage had no curtain, rather it used lighting to hide the performers from view. Right now the stage lights were dimmed to nothing, and the house lights were fully lit so the land-dwellers could find their seats.

Far above the stage, Aro and his fellow performers stood on the catwalk, leaning on the railing. An ocean of alien life to the three dozen watching from the catwalk.

The usual crowd of coastline people: otters, canines, rodents, gators. The tourists stood out among them: reptiles, coyotes, red foxes, wolves, cougars and bears. Then there were the foreigners: tigers and kangaroos to name a couple. Even after ten years, Aro still couldn't tell distinct individuals of a species apart. No one on the stage could. Everyone was equally alien, and Aro was keenly aware they thought the same of him.

This show was designed to combat that. A way to end the mystery. By presenting his world on stage for everyone to see, it would be that much less alien to everyone. He especially enjoyed this vantage point. His people were used to seeing the land creatures from below. This was the only place in the world where the perspective was reversed.

The crowd murmured amongst itself before the show. He'd come to view the audience as a school of fish: no real leader, but identical in behavior. Even though different people made up the theater house every night, they reacted the same to everything on stage. They cheered and clapped at the same time, got up, sat down and breathed as one. Fish. Thinking of them like this helped Aro deal with their alien stares. He shared this technique with everyone who joined the show, and it helped them adjust.

The house lights dimmed. As a single creature, the audience quieted down. The performers took position at the gaps in the railing and raised their heads. Now it was time to forget the people in the seats and concentrate on the performance.

The entire theater remained dark for a few moments. Then the stage lights brightened from both above and below, and the audience gasped in awe at what was before them.

There was no stage.

Suspended in midair over where the platform of a theater stage should have been was an enormous sphere of water. Below it, a crystal clear pool.

The audience chittered at the sight. Aro caught the usual reactions: "impossible," "how in the," "that's gotta be a trick," "projection or something." Aro smiled. They were always awed by the first image of the show, and the rest would only be better. The music started. Aro counted beats, waited for the right bar, and then dove into the sphere. As soon as his body touched the water, he was home.

On land, Aro's motions had to be carefully premeditated. In the water, he could move freely. He folded his arms down at his sides and righted himself. His tail stabilized him and he floated in the middle of the sphere, legs together, arms at his side, surrounding water absorbing the muffled sounds of the audience. They gazed at him, mouths gaping. Again. For most of them, it was their first time seeing an orca, let alone one like Aro.

A rare sight even among his own people, he was six-hundred pounds of solid muscle. He could bench press twice that much, squat three times, and easily curl half. He wore no clothes, but he had nothing to hide, unlike the land-dwellers. As part of the show, the audience was given a few moments to absorb his presence. He kept a stoic, dignified expression as he floated before them.

Then the other performers dove in. Dolphins, humpbacks, sharks, and even a few eels. They swam into position all around the sphere and hovered in place to let the land-dwellers absorb the sight of each performer. The audience orgasmed. Aro often wondered how they even survived being taken aback three times in less than a minute.

Creatures of the ocean tended to be massive. Nobody in the show was under three hundred pounds. Each of them was quite capable of lifting their own body weight. They were huge compared even to the largest land-dweller, but their bodies were still streamlined to glide through the water.

The entire cast was painted in their tribal colors, the same dyes and pigments used in their homewaters. The dolphins had green swirls. The great white had orange dots sprinkling his scales. The coral shark had deep purple crisscrossing his natural brown spots. Aro, the only orca in the show, was painted red between his black swatches.

The music cued them. The performers pivoted in place and began swimming around Aro. As they did, water stretched from the pool below. Like taffy, it rose halfway up the height of the giant central sphere. It pulled away from the pool, wobbled and collected into a perfect, hovering globe.

The looping dolphins dove out of the main sphere, arcing gracefully through the air and slipping into the smaller one. They swam in formation through it.

Meanwhile another sphere had been rising on the other side. It separated from the pool and collected itself into a second, hovering at the same height as the large globe. The sharks leaped into it.

Two more spheres rose from the pool and stopped above and just behind the large globe. The eels leaped into one, and the humpbacks into the other. Aro floated alone in the center.

The performers in each sphere swam in choreographed loops and twirls. Aro waited for his cue, then he glided through the water of the central sphere. His tail propelled him, his legs controlled his speed and rotation, his arms steered him. He swam in large circles, building up momentum. Then he leaped through the empty air and slipped into the shark's sphere. He curled up and glided through their formations. Aro looked like the erratic comet swirling around an orderly solar system, changing pitch and angle with every orbit, picking up impossible speed in such a small space and yet never touching a single shark.

On cue, he leaped straight up through the empty air into the eel's sphere and swam through their synchronized water dance as the music picked up. Aro leaped through the humpback's sphere, then finally into the dolphin's.

After building up momentum, he leaped through the air, straight towards the house and into the large globe. He didn't bend his path around to stay within it — he kept swimming towards the audience.

The people gasped as the orca flew towards them. At first he appeared to splash out of the globe and land on someone, but the sphere of water had stretched with him. It spread out into a sheet, a two-dimensional ocean hovering in midair over the seats. Everyone gazed up at Aro. Children pointed. Adults stared with open mouths.

While the audience had been distracted watching the massive orca somehow swimming over their heads, the other spheres merged with the sheet, and the performers glided through the hovering ocean. The dolphins and sharks swam in formation upside down, giving the people in the seats the illusion of viewing them from above. Some of the taller ones had to lean down to keep the fins from hitting their heads.

Gradually the ocean receded to the stage and re-formed a single globe over the pool. The dolphins gathered on one side of the sphere. The sharks on the other.

The choreographed opening was over. Now began the silent play. This was the element of the show that changed from quarter to quarter and kept the performers from getting bored with routine.

This quarter's play was a reenactment of the war between the sharks and the dolphins. Aro, the eels, and the humpbacks had discreetly left the stage. Most waited in the pool below for their cue. Aro had swum up to the top and waited on the catwalk, watching the house from his usual place.

It was his quarter off from this part of the show. He had performed in all three segments last quarter and was glad for a chance to relax for part of the night again. It gave him time to observe the aliens below.

He was always curious to see their reactions to the play. Aro himself had it memorized, and he'd watched audiences watch the play a dozen times by now, so he knew what their reaction would be before they ever made it. Fish were predictable. Land-dwellers in groups were no different.

One person caught his eye. Aro strained his eyes to see him through the darkness. He recognized the species only from photographs and books: lion. The first lion he had ever seen in his fifteen years on land.

The play was to the point of the battle itself. Every performer had small packets of a red substance hidden under their body paint. When struck, the packet broke and a trail of something that resembled blood poured out. But unlike real blood, it didn't dissipate. It stuck together and formed majestic strands in the water that swirled with the sphere's rotation. Aro wished real blood behaved so poetically.

He had raised objection to the romanticizing of this war while the segment was still in the planning stage, but the producers insisted it was just for the show. The story behind it would be well-known. Aro had been skeptical until he saw the reactions. To the land-dwellers, Aro's ordinary, everyday life was fascinating and poetic. It made him feel special.

The lion's reaction to the poetic blood was even more pronounced than the audience's. One of the performers let herself fall out of the sphere and into the pool below in theatrical death.

The lion cried.

Aro squinted, trying to get a better look at him. The rest of the land-dwellers watched with calm detachment. But not this creature. Aro had never seen anyone so absorbed in the show before.

The sphere was full of strands of poetic blood as the final two combatants swam and parried each other. The lion was the most attentive in the house. Aro wanted to see his reaction to the finale, but he had to be ready for his cue. As the show's star, he was part of every closing performance. Aro took his place above.

In the battle, the sharks won, and the last dolphin performer poetically fell to his death in the pool below. The last shark swam to the foreground and posed victoriously before the audience. In the silence, the blood swirled around them.

This was true. The sharks had won but had destroyed the territory they fought over and had to abandon it anyway. That was the reason Aro put on these silent plays. They may romanticize the battles, but they always preserved the poignant endings. The shark swam alone in the empty sphere with the blood for a minute. Then he himself fell to the pool below, leaving an empty globe behind for a few beats.

The stage lights dimmed. The house stood and applauded.

The UV lights switched on. The blood changed from red to blue. The sphere expanded into a sheet and flattened out like a tidal wave. Visually, it symbolized that out of the horrors of war came something wonderful. Mutual understanding and peace. The land-dwellers took their seats and gazed up in awe.

The lion gasped and sank deeper into his seat. That wasn't just a typical fish-gasp of amazement. The lion was enamored. Among an entire school of fish, this lion stood out in every possible way. Aro pondered it, almost missing his cue. He put it away and dove into the flat ocean. The other performers swam up, meeting in the middle.

The suspended ocean was low enough for the performers to reach down and touch the audience. Aro was always first to begin. He held his hand down to a wolf cub in a seat. The cub cautiously took his hand. Aro gave it a gentle squeeze and swam on as the music sped up. The other performers did the same to as many people as they could. It was tricky because they had to stay somewhat in formation to maintain their place in the choreography, but there was some room for variation.

To the people in the seats, it was like reaching into the water and touching a new world. Aro figured it was what gave this theater worldwide fame. No other place in the world allowed land-dwellers to touch another culture like this.

Aro glanced from side to side, looking for the lion. Alas he was on the other side of the theater; no way Aro could reach him from here. Too many ocean-dwellers were in his way, and if he broke formation, he could cause performers to fall out of the water and onto someone's head.

When the music reached a certain pitch, the performers withdrew their hands and crisscrossed through the sheet back to the stage. They jumped above, dove back in and never touched each other or fell through to the seats. The cheers and awe-inspired shouts were their reward.

Gradually the performers returned to the stage, the sheet receding with them and reforming into a sphere. They swam around for the finale. The UV lighting now highlighted their body paint, making them look alien even to the performers' eyes.

The ocean-dwellers stopped and floated in exactly the same positions in which they had begun the show. The music stopped. The audience jumped to their paws, hooves, and claws and applauded.

As one, the other performers did a loop, their own variation of a theatrical bow, and swam either above or below offstage, leaving Aro alone in the sphere for a few moments. Then he performed a theatrical bow in water, twirled around, and swam up. The sphere lowered into the pool, and the stage went dark. The applause lasted another five minutes. Aro leaned on the railing and watched.

The lion's mouth was agape at the spectacle, and he was panting. This wasn't an uncommon reaction, but in the lion's case there seemed to be something more authentic about it. Perhaps he had come from some faraway land and never even knew there were people who lived their whole lives in the ocean. The show would be much more intense to someone like him.

The theater-goers filed out. Aro watched until the lion left, then he crossed the catwalk and down the stairs to the performer's lounge.

Aro's room was on the top floor of the hotel adjacent to the theater. Each suite had been custom remodeled. Most everything a land-dweller would want in a room had been removed — the bedroom, the minibar, most of the bathroom, and so on. Instead, ninety percent of the floor space had been converted into a pool.

Made of transparent resin, Aro's pool was built right up against the exterior wall. The windows overlooking the city had been reconstructed to extend below the floor level. This gave Aro a bird's-eye window-view of the city even from the bottom of the pool. It was a view he had specifically requested.

The remaining ten percent of the suite was furnished with a couch, love seat, tables, and chairs facing a television. Aro occasionally watched television but seldom used the furniture. These things were for the land-dweller visitors.

Aro's was one suite of about thirty remodeled in this way. He had his own suite, and so did each of the sharks and the eels and the humpbacks. The dolphins, however, had a suite together, three rooms joined into a single unit.

The salty water was warm, constantly filtered and as pure as it could be. That was another thing he requested, as soon as he found out it was possible. It turned out to be the easiest thing for the land-dwellers to accommodate, which, fifteen years ago, was nothing short of magic.

Heated water, free of debris and all impurity, was the ocean-dweller's equivalent of finding the land of milk and honey. Countless stories of vain attempts to find this paradise were passed down from generation to generation. Nobody once put forth the idea that it would exist on dry land.

Among the ocean people, "luxury" was a concept that didn't exist. Everyone in the sea was the same. The mobility water permitted meant there was no way for one group of people to separate themselves from another group. Kings and queens were the same as paupers and generals. To have heated pools filled with filtered water, air always in easy reach, separated from everyone but a privileged few was luxury in every sense of the concept. It was as unfathomable to an ocean-dweller as sleeping in the clouds, and yet here he was.

Aro floated gently to the surface and rested on his back. The show always took a lot out of him, and coming back to this pool of filtered water was the only reward he needed. About an hour after the show concluded there was a knock on the door.

"It's open," Aro shouted.

A spindly lapine wearing usual business attire walked in. Aro raised his head from the pool and welcomed him.

The Cast Assistant, Olis, carefully stepped around the pool, turned a chair to face the orca and sat down. He set the tiny computer on his lap, opened it, and ran down Aro's messages. The orca turned over and swam casually around and through the pool as he listened.

Aro didn't know how to use a computer. He couldn't even read, but he didn't have to; Olis had been hired to take care of these matters for him. His assistant read him official communiqués from award ceremonies, royal banquets, celebrity events and the like.

Today was more of the usual invitations to visit faraway places, and Aro listened with casual interest. Just last month he had taken a trip out west to visit film studios and meet some of those performers. He was in negotiations to get the cast involved in motion pictures. Aro was thrilled at the idea of a film adaptation of the stage show. Finally a chance to put every element of the show together and present it to everyone who couldn't see it in person.

It was a lot to arrange, as transporting the cast over long distances was no easy task. Trucks had to be equipped with pools and water systems. As of now there were only two such trucks available. Aro was usually the only one who traveled, as he had been told it was too expensive to transport everyone.

That's what the negotiations were about, and it was the message Olis was reading to him now. The theater's producers were trying to convince the film studio to split the massive cost of transportation and housing. The film studio's counter-counter-proposal was to pay for one truck, one room, and the entire cast would simply be housed in one of the community pools.

Aro did a loop through the water, considered it below the surface for a minute, then came up and said, "I don't like that. It's not wise to keep sharks in crowded places for too long. Dolphins can get away with it, but sharks get agitated."

As Aro spoke about the generations of war between sharks and dolphins, and between orcas and sharks, Olis typed. Right now it was only the show that kept them together in peace — they were in this for a common good — but if cooped up together for too long, old rivalries would bubble up again.

Olis finished typing almost as soon as Aro finished speaking. He nodded and continued on down the list of messages. Aro agreed to a few public appearances, other invitations to meet various kings, queens, and presidents across the world. As usual, he would go alone and speak for the group.

It was amazing. Countless opportunities laid out before him. All he had to do was say yes, and he was easily transported over vast distances to meet powerful people.

When he had answered everyone, Olis closed the computer and said goodnight. Aro wished him goodnight as well. The rabbit walked out and closed the door behind him. He didn't bother locking it.

Aro folded his hands behind his head and floated between the surface and the pool's resin bottom. He rolled over to his side and gazed out the window at the city. An endless nighttime vista of lights greeted him. He never tired of it.

Since Aro had left the ocean fifteen years ago, every land-dweller lifted him up on a pedestal and marveled at him. In the ocean, he had just been an orca, unable to change or influence anything. None of this would have happened in his homewaters, and he was thrilled for the chance to reach as many land-dwellers as possible and tell them about his people. It was working better than he had ever hoped.

The lion was in the house for the next night's show. And the next. And the next. For five straight performances Aro watched him from the top of the stage. Most people only came to this theater once. Tickets were too expensive to buy on a whim; this show was something people planned ahead for months to see.

It wouldn't have been so unusual if he had more people with him each time. It wasn't uncommon for people to bring a friend or family member to see the show the next night. That was the usual reason anyone saw the show more than once, but the lion was alone. Night after night he found his seat by himself. No one shared his awe and fascination during the performance. No one joined his side as he filed out of the theater.

Aro watched him closer during the performances. After the play, the lion leaned out of his seat and gazed up at the ocean above. One of the sharks happened to swim over his seat, and she reached down and held a hand out to him. The lion eagerly reached up and took the hand. He grasped it hard, she would later tell Aro, like he was trying to pull himself up into the ocean. When she swam away, the lion turned around in his seat and watched her go. He watched everyone at once, following every performer.

He seemed more and more in awe every time he saw it. Aro wanted to arrange it so he could shake the lion's hand, but the lion's seats were always too far away from Aro's reach. The blocking was ironclad. Any deviation from it would be disaster.

While standing offstage during the silent play on the fourth night, Aro wondered if this lion really was from that distant continent whose name escaped him. He remembered it lay in waters that were foreign even to Aro. What must the world be like over there for him to be so fascinated by ocean-dwellers?

On the fifth night Aro found the lion in the audience again, and as usual he was not in a seat under Aro's path. The lion watched the silent play intently, hanging on the performers' every action.

Aro had met kings and queens, dictators and presidents, celebrities and titans of industry, but never in his fifteen years on land had he seen this kind of reaction from those land-dwellers. The first person to be truly touched by the ocean-dweller's everyday, ordinary life. The first real sign that people were getting the message. Aro wanted to thank him, but not in the same way he thanked the rest of the fish. He wanted the lion to know what it meant to him.

The finale ran like clockwork, and as soon as he was out of the sphere, Aro clumsily ran across the catwalk, down the steps and through the door to the lounge. He quickly wiped the UV blood off his hide, grabbed a towel, and dried himself off.

Aro couldn't understand the value of being dry, but Aro was used to this since the theater and hotel staff balked at the performers whenever they walked around wet. Or naked.

Aro didn't see the point in clothes either. He had no "offensive" parts to flash anybody with, but he and the other performers were instructed that when they went out in public, they must be dry and clothed.

As dry as he could be, Aro threw on the shirt and shorts he had stashed behind a trash can before tonight's performance. He walked out of the lounge, through the office area, and out the far door.

The people in the hall were just exiting the theater. When an enormous orca stepped out the employee's only door, they were even more stunned than they had been during the performance. Aro smiled as best he could. A crowd gathered immediately.

Their producers didn't discourage unplanned appearances between shows, but it was seldom done. Aro himself hadn't done it in two years; things had become so busy he didn't have time to go out and meet people.

As graceful as he was in the water, on land he was just a big klutz. His muscles, invaluable in the water for twisting and looping through the currents and fending off predators from all angles, on land they tended to grind against each other and get in the way. He had been warned that it could ruin the magic, seeing an ocean-dweller on land, which would damage the show's reputation.

Still, connecting with the fans like this could help the show, so the producers didn't mind the occasional surprise meet-and-greet as long as they refrained from any activity that would make them look graceless.

Even for all that, the main reason it was a rare occurrence was because ocean people spoke in an ultrasonic vocal range. Most of the performers couldn't speak the land-dweller's languages. Aro was one of only three who could. He was not only the star performer but the primary translator between the choreographers, directors, producers, and everyone else on land who had to be part of their lives. It had taken four years for Aro to reach this point. Most of the others were just starting.

The crowd filed out of the theater and congealed around Aro. The orca towered three feet above them, reaching down to shake hands of the tiny land-dwellers and answering questions.

"Absolutely love the show!"

"You guys are beautiful up—"

"How do you get the water to do that?!"

"Oh, I know, right—"

"—amaz—"

"—takes my breath away!"

Aro laughed a little. "Thank you, thank you for coming. I'm glad the show thrilled you, but I'm not allowed to talk about the water effects. Trade secret."

"—it true all of you got cut off in some lake that dried up and now you're trapped here?"

"I heard that, too!"

"Everyone's sayin' it—"

"—how did you—"

"No, it's not true. Fifteen years ago I decided to venture onto dry land. As a youth I'd heard rumors of people who live their lives above the surface, and I wanted to find out if they were true. I found a whole civilization of billions right above our heads. I was always told if I showed myself I'd be killed, but I didn't believe it. Communication was difficult for a while, but there had been other sea people who'd made the same leap I did years earlier. They had already figured out how to communicate with my kind, to an extent. I gave my story and wanted to know as much about the land as I could. About ten years ago someone approached me with the idea for this stage show as a means to tell the world who we are. The others joined the show pretty much for the same reasons. They'd heard the rumors and wanted to find out for themselves."

Aro always marveled at how everyone quieted down and listened whenever he spoke. The fish murmured, tittered amongst themselves.

"How much can you bench?" someone asked.

"I heard you can lift a car; is that tr—?"

"—is it just for the show?"

Aro smiled charismatically. "We exercise to maintain it now, but in the open water, we get like this just swimming against the currents and fighting off predators."

"What's the blood made of?"

"—rade secret, too?"

"Yes," Aro said, shaking a few more hands. "It's another secret. It's similar to our body paint. We really do paint our bodies like this; it's for tribal identification. I'm from the tribe of," Aro made a few ultrasonic whistles. "It happens to glow in UV light. Sea dwellers' eyes are sensitive to it, so it means a lot more to us."

"What's it made of?"

"—is it true it takes six hours to put it on?"

"How much do your makeup people get paid to put that stuff on?"

Aro sighed. Typical fish questions. They kept coming. Aro stopped giving historical and cultural details and focused on the rumor and the stage. It's what the fish wanted to talk about, and if there was one thing he learned in the water it's that you can't steer a school of fish by yourself.

He found the lion in the crowd, listening eagerly but struggling to keep a position in the crowd. The lion stood a foot taller than everyone else. Aro's eyes met the lion's.

Aro smiled at him, leaned close. "I see you in the house a lot lately."

The lion was speechless for a few breaths. He'd been singled out; one of the performers had noticed him, and the lion had gone into fanboy lockup, no doubt. "It's... Beautiful."

Aro smiled. He leaned close to the lion's ear and whispered. "Go back inside the theater. I'll meet you there in twenty minutes."

He straightened up and addressed the crowd again. The lion stood there stunned. Aro made eye contact again and nodded, hoping that was the correct gesture for "you heard right, now go."

The lion slowly turned and walked against the flow into the theater again. Aro smiled and mingled with the audience for another ten minutes, answering more fish questions. Then he started to back away to the door. The fish objected as one, following him as he retreated.

"I'm sorry, I'm sorry. I can hold my breath for an hour in the water but I can only be out of it for a short time. My skin starts to dry out after just half an hour."

The fish were disappointed in a very understanding way. Aro shook hands as he backed up to the employee's only door. He punched in the code, slipped inside, and shut the door behind him. He paused. Listened to the murmur on the other side.

The fish were comparing pictures they'd taken, showing each other videos. Others were telling their children how lucky they were to see the orca offstage. Aro caught his breath and smiled at his position. No one back in his homewaters would believe that on dry land, the fish chase you.

He lumbered down the hall and into the lounge. The other performers were in here already, lounging around or swimming along the bottom, imagining they were back in the open water and not in this tank.

Aro stripped off the clothes and plunged in the pool. Ultrasonic questions of why he'd gone out and met the people tonight of all nights filled his ears.

He told them he had to meet the lion.

The others still questioned why he should single this one out.

Aro replied that he had never seen someone so touched by the show before. It meant the show was working. It was removing the mystery — introducing the land nations to the world under the waves. Ten years of work, and it was finally starting to pay off. He didn't want to let this lion slip through like the rest of the fish. He had to thank him personally.

Aro allowed himself only two minutes to recover, then he got out, dried himself off, and slipped the clothes on again.

He didn't climb the stairs to the catwalk, instead he used one of the stagehand exits to the house. He grabbed the undersized handle gently and twisted it. The door opened inward, and he stepped into the empty theater. Sitting in the same seat from which he had watched tonight's performance was the lion, all alone. Aro walked up the aisle and sat next to him.

Sitting was one of those inelegant actions ocean-dwellers were encouraged to avoid. His body was not made for it; his tail got in the way and his muscles bunched up like cement balloons. The movement just wasn't part of an ocean-dweller's life. But Aro wanted to meet the lion on his terms, so he risked looking like a clown.

"Wh... Hello," the lion said.

"Hello to you."

"Oh I can't believe you were serious! I love the show! It's really beautiful I can't get enough. All of you are so wonderful and... And uh. You're even bigger in person. B—but why did you ask me to meet you here? I'm, um, mm..."

Aro understood the nerves. Everyone was nervous talking to someone as alien as an orca. One thing he learned was to prompt the other person to talk about himself.

"You never saw an ocean-dweller before?"

"Oh, no, no, never! Until this week I didn't even know there were... Uh. So it's true? It's not just a show? There really are people who live their whole lives in the water?"

"Of course it's true."

"How... It blows my mind every time I think about it! Especially the water! Oh, please can't you even give a hint on how you get it to do that?"

Aro chuckled. "No hints. They'd harpoon me if I uttered one word."

The lion blinked. "They would...? Seriously, they'd do that?"

It caught Aro off guard. It was the number one question he got in interviews and normally people laughed when he told that joke. The press always did. Aro recovered quickly, smiled and patted the lion on the back.

"I'm kidding, I'm kidding. But I still can't say."

"Oh, I understand, I'm sorry. It's just... I can't help but wonder if..."

Aro waited for him to finish. He didn't. So he held out one hand. "I'm Aro. What's your name?"

"Jhor," the lion answered, taking his hand. "And—and I gotta say it again — I absolutely love all of you. Just the idea of whole races of people living their whole lives underwater. I never imagined. There's so much about the world I don't know I'm overwhelmed, and it's an honor to meet one of you. B-but why did you want to meet me? You must see thousands of people every day!"

Aro released Jhor's hand. "I've been watching you from offstage all week. I created this show to introduce the land-dwellers to my people, and it makes me so happy to see someone enjoy it as much as you have."

"Oh it's too fascinating to pass up! I can't get my mind around it! Entire civilizations of people living in the water and we never knew about you until a few decades ago! It just doesn't seem possible!"

"I've often thought about that myself. You see, ocean people are taught from a very early age to avoid the surface people. Venturing onto dry land is forbidden. Anyone who does will not be allowed to return, fearing they'll lead land-dwellers to the tribes to exterminate their enemies and claim more territory."

"Really? Sounds pretty harsh."

"It is harsh. That's why I waited so long to do it. But I had to try. It amazes me that we haven't made contact sooner. If I were to return now I'd be an outcast, and an orca without a pod is all but doomed to die."

"Oh. So... you're trapped here?"

"In a sense. But I've been lucky."

"I'll say! You're world-famous! Hey, I'm sorry but I have to ask. Is it true you're only twenty-six years old?"

"Actually, yes. We don't age quite the same as people of the land."

"And did you just happen to come up to the surface in Orlando, or did you come up somewhere else?"

"Believe it or not, this is where I came to the surface."

"Why here? Of all the places you could've ended up, why here?"

"The rumors went that land people tended to gather where water was warm. I happened to choose this place. And you? How does a lion end up here? I thought lions only lived far away from here."

"Oh, I'm attending school. I'm on holiday with some of my other classmates. We won this contest for an expenses paid trip to Orlando."

"Ah, that's how you can afford five tickets," Aro said. "And you chose to spend your evenings here night after night instead of the other attractions?"

"I offered the others to come see the show. A couple did, and they loved it. But they didn't want to come see it again."

"And yet you did."

"It's like a work of art! You can't see it just once! How do you rehearse? How do you teach new people to swim in water so thin like that? Has anyone ever been injured?"

Aro was starting to feel dry. "Swimming in suspended water is an exotic experience, even for us. It takes a lot of getting used to. The theater shuts down for a couple weeks every quarter, and that's when we prepare new segments. It's rare we get any new performers though."

"When was the last time you had one?"

"Two years ago. One of the eels was the last to join. He is actually an outcast from the ocean. Please understand, his people are very strict about even going near the surface creatures. He went too close and was chased away. It's very sad."

"Why strict? Don't you need air?"

"Air is critical among our civilizations — we always establish settlements in places where air is plentiful, but it's never near surface creatures, if it's ever close to the surface. The show is often a safe haven for the desperate and—"

"Hey, there's a rumor going around that you have someone in the wings! Is that true?"

"What do you mean wings?"

"A new performer in training. You're saving him — or her for a big reveal soon. Are you?"

It was not true. Aro was about to state it directly, but he had a feeling he should withhold an answer.

"I'm afraid I can't talk about that either. Another trade secret."

The lion laughed. "Oh, I understand, sure. Sorry, since I've been seeing the show I've been talking to a lot of people about it. People say things. Hard to know what the truth is."

"Is that so? You hear these things a lot?"

"It's just a fraction of what I've heard in the last week! There's a lot more! Hard to believe isn't it? You're famous all over the world and there are still so many questions!"

Aro didn't respond. Jhor picked up the thought immediately.

"Like that play! For something without a word of dialogue, it's amazing how much of a story you can tell! And it's so basic! There's nothing to it, but seeing it in person, right in front of me..."

"What did you see?"

"What did I see? In the play?"

"I'm curious. What happened?"

"Well, there was a battle between the sharks and the dolphins. The sharks won, but there was nothing left."

Aro waited for him to continue. When he didn't, he said, "Is that all?"

"Yeah. Is there something else?"

"Well there's a good deal of history behind that play. I wrote it in the program."

"Oh, that. I'm not much of a reader. The play is much more beautiful."

"Beautiful... It represents a great war, not a battle. Thousands of dolphins and sharks died in it. All over a parcel of territory about the size of this theater and hotel. It was over the right to catch fish. Thousands dead... over hunting grounds. The fighting scared away all the fish, and they never returned. I witnessed that war. The bodies floated just above the ocean floor so thick both sides didn't swim. They grabbed bodies and climbed through the water to fight each other. They used their fallen to shield themselves from attack. It was the most gruesome thing I've ever witnessed. I designed the play to convey that."

"Oh. Yeah, I'm sorry. It does represent a war. I did read that part. But it's just beautiful. It's a powerful experience. You should be proud. Were any of the dolphins in the show in that war?"

Aro stared at him. The longer he sat with the lion, the more he felt like he was evading a fish. "Every dolphin and shark who fought in that war is dead. Orcas and the other neutral people are the only ones who can tell the story. I wanted to share it with the land people. It's a very... solemn and tragic tale. One that hurts me personally."

"I understand. Oh, and you know another rumor that's goin' around? That the dolphins are all gay and they... you know... after every show. They have a room in the hotel together and when they're not performing they're always—"

"Trade secret," Aro said.

"Sure, sure! Hey, uh, uh, do you mind if I got a picture of us together here? I wouldn't forgive myself if I didn't ask."

Jhor was a fish.

Aro habitually switched to fish-handling mode. "Of course." Aro raised himself out of his seat, stood and posed the way he always did for photo ops. Jhor pulled a phone out of his shorts, snapped an image of Aro by himself in the theater house. Then he stood beside Aro, held the phone at arm's length and took a quick shot.

"Oh, thanks. That alone made this trip worth it! Thank you so much!"

Aro smiled. "You're quite welcome. And thank you for coming. I have to end this now. Have a very good night and the rest of your trip to Orlando."

"Can't get any better than this! Thank you so much you've made my year! Didn't even know your people existed a week ago and now I got to talk to you! It's been an honor! Thank you!"

"You're welcome." Aro backed away from the seats and walked down the aisle to the exit door on the side.

Jhor waved to him. Aro waved back as he pushed the door in. He let it shut behind him. Aro lumbered heavily to another closed door off to the side. Aro punched in the code and walked to the lounge. Everyone was still here. The sharks swam in circles above and around the dolphins. The eels lounged on the bottom. The humpbacks mingled with everyone. Aro stripped his clothes and dove in. That was the most terrifying fish he'd ever had to deal with.

The ultrasonic questions slammed him like boat anchors.

Aro answered simply. "I was wrong."

The day after meeting Jhor, he asked for a computer, and for Olis to show him how to use it. Olis turned on the screen reader feature, then showed him how to use the speech commands to control the system. It reminded Aro that he needed to learn how to read.

It took Aro a week to get used to using the machine to accomplish even simple tasks, but he had to find out for himself. All of a sudden he didn't trust what everyone told him. By the second week he was proficient enough to search for articles and news broadcasts on the theater.

The computer read what people were saying. He listened to interviews he'd given. It was eerie hearing words he'd spoken repeated by a computer voice, but it gave him a unique opportunity to hear the interview from a new point of view. He listened to the questions now. He noticed his answers — the same kind of answers he tried to give to Jhor and the rest of the fish. The reporter or king, or prime minister, or other person of media always followed up with another question about the show. Usually rumor control.

Even the comments on these stories never discussed the history Aro spoke of. Nobody read the programs outlining the significance of each silent play. Everything was about the performance and the performers.

Gossip. Hearing the interviews for himself now, he realized that was the majority of the questions he answered. Rumor and gossip.

Aro had also taken to sitting on the couch and watching television. It was the first time in years he used the couch. He fumbled with the remote control, far too small for his hands, as he flipped through the channels. He watched news programs mostly, and occasionally he caught mention of the show in some form. He watched his own interviews. He watched specials on the theater and its performers.

Tonight, a month after meeting Jhor, Aro had only been watching TV for ten minutes, but already he felt dry and smothered by the air. He backed away from the TV and jumped into the pool. As he floated just below the surface, his eyes drifted to the nighttime view of Orlando.

Over the last ten years Aro had dismissed these as the reactions of fish. Just the normal groupies other actors and celebrities warned him about. Surely there were people out there who understood why he was here.

Everyone he met was a fish. Every world leader, every actor, every creature on the land saw him as a spectacle. An exotic species from a faraway world for sure, but merely entertainment.

They told Aro the show was designed to end the mystery. By presenting his world on stage for everyone to see, it would be that much less alien to everyone. Things would change. With understanding, the separation could end.

It was a lie. They weren't interested in helping people understand; the show was a spectacle, and Aro had let it happen.

Aro suddenly became conscious of the filtered, heated water and the beautiful view from a swimming pool eighty stories up. Extravagance beyond anything that was possible underwater.

He had become complacent in land-dweller luxury. The prestige, the popularity and admiration of standing on this pedestal.

He had found utopia, and he had let it become his reward for venturing out of the ocean, but that was not why he was here. Just like the fish watching him from their seats, he had been observing the world of the land-dwellers but not making an effort to be part of it.

Aro twirled upright and propelled himself out of the pool. He slid up the tile floor on his belly, halted himself and stood on his feet. He dried off quickly and picked up the phone. Speed dial number one was pretty much the only number he ever used.

Olis answered. "Hello, Aro?"

"I need to speak with you immediately."

"Of course. What's happening?"

"The film deal. What's the status?"

Olis didn't have the latest information, but he told Aro what he knew right now.

"If I'm going to put my performers through this, there will have to be some changes."

"What kind of changes?"

"It will not be a film adaptation of the play."

"What do you mean?"

"It needs to be a documentary."

"With respect, Aro, the producers will insist on—"

"They are missing the point!" Aro shouted. "There is a whole civilization down there, and nobody cares! It isn't entertainment! Millions of people live and die in the ocean, and it's time the land-dwellers saw it how it really is!"

Aro didn't even listen to the lapine's objections of how documentaries make only a fraction of what a high-budget spectacle production would earn. Aro cut him off.

"I'm tired of this machine between us. Please meet me."

Aro hung up. Immediately he dove into the pool and swam in circles. He felt like he was hunting again. Yes, he was supposed to chase the fish. He was the hunter. Not them.

Born to Die

By Nenekiri Bookwyrm

"Are you sure this is safe, Carl?" the very nervous hermit crab said.

"Absolutely not! You should know better than to ask me that by now, Sadie."

Carl was suspended over the end of a sheer cliff that dropped down to a deep dark part of the ocean. The view was giving Sadie a case of vertigo the more she stared into its inky blackness. Carl had a piece of seaweed tied firmly around his waist and looked confidently over the side of the cliff. He didn't seem fazed by the large drop at all. As a krill he was used to being in near death situations. Bungee jumping into the deep sea was nothing comparatively.

Sadie wasn't convinced though. Even though she'd known Carl for a long time, she could never get used to his insatiable appetite for danger. She had a hard time reconciling how he lived his life with all the imminent danger around him. To her, he was inviting trouble at every turn. She felt much better curled up inside her protective shell. In fact, the closer he got to the edge of the cliff, the more she unconsciously curled up inside her shell. Still, she kept her eye stalks uncovered so she could see what happened to Carl. As much as she hated to admit it, half of the reason she went along with Carl's ludicrous stunts was because they were immensely entertaining.

Carl secured the seaweed around his waist one last time with his many forelegs, winked at Sadie, and fell backwards over the edge of the cliff. Sadie couldn't help but let a gasp of bubbles out as he plummeted out of sight. She came out of her shell to scuttle up to the edge of the cliff, kicking up sand and debris in the process.

When the sand had settled back down on the seafloor, she leaned over the edge. It was hard to make anything out in all that blackness, but she did see one little blip of light traveling down, down, down. Carl was slightly bioluminescent. His natural green light was the only trace of him. But just before Carl's light got out of sight, another light joined him. This one was white and faint in the distance.

The seaweed line next to her started to gain slack at an incredible speed. The white light was getting brighter too, rapidly growing in size as it got closer.

Sadie pulled herself back from the edge right before a huge fish with rows of jagged teeth rocketed past her in a torrent of bubbles. Laughing the whole way was Carl, riding on top of the anglerfish by hanging on to the long dorsal spine at the top of its forehead. The anglerfish bucked up and down, trying to throw Carl off from its back, but he hung on tight.

The light on the end of the anglerfish's forehead bounced wildly around, leaving trails of bright light in its wake. Sadie would have been impressed with the laser light show if she hadn't been afraid of the anglerfish eating Carl.

"Get off that thing Carl! It's going to eat you if you're not careful!"

Carl's hooting and hollering drowned out Sadie's warning. The angler had enough of the bucking bronco bit and decided to change up its tactics and thrashed side to side. Carl managed to hang on, but his forelegs were starting to give out under the immense strain. The anglerfish wrenched its body to the right and Carl flew away. Sadie gasped.

The anglerfish spun itself around so it could face Carl and smiled. Well, it made whatever facial expression passed for a smile on an anglerfish's broad, toothy face. Carl didn't seem to have much of a reaction at all. If anything, he just seemed disappointed that his ride was over. He shrugged and crossed his front forelegs over his chest, daring the anglerfish to do his worst. The anglerfish opened its massive jaw, getting ready to lunge forward and bite down. Carl waved a quick "goodbye" with his right forelegs and shot straight backwards in a powerful stream of bubbles. When the anglerfish bit down, all it grabbed in its teeth was the seaweed line that Carl had slipped out of.

On his backward trajectory Carl crashed into Sadie's shell. Sadie poked her eyes out to glare at him. She seemed mad, but Carl couldn't tell why.

The anglerfish spit out the seaweed, scowled in their direction, and mumbled something before swimming back down into the depths.

Carl waited until the light faded from view before bursting out laughing.

"Did you see their face? Salt and silt, that was glorious. I haven't had that much fun since I played chicken with an electric eel."

Sadie had come all the way out of her shell by now and was looking worriedly toward the depths. She put a claw up to her mouth and squinted.

"You aren't worried about what the anglerfish said?"

Carl stopped laughing for a moment to reply. "I figure they just called me a name or something. Did you understand them?"

Sadie shrugged with her claws. "No, but it bothers me. Something about the way they said it creeps me out."

"I wouldn't worry about it," Carl replied.

"You never worry about anything," Sadie said.

"That's why we're such a good team!" Carl extended his antenna out to his sides dramatically, as if he was about to say something terribly important. "You worry enough for the both of us."

"Someone has to," Sadie said snidely.

Carl's whiskers drooped a little at her remark. He held his mandibles with one of his forelegs and thought a moment before saying, "I know what'll cheer you up. Let's go get some food. I found a new patch of algae up at the end of a shoreline not too far from here."

Sadie sat up on her legs a little at that. She did feel a bit peckish. Mortal danger had a tendency to make her appreciate a good meal more than usual as well. Her eyes lit up as she waved a claw through the water with a flourish.

"Lead the way!"

Carl and Sadie swam through the ocean for about an hour, with Carl stopping every so often to wiggle his antenna and adjust their course. It was during the fifth readjustment that Sadie decided to say something.

"Are you sure you know where you're going? I thought you said the place we were going to was close by?"

"It is close by, relatively speaking. The ocean is a big place after all! I just need to try and pick up the right current and we should be there shortly." He closed his eyes and twitched his antenna again, feeling the water shift underneath them. He held this pose for a few minutes, to Sadie's surprise. She hadn't seen him stand this still in years.

Sadie crossed her arms over her chest and huffed. "If I wanted to wait around for something to happen, I would have stayed back home in the hermit crab commune. Those old crabs never do anything fun."

Carl half-opened one of his eyes and said, "Trust me, I'm just finding us a faster route." His right antenna began to twitch and jiggle and Carl opened his eyes all the way. He motioned with his right forelegs over to Sadie.

"Can you move a smidge to the right?"

Sadie cocked her head to the side, wondering how that would possibly help them get to the food any faster. Out of curiosity more than compliance, she shuffled her legs along the ground until she was a few inches to the right.

"Like this?"

Carl turned around and nodded at her. There was a mischievous gleam in his eye that she didn't trust. Before she could say anything, he whipped back around and flung himself backwards into her claws.

"Hang on tight!" he shouted as an enormous yellow beak broke through the surface of the water above them.

Sadie had just enough time to reflexively curl into her shell before the seagull scooped her and Carl up. They quickly gained altitude as the seagull flapped its wings, making its way back to its nest. Carl hummed a song during the ride and seemed content with the seagull's occasional jostling when it would flap its wings to stay airborne. Sadie, on the other claw, was screaming.

"Oh, calm down. I can see the algae patch coming up in a few feet."

Sadie was too busy screaming to hear him or to notice as he scrambled up her shell towards the seagull. A beady yellow eye swiveled to look down at him, or rather attempted to look at him. Carl was quite small and the seagull was having trouble focusing on something so close.

The seagull tried to squint to focus on what Carl was doing, but by that point, he was already using his delicate antenna to tickle at the seagull's nostril. The seagull jerked a little in the air and lost some height as it stopped flapping for a second. It righted itself and managed to ease into a steady glide. Carl reached out and tickled it a second time, causing it to dive down further to the water. Carl kept an eye trained on the surface of the water and when he saw a patch of bright green floating on the surface, he tickled it for the third time. Immediately, he jumped back down onto Sadie's shell and grabbed onto one of her ridges. The seagull let out a sneeze that shot them both down into the ocean below.

They passed through the algae cloud in a spectacular shower of bubbles and drifted to the ocean floor covered in a thick green film. For a few seconds, everything was quiet. Then Sadie erupted back out of her shell with a desperate gasp.

"What were you thinking, sand for brains?" She waved her claws excitedly but snapped her mandibles in Carl's direction.

Carl drifted from around the back of her shell and waved his forelegs dismissively. He reached out for some of the green algae that had come off of Sadie's claw as she was gesticulating and started to chew on it.

"We weren't in any real danger. I had the whole situation under control."

Sadie's eyes just about rocketed off of her head at that comment. She stamped her feet and swished her shell, shedding more of the algae cloud in the process.

"Under control? That's what you call under control? We were outside the water Carl!"

"It's not really that big of a deal. I don't know why you're getting this upset."

Sadie put her claws above her head and said, "We can't breathe outside the water!"

"Well, you shouldn't have been screaming then. Terribly inefficient use of the air you did have."

Sadie held up a claw as if she was going to say something, and then let it drop back down. She thought for a moment and squinted her eyes at Carl before her mandibles returned to moving normally again.

"You wouldn't even understand if I could explain it to you."

She turned around and started shuffling back the way they came. Carl was busy eating some of the kicked off algae but stopped mid-bite to look over at Sadie.

"Hey, where are you going?"

Sadie didn't turn around but answered over her shell with, "I need a break. I'm going home. The long way this time."

Carl tried to swim in front of her to get her attention, but she shuffled away from him. He tried to clean some of the algae off of her shell, but she shook him off. After a few minutes of the cold shell from her, he finally got the hint and swam back over to the algae patch to finish eating.

By the time he was done eating, Sadie had made it over the nearest sand pile and was steadily getting further away. He wanted to go and say something to her, but knew that if he did, it would only make things worse. Even if he thought she was overreacting to his stunt from earlier.

So what if he couldn't absolutely guarantee that they wouldn't be eaten? Carl had to live without that guarantee every day. And he had to do it without a way to protect himself from predators.

He swam for a few days in no particular direction, just coasting on the currents with his thoughts. It'd been a long time since he was left with his thoughts without something to distract him. He didn't like it. Not one bit. The ocean felt too big for him.

While he would never admit it to her, Carl felt safer with Sadie around. She wasn't the biggest hermit crab, but she was bigger than Carl. And her shell helped to make Carl feel safer. He knew that she would be protected from whatever dangerous stunt he did, so he wound up doing more dangerous things as a result. But more than that, she had pulled his tail out of more riptides than he could count on his forelegs. Now that he was treading unfamiliar water all alone, he started to realize how much she cared about him staying safe. He knew with a horrible certainty that he wasn't treating her the same way she did him. He had to apologize.

Carl had a pretty strong idea where she might be, but it would take him the rest of the day to swim there. He needed to find a faster ride. He twitched his antennas and tried to feel out if something bigger was swimming in the nearby currents. He picked up on a few fish, a lobster, and a sea urchin. None of which were going to be fast enough. Then his left antenna nearly bent off his carapace as he picked up on something bigger. Much bigger. And more terrifying to Carl personally than anything else in the ocean. A blue whale.

It was approaching fast and he had to make a decision quickly. There was a short window where he could try and hop on, but his forelegs trembled at the thought of it. He'd seen whales eat entire clusters of krill in one gulp before. Was it really worth the risk just to make it up to Sadie? Would she even accept his apology after the way he acted?

He would never know if he didn't try. He steadied his forelegs, took a deep breath, and shot himself backwards into the current closest to the whale.

The current was massive. A huge channel of water that parted to the sides of the blue whale as it swam. Carl had entered close to the whale's midsection, hoping to avoid the large cavernous mouth at its front. He needed to find a spot where he could hang on without the water carrying him away. Unfortunately for him, the whale's skin was smooth. He didn't think his forelegs could grab and hold onto a surface like that for very long, let alone the time it would take to make it to Sadie. And with the speed he was traveling through the current, he didn't have time to be indecisive. He saw white specks on the edge of the tail as it raised up and flopped back down into the water. Carl was pretty sure he knew what those specks were and started swimming towards them.

He reached out all of his legs to grab it as it went past, nearly losing a few in the process. The wrenching motion wasn't great for his carapace, but he'd managed to hang on. The barnacle he'd grabbed onto didn't seem to mind him holding onto it. Either that or it didn't care. Carl thought it might have been the latter since they didn't seem to mind being dunked in and out of the water repeatedly.

He held onto the barnacle until he could see the shelf that led to the deeper sea that he and Sadie had been at just a few days ago. He wasn't sure if she'd go back there after his most recent stunt but was glad to be right.

Sadie sat on the edge of the shelf with her claws to her sides, staring out into the open ocean. Carl blinked. Now a massive tentacle rested on the shelf next to Sadie. Then another on her other side. The tentacle to her left swept inward, grabbing Sadie up in one fluid motion.

Carl's eyes went wide and he let go of the barnacle. The whale's tail came down, the current blasting him toward the shelf.

The giant squid's head was visible now, staring angrily with one giant eye at Sadie, completely wrapped in its tentacle. Sadie was fully curled inside of her shell as the other tentacles tried, and failed, to pull her out of it. The squid was the largest sea creature Carl had ever seen. Its head was easily as big as the shelf it crawled out of and the tentacles seemed to be able to reach across the entire sea floor. Next to the squid was the anglerfish, cackling at Sadie's misfortune.

The squid was getting tired of trying to pry Sadie out of her shell, so it opted for a different approach. It let the other tentacles fall away from her shell, then it slowly raised the remaining tentacle up and went to slam it directly into the ground.

"No!" Carl shouted, bursting into a sprint, swimming so fast he couldn't see with all the bubbles in his vision. He was aware of something behind him. Following him and gaining speed as he tried to make it to the giant squid in time. She had to be fine. He'd survived worse, she could too. She'd have to. How was he going to apologize if she didn't?

His thoughts were interrupted by a screech of pain so loud he veered sideways. The anglerfish that had been chasing after him was blown back as well. Whizzing past him was a familiar hermit crab shape. It bounced a few times on the seafloor before skidding to a stop next to a nearby outcrop of coral.

Carl shook his antenna a few times to get his bearings straight and swam over to her. Sadie was a little dazed from the fall but otherwise seemed to be fine. When her eye stalks adjusted to the ocean being level again, she squinted at him curiously.

"Did I hit my head that hard or are you really here Carl?"

Carl had a hard time keeping tears from his eyes, but he nodded a yes to her.

"How did you even get here so fast?"

"I found a blue whale going this way and hitched a ride."

"Salt and silt Carl! What would possess you to do that?"

"I wanted to apologize for the other day. You wouldn't be in danger if it wasn't for me."

Sadie put her claws together nervously and Carl could see a bit of squid tentacle hanging off the right one. "That's sweet Carl, but could we do this when we're not about to die?"

Carl desperately wanted to point out that he was always in danger of dying, but thought better of it. "Yeah, we can."

The anglerfish had come to its senses, and the squid's tentacles frantically combed the ocean floor for Sadie, stirring up the sand. She peered around the corner of the coral and then turned back to Carl.

"I have an idea of how to save our shells, but it's going to be dangerous. Are you up for it?"

Carl struck a dramatic pose with his forelegs holding his waist and his head held high. "I'm insulted you thought you needed to ask. What's the plan?"

Sadie pointed with her left claw over to the anglerfish, which was now swimming in frantic circles trying to find Carl in the swirling sand. "I need you to lure them over to the squid and shine the light through your body. Can you do that?"

"Yes, I can do that. Not sure what that'll accomplish but I'll lure them. What are you going to be doing?"

"I'll distract the squid and try to avoid the tentacles as long as I can. I don't know how much time that'll buy you, but hopefully it'll be enough. Good luck."

She scuttled out from the coral and waved her claws as she ran. The squid noticed almost immediately and waved its tentacles closer to her.

Carl peeked his head out from the coral to see where the anglerfish was, only to find it was barreling toward him. He jumped back as the sharp teeth sank into the other side of the coral, then swam directly for the squid. The anglerfish spat out the chunk of coral and followed after him. While the anglerfish could swim faster than Carl, he could outmaneuver it with his quicker reflexes. Each time the anglerfish was close to biting him, he would jet away and reposition to keep out of its range. He was almost to the squid when he saw Sadie get picked up by one of the tentacles again. If he was going to save her, it had to be now.

He stopped swimming and held out his legs as the anglerfish

swam past him. He grabbed onto the angler's light and wrapped himself around it as best he could. The light was intensely bright this close and he had to squint his eyes to keep from being overwhelmed.

The anglerfish thrashed, trying to pull it's lure back into its mouth. But every time it would go to pull Carl closer, he'd rocket his body away with a squirt of water, pulling the lure with it. It was a battle of stamina and Carl was close to his limit.

Through his squint he made out something very big swimming toward them and it all clicked. Sadie was using Carl's bioluminescence to bring the whale back. With the light shining through his body, it looked like a swarm of krill right next to the squid.

The anglerfish lunged at Carl once more. He pushed back, but didn't make it as far this time. The anglerfish bit down on Carl's left antenna. Pain exploded along the left side of his head and he fought back the urge to black out. He couldn't let go now, even if he was moments away from being eaten. If he could save Sadie, it'd be worth it.

His right antenna twitched. At first Carl thought it was a reflex from losing his other antenna. But then a massive wave hit the both of them as the blue whale and the squid collided. Carl was thrown out of the angler's mouth in time to see the squid's tentacles wrapping around the blue whale as the whale tried, and failed, to suck in the swarm of krill that had mysteriously disappeared.

The tentacles along the ocean floor pulled back toward the squid to deal with the blue whale and the angler had gotten caught up in one. As it squirmed around it shot a final glare at Carl before vanishing under the inky darkness of the shelf.

Carl found Sadie scuttling away as the squid and the whale fought behind them. He followed her until they both felt like they were a safe distance away from the chaos. They floated there for what seemed like hours before Sadie broke the silence.

"We made it," she said.

"Somehow, thanks to you," Carl replied.

Sadie brightened at that and ventured a bit out of her shell before noticing Carl's missing antenna. She winced a little before asking, "How are you feeling?"

Carl blew out some bubbles and said, "Exhausted, but alive. I'll find a way to manage with only one antenna. Though there's something I wanted to ask you."

"Sure, go ahead."

"Can you lead the way to the hermit crab commune? Boring and safe sounds really good to me right about now."

Dry Skin

By Kary M. Jomb

My skin is drying out. I can feel the withdrawal symptoms. I want to go back home and run a bath, lace the water with sim-dopa66, and soak, soak, soak up the delicious chemical through my salamander skin. Without the magic chemicals, I'm withering, drying up, shriveling like a water lily in the desert.

That's me. An orange-skinned water lily in a desert of fuzzy creatures ... bears, badgers, dogs, cats, weasels, ferrets, mice, moles, rats... They all have more in common with each other than I do with any one of them. They look at me, and no matter how many clothes I'm wearing, no matter how puffy my jacket, no matter how long my sleeves, how high my turtle neck, all they see is the naked skin of my spade-shaped face, my smooth jawline, the expanse of dimply skin between my eyes. It's all naked. No fur. I'll never fit in.

But I can't give up and go back to my apartment. I can't run that blessed bath. I flushed the last of my sim-dopa66 down the drain. I swore I'd get clean. I'd dry out. Hah. I hadn't realized how literal that would be. I know these symptoms will only last a few days, maybe a week or two, and then my body will readjust. But I feel like I'm dying without the sim-d. No amount of fancy almond cream or apricot body oil makes a difference. Natural products can't touch the deep dryness of my body screaming out for more sim-d.

My skin feels flaky, like it could fall right off, shedding like orangey-brown leaves falling from the trees in autumn, leaving me more naked than naked. Raw musculature; shining white bones. A skeleton covered in glistening red meat. That's all I am. Everyone else in this restaurant is coiffed in thick, luxurious, velvety fur. And I'm just meat.

But I let the ferret waiter guide me to the table. I gulp down the water, trying to fill my body with the moisture I can feel gone from my skin, but it sits in my belly like lead. I slurp up an ice cube from the sweaty wet glass, juggle it around inside my mouth, playing with it using my sticky tongue. Freezing my tongue; melting the ice. The beads of sweat from the glass feel like an affront on the dry skin of my bulbous fingers, making them feel only more raw. My skin doesn't absorb the moisture. Not like it should.

I hate withdrawal. Sim-dopa66 isn't the most dangerous drug, but it sure as hell ain't easy to quit. I know that if I can hold out long enough, my skin will regain its natural levels of moisture. But I don't think I can make it.

I'm seriously considering going home, selling my TV, and seeing if I can buy some more sim-d. Then I could bliss out for another week. My TV should buy that much. After a week of sheer joy, I'm sure I could find something else to sell. I think faster with sim-d zipping through my veins anyway. I'm sure there's a better solution than drying out. What was I thinking? Without sim-d, I'm nothing but a ball of nerves and raw skin, unable to think straight or enjoy anything. I'll never find a natural high. Only the chemicals work for me.

Then I look up, and I see my blind date is already here, another addict I met online and bonded with through the veil of a furry avatar, someone else trying to get clean. My spade-shaped jaw drops open when I see him. My skin-covered, furless spade of a jaw. Orange and raw. And dry. But I feel a tiny wellspring in my heart.

He is gorgeous. The roundness of his snout. The jaunty flip of his little ears. The fullness of his figure. And the bare, naked, pinkness of his skin. Bare and naked. Like me.

"Hi," he oinks and smiles at me.

Maybe I'll give this a try.

So, I say, "You're Greg? I'm Lily."

"Somehow, I could tell," Greg says, sitting down in the chair across from me."

I laugh nervously. Looking around the room, I can see what he means — everyone else is happily grouped together, tables of two, three, four, or even larger. Talking, eating, and not fidgeting restlessly with their water glass like they wish they could crawl inside it and melt into a liquid themselves.

"Have you been here before?" Greg asks.

I tell him that I haven't, but I've been studying the menu while waiting for him. It's sort of true. I did glance at the menu while trying to foist off my panic attack. To prove myself, I point to some of the things that look good — mostly artificial proteins and vegetable plates — and ask if he knows if they're good.

"My ex-boyfriend was a salamander," Greg says, "and he introduced me to this place." The handsome pig takes my menu out of my hands, turns it over, and points with his keratinous hoof-hand to a special on the back I hadn't seen. "This was his favorite."

Candied flies and roasted earthworms. That does sound delicious, like it was designed exactly for me. "So few places serve dishes like this..." I don't say, "with actual dead animals." Sure, they're only flies and earthworms, but there was a time when pigs and salamanders weren't considered so differently.

I put the menu down, tilt my head, and stare at Greg as he studies his own menu. When he puts it down and smiles at me, I say, "So, ex-boyfriend?"

He shrugs. "Yeah, I'm bi."

"Cool," I say. "But... salamander?"

He shrugs again. "We furless species are... way overrepresented on... um... you know, the forums where we met. No matter what avatars we might choose to hide behind."

"That's true," I admit, trying not to see it as a red flag that Greg has dated a salamander before. There aren't that many of us in this city. It'd be weird if he was seeking us out.

Wouldn't it be?

Or maybe that's just the paranoia side-effect caused by coming down from sim-d.

Greg and I order — the special for me, and a vegetable plate for him — and settle into the awkward conversational dance of getting to know each other as real live people, who have to say words with our clumsy tongues, and think of them on the spot, instead of carefully crafting blocks of text to each other over the course of days, polishing and refining them like diamonds.

It's a struggle, and yet, I feel more comfortable with Greg than most people, even people I've known a long time. He seems okay with the awkward silences, and he grunts appreciatively at everything I say, like he gets it, really deep down inside of him, he gets it.

By the time our plates are empty, I'm starting to feel terror at the idea of this blind date ending. What if I'm mis-reading everything, and he'll actually be relieved to get away? What if Greg makes everyone feel comfortable, and I make everyone uncomfortable... so, of course I like him, but it doesn't mean anything about how he feels about me.

Greg draws a deep breath, sighs it out, and I can hear the words ready to come: goodbye, see ya later, so long, catch ya on the forums. And then we go back to being blocks of text, and I never get to touch his pink, nearly glowing skin.

"You don't get out much, do you?" Greg says.

My eyes widen. I know my spade-shaped face looks especially uncanny when they do that, so I try to stop it. How did he see right through me?

He puts a hoof up and says, "That's not a condemnation. I just mean... you seem uncomfortable."

I don't know what to say to that, but it makes the burning, flaky feeling all over my skin so much worse, and I think he can tell I'm stumped for words, because he goes on:

"Can I take you somewhere? It's kind of underground... well, not literally, but it seems like a lot of people don't know about it. And I think you'd like it."

I nod, mutely. All I want right now is for this date to keep going on... or maybe to run away, sell my TV, and bliss out in a bathtub of sim-dopa until I die. That might be easier.

But letting Greg take me by the hand, lead me out of the restaurant, and onto a subway train heading to Little Oceania is more exciting. His skin is warm in a way mine isn't, also in a way that fur never can be. The warmth is part of the skin, radiating out from the blood rushing underneath. There's no layer of fur between his skin and mine. Creatures covered in fur can never feel this close, not just by holding hands.

Sure, they might have paw pads, little islands of skin in their great grasslands of fur. But it's not the same. Greg's bare arm presses against mine in the crowd on the subway train, the smooth concavity of the inside of his elbow, the length of his forearm.

When we get off the train, I feel like we've been flirting indecently in such a public place, even though we were just holding hands.

Having bare skin doesn't feel so bad when I'm not the only one.

And when someone else seems to want to touch it.

It feels less like a mark, a brand, something that screams to the world: there's something wrong and different about this one!

Greg leads me through the streets of Little Oceania, a small and strange part of town. Many of the windows here are filled with aquariums; sea green water behind them bends the view in the wavery way that water has. Light from inside the buildings falls on the concrete outside in dappled, twisting ways. I start to wonder whether the windows are filled with aquariums, or if that's just the inside of the buildings. Are the buildings here all filled with water?

"I've always been curious about Little Oceania," I say, quietly, not wanting to sound like a rude tourist to the sea animals we keep passing — mostly otters, seals, and sea lions in rolling chairs. Fuzzy mammals, just like everywhere else. Though, there are sharks, dolphins, and fish too. Some of them using wheelchairs; others have prosthetic legs. I think, there are more creatures with furless skin here than elsewhere.

"Oh yeah?" Greg says. "Why haven't you checked it out?"

"It didn't seem like it was for me," I say, peering through the windows we pass as intently as I can while seeming casual. I'm almost certain I'm not pulling "casual" off, and my anxiety starts to sky rocket, like a buoy when you try to pull it deep under water, and it just screams to go flying back up to the surface.

But for me, the surface would be my own apartment. And that bathtub. The one that's empty.

These buildings aren't empty. I see shapes behind the windows — figures moving in the shadowy depths of the water. Could Greg and I even go into these buildings? Or would we drown? If I pulled open one of the doors, would water come rushing out onto the street while sharks and seahorses yelled at me in squeaky underwater languages?

95

"I think... I'm getting tired," I say. "Maybe I should just go home."

Being here feels like a punishment for wishing my skin didn't feel so dry. Now there's water everywhere — too much, and also, too out of reach.

"Just one more block," Greg says. "Then you'll see what we're here for."

So, I hold his hand for another block, and we arrive at the unimpressive entrance to a community rec center. There's a banner hung over the double front door with bright blue, cursive writing, surrounded by wavy lines, presumably to represent ocean waves. The banner says: "Welcome to the Undersea Ball!"

A smaller banner in a more plain font underneath reads, "Every 1st and 3rd Tuesday of the Month. All welcome."

"Undersea Ball?" I ask, voice getting embarrassingly squeaky. "A party?"

I stop walking, and since Greg keeps walking toward the door to the rec center, he ends up pulling on my hand.

"Oh, come on," he says, when he see my reluctance. "You said you were worried about not belonging, but look!" He points at the banner with his free hand. "All welcome! Also, how could you belong here less than me? I'm a pig. You don't get much more landlubber than that. Salamanders at least lived in creeks and ponds originally."

"Have you been here before?" My voice is less squeaky now, but quavers in a way I don't like. Almost gravelly, rough with all the feelings I'm trying to hide. Or contain. Shove down and swallow until they don't exist.

If only I could let my feelings swirl down the bathtub drain like I did with my stash of sim-dopa...

Greg is talking, and I try to shake the thoughts — the cravings — of sim-dopa out of my head and focus on his words. He's telling me stories about all the times he's come to this Undersea Ball. I can't focus on much of it, but his snout is really cute, and he's trying to coax me. Imagine that. A good-looking, well-adjusted pig like *him* is trying to coax *me*.

It almost makes me feel like I'm worth something.

Then I remember that I met this guy on a sim-dopa forum in the first place, and he's just as much of an addict-loser as I am.

But somehow, he's getting by okay.

He's walking around town, going to parties, and making it through entire dates without trying to run home and sell his TV.

Maybe... there's something to this rec center party, if he believes in it so wholeheartedly. Because through the fog of my panic and cravings and anxiety and longing, I have managed to piece together that Greg is saying he finds this party helps him stay off of sim-dopa somehow.

Somehow.

I don't see how. But... Giving it a try is better than any of the strategies I've been using. Especially because I've run out of strategies. So, I relax into the gentle tug on my hand, and I let Greg pull me inside, through those double doors.

The rec center is one of the few buildings around here without water right behind the windows. Crepe paper in shades of blue flutters along the hallway walls, just below the ceiling. We follow the crepe paper. I hear echoey noise up ahead. When we get to the end of the hall and Greg opens the door, I see a standard rec center swimming pool. That's why the sound echoed so badly. Something about the water just works that way.

But all around the pool, there are bouncy castles and inflatable water slides set up. There are tables laid out with food and fliers — the fliers look like they've been laminated to protect them from the water. Everything is wet, and everyone is splashing. The pool is filled with more of the kinds of animals we saw outside walking the streets of Little Oceania, but also a random cow, a couple chickens hanging out with a group of ducks, and even a lion with his mane done up in braids. He's standing in the middle of the pool, splashing his big paws against the surface of the water more than anyone else. It looks like the braids are meant to keep his long wet fur from hanging in his eyes.

"The lion's named Bruno," Greg says. "He comes every month. Says he's a sea lion now."

"Is that..." I don't know if I want to ask if it's weird or offensive or what. I just don't know what to make of any of this.

Greg shrugs. "None of the actual sea lions seem to mind. They throw this party to draw us landlubbers in." Greg looks at me and adds, "Well, not necessarily landlubbers. I still think you're at least halfway to being an ocean animal."

I point at the tables of food. I'm not hungry after the delicious dinner, but I ask, "Is the food good?"

"Oh, it's the best. I don't usually eat before coming here." Greg looks down at his hind hoofs, his pink cheeks growing pinker. "But, you know, tonight was kind of special."

"Yeah?" I ask

"Yeah," he says. "I mean, wasn't it?"

"I guess so," I say. "I'd been really looking forward to meeting you."

"Me too," he says. "Talking to you these last few months... it's been the only thing that's kept me from... you know, going back. Well, you and—" He gestures around us. "This."

I stare at the chaos around us, and I feel the chaos inside myself subsiding. There are dolphins and sharks swimming circles in the pool, just under the surface. A pair of seahorses are sitting on deck chairs by the edge, their long, curving tails draped into the water. Under the noise of voices and splashing water, I hear strains of music, and I look over to see a band made up of lizards, a river otter, and a pufferfish playing waterproof instruments.

This time, I lead Greg, and we go over to the edge of the pool. I sit down and dangle my feet in the water, and he sits down beside me, still holding my hand.

The water feels cool and soothing, completely natural, and his hand feels warm. My skin still itches from my withdrawal, but there's too much joy here for me to pay attention to it.

Greg points out everyone. He seem to know them all by name, and a little bit of each of their life stories. He's a really friendly guy. Even his ex, the other salamander, is here, and they seem to still be friends. There's a whole community here that I never knew about. That I would have been too afraid to try on my own. I'd have never walked through those double doors and down that long hallway alone, without Greg's hoof holding my hand.

But now I'm here.

And I can feel the currents in the water from the dolphins and sharks swimming by, pulling me, teasing me, asking me to jump in. Get to know people. Try out this place

"Next time," I say, "we should bring swimsuits."

"Oh, absolutely," Greg agrees. "Swimming here is the best." And then the smile under his snout grows really wide, making his cheeks as round as apples, when he realizes I've just said there'll be a next time.

The Net

By Kittara Foxworthy

"Ss'ook, wait up!" Coral called over the growing rumble of a far off engine as she raced behind her cousin. "Just because you're bigger than I am doesn't mean you can leave me behind." She sounded whiny but she couldn't help it. Patrolling the area surrounding a school of yellowfin tuna that the clan had been farming was boring work. These fish, almost ready for culling when the mature were separated from the young to feed the clan and its allies, showed little likelihood they would try to separate and make their guards have to chase them back together. It was a moonless night but that didn't matter to her or any of the other calves. She could find the fish even in the blackest of waters. Through all the songs and sounds that traveled kilometers through the depths she could track down a single fish if she wanted to.

Coral, at thirteen years old, was on the cusp of puberty. She was one of the new special dolphins that had been given hands and feet by human scientists. Over four decades ago her granddam, Kelp, was the first dolphin born with the modifications. In addition to hands and feet, they had longer flippers with joints they could lock into place at the shoulder, elbow and wrist. Their flukes were split into two legs with the same kind of lockable joints at the ankle, knee and hip. There were still dolphins like her older male cousin Ss'ook who had the original body type. Ss'ook took out his disappointment on Coral every chance he got.

He kept swimming ahead of her, showing no signs of slowing down.

"Ss'ook, please, you're supposed to be showing me how to herd. Not showing off how much bigger and faster you are."

Her reminder of his duty only seemed to annoy the older dolphin. He surfaced, then did a long dive down to check out the lower edges of the school. Coral rose to the surface. There was no moon tonight. No light anywhere to be seen — not that it mattered to a dolphin. She took a deep breath to follow him, and noticed as she inhaled that there was something foul in the air. There had been a subtle rumble in the water for some time now that didn't belong with all the songs of the other sea creatures. It could just be one of the big cruise ships whose engine noise could be heard from kilometers away. Besides, any ship that was on the water was required to have running lights so it wouldn't accidentally run into another ship.

Before she could dive more than a few meters, something dark was thrown into the water. It spread out around her, moving fast, partially circling the school then pulling it along. Coral tried to swim free but the tuna started to panic and she couldn't get past all their shining silver bodies.

Suddenly Ss'ook was there on the other side of the net, for net it was.

"Coral! I'll get you out!" His words were rushed with panic — they'd all heard what happened to dolphins who'd been caught in fishing nets from the time they were babies. "Just hold on!" He started frantically chewing at the fibrous rope the humans used to make the huge nets strong enough to pull tons of fish out of the water in one haul. He grabbed a hold of the net and pulled back as hard as he could with all his might, but it didn't stop. It didn't even slow down, pulling Coral along with the fish.

She grabbed onto the rope with her hand-like flippers and hooked her foot-like flukes through lower down to hold herself stationary. Dolphins didn't have the same kind of hands that humans had: theirs folded back to the side so that when their fingers were pressed together they made an almost seamless curve at the end of their wrists. This made grasping the net a little difficult, and her grip was tenuous at best. The fish around her were panicking as they realized they were caught, swimming every which way, bodies pressing against each other and Coral so hard that it was nearly impossible to speak.

Ss'ook bit at the rope over and over but dolphin teeth weren't meant to tear things, and all he could manage was to push the fibers apart a little. When he let up the holes closed as if he'd never bitten the rope at all. Frustrated he tried a piercing whistle that was supposed to scatter the tuna but it just made them more frantic, shoving against Coral even harder.

Three more dolphins appeared beside Ss'ook — most of the others in the herding team. The eldest, Conch, another special, wasn't with them.

"How did Coral get inside there?"

"What are you doing? You know you can't get her out!"

"It's no good, Ss'ook! You can't free her. Conch sang to go back and get help!"

Coral couldn't tell which of them was talking, since she was too busy trying to avoid getting tuna fins in her eyes.

"Go then!" Ss'ook sang. "I can't leave her! She's my cousin!" Ss'ook's cool was starting to crack, letting the fear he felt start to seep out.

"How'd she get in there? We just thought the tuna were in danger. Is there any way we can get her out?" Stingray sang.

"You know as well as I do that there are only a few ways to get her out and we can't manage any of them on our own! Go get help!" His song had a discordant sound to it now, showing the fear that she knew he was trying to hide from her.

"We'll hurry! Conch stayed up near the surface, he's using that knife he carries to try and cut through the anchor rope on one side of the net." Then they were gone, leaving her with Ss'ook and the panicked tuna.

Coral could hold her breath for quite some time, fifteen minutes under normal circumstances, but with the added pressure of the fish shoving her into the net and her fear of dying it was being forced out of her faster than usual.

"Can you get to your knife to use it?" Ss'ook asked her, trying to sound calm though she could tell he was just as frightened as she was.

She let go with her right hand but couldn't move it. The fish pushing at her forced her hand and flipper right through a hole in the net.

"Do that with your other flipper, maybe once they're free of the net you can get it loose." It was a good suggestion so she pushed her left hand and flipper through the netting. She could just reach the little knife strapped to her left flipper. She managed to unfasten the snap that held it in place but it slipped out of the sheath and spiraled silently downward in the water.

"Wait here, I'll get it," Ss'ook sang, diving fast after the disappearing piece of metal.

Kelp and her squad were just heading toward their assigned patrol to relieve the six who'd stood the last eight-hour shift, when the calves' song for help reached them. They came barreling into the midst of their elders out of breath and frightened to the point that they were blowing spouts of water up from their blowholes when they breathed.

They all sang at once so it was hard to make out who was singing what, the calves not having settled into their individual songs yet. "The net came out of nowhere!" "Conch sang to come get help!" "Poor Coral's going to die!"

"Hush!" Kelp's voice rose above the babbled terror and quieted them. "Where?" She was one of the oldest matriarchs of the clans and respected as such. Her single question calmed them enough to get a coherent answer from the eldest.

"The yellowfin tuna school," Stingray, one of the two special calves in the trio, answered.

Kelp nodded her head a few times, then addressed her squad. "Cuttlefish, take the calves back to the clan. The rest of you, you're with me." Having given her orders, she surfaced and began racing along the top of the water, leaping and diving to gain speed. Behind her the four remaining members of her squad followed in her wake. Every third dive or so she sent out a location signal to maintain a course for the school and the boat that was above it.

They weren't far, that was a mercy. Legal trawlers that fished outside the Eastern United States coastal waters tended to stay along the edges of dolphin territory, ever since their government had begun levying fines and impounding ships for infractions. These fishermen had invaded far inside those borders, where the calves should have been safe. In the space of four kilometers they came upon the scene. With its running lights off the boat was nearly invisible in the moonless night. It looked in bad repair: Kelp could feel the acrid sting of gas on the water as she came up behind it and the oily film that was spreading out from it when she was still five kilometers out.

"Arame, go under and see how Coral is, let her know we're going to help. Cod, Pearl, circle under and come up on the far side. Tarpon, stay close." She headed toward the ladder that extended almost all the way into the water on the nearer side of the boat; in the darkness, she found it only through echolocation. The boat was one of the big mostly automated ones that only required a crew of five, the same kind that the dolphins usually sent their schools into the nets of when it was time to harvest the fish. A small jump had her grasping the lower rungs and pulling her considerable bulk up. The rungs were rusty and slippery with built-up algae. One of the modifications the original dolphin scientists had requested was additional muscle mass in the arms and legs to compensate for the size of a dolphin body as compared to a human. That extra strength came in handy now as she scrambled up the loose metal rungs of the ladder.

Kelp was halfway up the side of the boat when she felt it rock gently, telling her one of the other three was also making the ascent. She paused at the top of the railing, looking over the side to see that four humans were standing around a winch at the back of the boat. A quick check and she saw the back of another standing in the control booth at the top. When Cod waved to her from the far side of the boat, she slid up over the railing and motioned Tarpon to head up into the control booth.

Purchasing that old fishing boat a few years back had been a blessing. Now almost all of the special dolphins could pilot a water craft of any kind, which made dealing with these humans that much easier. They could just tie them up and cart them back into their own waters, leaving them for the Coast Guard to deal with. Much as Kelp wanted to take a personal hand in dealing with their punishment she knew it was a bad idea for her to do anything else.

Cod began moving toward the humans when Kelp did, leaving Pearl to bring up the rear as they approached. With their larger size and odd shape they would look like looming figures in the dark, something that had helped them in the past when dealing with poachers. Humans were frightened of things that lived in the darkness; it had something to do with their poor night vision and lack of echolocation.

Usually when they found a poacher in their waters they tried to talk to them and if that didn't work they contacted the Coast Guard to come and deal with them. But with Coral caught in the tuna net they didn't have time for niceties.

Kelp pulled the small dart gun from the holster on her left fluke and shot the first of the fishermen in the back of his neck with a paralytic-laced dart. He fell to the deck like a stone. Cod and Pearl took out two more but the fourth rushed toward her as if he could knock her off the boat. Without thinking, she lowered her bulk, presenting her side to him, and let him hit her. He slid on her still-wet skin and fell over the railing into the midnight black water.

Two soft clicks from the control booth told her that Tarpon had taken out the human at the helm. The human in the water started screaming and thrashing around, making more noise than a playful calf.

"Cod, make sure there aren't any more. Pearl, tie these up so they don't get any ideas when they can move again." She moved to the hauler's net controls and shut off the lift. Then she threw it into reverse, unspooling the thick cable back down into the water. "When you have these taken care of, fish that other from the sea and tie him up as well." She spared a moment's thought for what her grandcalf was going through. "You don't have to be gentle about it either."

She took a deep breath and dove over the side back into the ocean. She found Conch first. "It's over, youngling." Kelp had to take the knife from him before he'd stop sawing at the rope. He'd made a fair dent in it, though he would never have gotten all the way through before the rope was hauled above the water. "You will be honored for your strength and bravery. Come now. It's time to set the tuna free." She led him down toward the other three dolphins at the back of the net. The tuna, with nothing holding them back, had begun to swim free on their own. She could only hope they were in time.

Arame heard them coming and whistled a position signal. Kelp swam faster, leaving Conch behind to catch up to her. As she reached the back of the net she saw Ss'ook waiting with Arame, watching the thick strands of rope.

"She's holding her place on the net but the fish are still pressing against her," Arame reported.

"So why don't you just clear the fish?" Kelp asked, watching Ss'ook and knowing that he needed to do something to help save his cousin, even though it wasted precious moments.

"I... don't know how to do that," Arame responded. He'd never been on herd detail as a calf, she remembered.

Ss'ook's eyes widened and he let out a piercing blast of sound that startled the tuna and made them all dart away from him. Now Coral was visible inside the net, her hands curled around the rope as if she held to life itself. There were still too many fish around her for her to swim up and out.

"Coral, you need to let go. Climb up the net. One hand over the next." Kelp kept her voice soothing, reaching out to touch the calf on the hand. She had to keep Coral calm so the calf didn't try to inhale while she was still underwater. "Let go with this hand, then reach up." She could see the net falling and she feared that it would come down around the girl and pull her into the depths.

As Pearl and Cod joined them, it only took a few heartbeats for them to see the problem; they swam up to the top of the net and tried to hold it straight so it wouldn't fold over the calf.

Coral shook like a tree in a hurricane, her grip on the net growing less sure each time she reached up to grasp it again. It was understandable: she'd just been nearly crushed to death by the weight of the tuna pressing against her. Kelp stayed with her while Arame, Conch, and Ss'ook, who still needed to be doing something to free his cousin, went up to help hold the net upright as it sank down between Kelp and Coral.

The smaller dolphin followed her granddam's instructions mechanically, lifting one hand and moving it higher before lifting the other, like she was climbing a ladder. It took too long for Kelp's liking to free her: Coral was going to breathe in soon, even if they didn't get her out of the water. It was slow going with the weight of the net drawing it down and Coral lifting herself higher. As soon as the tuna cleared out, Kelp was over the net and pulling Coral upward.

As they breached the surface, Ss'ook joined them, helping to support Coral's weight on one side as Kelp held her up on the other.

"Breathe, Coral," Kelp directed, waiting while the calf took a few gasped breaths, shooting water up a half meter from her blowhole. It was a good thing Kelp had arms and hands, Coral was so exhausted from her ordeal that she kept wanting to slip below the water again. Only Kelp's strong grip on the calf kept her from the same fate the net would have caused if she hadn't been freed.

Ss'ook wasn't helping things much. He trembled almost as badly as his cousin, his breathing just as ragged. Kelp had her hands full just keeping the pair of them afloat so they didn't drown themselves now that the danger had passed. She wanted to ask Ss'ook what had happened but she held her tongue. He would sing when he was ready, just like Coral.

Arame surfaced beside Kelp, holding Coral's knife. He nodded at Ss'ook. "He was holding this in his mouth, trying to saw through the net to get her out." He passed the small knife to Kelp then dove again heading down to make sure the net didn't take too many of the tuna with it.

Dipping her head under the water, Kelp sent out a long-range signal asking Ss'ook and Coral's mothers to come to them. The calves would need the emotional support of their dams after this. Besides, she still had work to do.

Her message told the cows they were urgently needed, so that they didn't take their time getting to her. Each brought along another dolphin to help guard the calves as Kelp had requested.

"Coral was caught in a tuna net that shouldn't have been here and Ss'ook stayed with her trying to cut her free. They need you right now." She brushed her rostrum against each of her daughters. "Cod, you're with me."

She swam back to the side of the fishing trawler, confident that Arame would take Conch back when the net was too deep to cause any more harm. By the time she returned to the clan the news would have spread through the entire Atlantic. This was an incident that wouldn't soon be forgotten. She'd have to be careful how she handled it.

Again she climbed the ladder. This time the lights were all on: from the forecastle to the stern, the craft was lit up like the stars above in the cloudless sky. Tarpon was still at the controls but he'd changed the boat's course to head toward the closest port known to have a Coast Guard presence that, if not friendly, was at least on good terms with the dolphins. That was standard operating procedure when they captured a craft that was fishing in their waters. Cod also climbed aboard the craft, standing over the prisoners in the back while Kelp stood at the prow like the bowsprit of a ship.

The three dolphins took turns diving back into the ocean to keep their skin wet on the long journey back toward land. No more than half an hour in the wind would start to make their skin slough off. They each took a final dive outside the harbor before Tarpon guided the boat to the mooring that he was assigned by the harbor master. The Coast Guard met them at the dock.

Kelp took a small black device on a long elastic band out of the pocket on her right flipper cover. She slipped the band over her head as she leaned over the railing to greet the humans.

"We found something that belongs to you." The small device on the side of her head translated her remarks mechanically into English, the dominant language on this side of the Atlantic. Her song sounded discordant to her ears without the diffusing effect of the water.

"I see that," Buster Cobbler replied. He was a large round man with dark hair in a uniform with the fancy decorations she knew indicated a Captain. "I take it they were out where they shouldn't have been?"

Kelp nodded her head. "Yes, the boat was trawling in our waters with no lights showing. I believe that is illegal by your laws. This time in addition to taking fish they were not entitled to, they nearly crushed one of our calves in the process." Buster was a good human who had treated them fairly in all their past dealings, so she felt no apprehension about passing these monsters off into his hands.

One of the fishermen behind her, able to speak now that the drug had worn off, gasped, then swore viciously. She heard a thumping sound that was likely Cod kicking the human into silence.

The humans on the dock started looking at each other with wide eyes. Finally Buster asked, "Is the calf alright?"

Kelp made them wait, knowing that it would only increase the uneasiness. Before the Atlantic and Pacific oceans had become recognized members of the world nations in their own rights, humans had had a taste of what it would be like to lose the sea and do battle with the special dolphins.

All it had taken was a group of scientists offering this new modification technology to a team of dolphins they'd been working with to break the language barrier. Once the special dolphins began breeding true on their own, it had been a simple step from there to removing unwanted crafts from their waters. Most of the coastal nations had been understanding, taking these infractions seriously. However China and Japan hadn't subscribed to the initial program and resented having their use of the ocean dictated to them by 'fish'. Tensions rose, lines were drawn, alliances made, and the inevitable war began.

Bringing herself back to the here-and-now, Kelp studied the effect her silence had had on the group of humans below her on the dock. Satisfied that they were sufficiently worried about her answer to come down on her side in this little mess, she pushed herself up off the railing to stand straight above them.

"The calf will live. However it will be some time before she heals of the injuries she suffered both physically and mentally. It could have been much worse." Kelp let her words have the desired effect.

"The yellowfin tuna school this crew was after was one of our farms. It is almost ready for harvesting. In another few days we would have herded some of them into one of your lawful trawler's nets. Now the school is scattered and it will take a week to gather them back together." Her skin was starting to feel dried out; she needed to get back into the water soon.

"A detailed description of this ship and crew will be circulated through the clans. If it is found in our waters again you will not be coming to the docks to take charge of it." The small device at her neck did nothing to convey the menace she wished she could imbue those words with. Maybe that was why China and Japan didn't take the Pacific dolphins seriously. The emotions behind their words weren't clear to the human ear. She heard two splashes on the far side of the craft and knew that Cod and Tarpon were safely out of harm's way.

The human behind her swore again. Those in front of her paled a little but the captain nodded. "Can I come aboard and take charge of the prisoners? I'll see to it myself that they are held accountable to the extent of our laws, including endangering a minor." Buster reached out to touch one of the lower rungs of the ladder.

"Certainly. Once I leave them in your custody I may return to my clan to be sure my grandcalves are well. Take care, the rungs are not sturdily attached to the hull." She backed away from the ladder, letting the large man climb onto the boat. "The criminals are secured there." She motioned with a flipper at the group of men, their backs to each other surrounding the winch stand.

The large human bowed his head slightly. "Thank you Matriarch." He then added, "Did I understand correctly that there was more than one calf affected and that they are your grandcalves?"

Kelp nodded even as she made her way across the boat toward the far side where her people were waiting for her. "You did. There were six calves guarding the school. The one that was caught in the net is my granddaughter. My grandson stayed with her, as did another, while the remaining three went to get help." She thought she saw compassion in Buster's eyes but it was hard to tell things like that in a human face. Her skin was really itching now and she could feel bits of it starting to slough off. "Is there anything more you need from me?" She lifted her hands to the band that held the translator in place.

"No, no, that's everything. Thanks again for bringing this to our attention." Several more humans in the same uniform were on the boat now, with another coming up the ladder.

"Then I will take my leave of you." Deftly, she folded up the elastic band and put the little device into its pocket.

The man who had been in the control cabin started talking.

"It's been eating puffer fish!" An allusion to the intoxicating effect of the fish on dolphins. He spat on the deck. "You can't trust a word they say. We was in our waters b'law."

"Was your transceiver on?"

"S'broken."

"We'll be checking on that. You know if you're running without a transceiver you're running illegal anyway."

He spat again, "An' there weren't no calf in the net! They was wild fish!" He would have gone on but the captain cleared his throat.

"I'd shut up if I was you. They have quite good hearing and that device is so we can understand them, not so they can understand us." He waited while Kelp finished tucking away the device and dove into the waters below. When her head breached the water she could hear him again.

"... wouldn't expect to get your boat back, and your license is also forfeit."

"You're gonna take the word of a fish?" the belligerent man from the control booth said.

"If you ask me you're lucky to be alive. They've been know to sink ships caught poaching repeatedly. Imagine what they'd have done if you killed the calf."

Plenty of Fish in the Sky

By Daniel Lowd

They say there's plenty of fish in the sea, but Murkfin had to disagree. Strongly. Sure, there were *many* fish in the sea. No one was contesting that. But plenty? That's a matter of perspective. The sad truth was that most fish in the sea had at least one of the Four Fishy Flaws:

1. Too difficult to catch. Murkfin was a capable shark and could swim well enough, but she had better things to do than race around the reef all day, exhausting herself in pursuit of a swimmy snack.
2. Too small to be worth the trouble. Murkfin wanted fish she could really sink her teeth into. All of her teeth. Some fish would barely merit a single tooth, and Murkfin could never decide *which* tooth.
3. Too unpalatable to enjoy. Like most sharks, Murkfin had a sensitive nose for smelling out prey from miles away. Unlike most sharks, Murkfin had a refined sense of taste and refused to eat fish that were too bitter, too salty, too stringy, too sour,

or even too fishy.

4. Too friendly to kill. That would include Sully, the remora that followed her everywhere. It was kind of pathetic, really, but she had to admit she appreciated his company. Well, she had to admit it to herself. No need to admit it to Sully. He was enough of a pest already without any extra encouragement.

So, no, there were not "plenty" of fish in the sea. In fact, the sea was a great big watery disappointment. Murkfin expected more. Murkfin demanded more. And as a great white shark, Murkfin believed it was her birthright to get what she wanted.

"Nice ocean, isn't it?" Sully rarely had anything important to say, but somehow that never stopped him from saying it.

Murkfin took the bait. "It's the *only* ocean, Sully. Nice or not, it is what it is." She didn't mean to encourage his inane banter by responding. Some days she managed to hold her tongue for hours. Alas, the silence never made Sully more clever or interesting.

"But it is nice. I think it's nice." Sully's enthusiasm for water could not be dampened.

On a typical day, this conversation could proceed in four different directions:

1. A Sully monologue. A more sophisticated fish would have an internal monologue, but for this simple remora, every passing thought became external.

2. A Sully dialogue. When Sully was of two minds about something, he could argue with himself for hours. Neither mind ever won.

3. Murkfin attempting to change the topic. If she was going to talk to Sully, she may as well discuss something more interesting than, say, the subjective quality of the ocean.

4. A distraction. This was the preferred option, when the conversation was interrupted by something more interesting or important. And almost everything was more interesting and important than Sully.

Today was not a typical day. Murkfin stopped swimming and spun around to face the little suckerfish, who had been shadowing her like an irritating ray of sunshine.

"It is what it is," Murkfin expounded, continuing the conversation in spite of herself. "But... what if it weren't what it is? What if it were what it *isn't* instead?"

"What if the ocean weren't nice? Well, gosh, I've never considered that." Sully's bug-eyed face twisted slightly as he attempted to think the unthinkable.

"No, Sully — what if the ocean weren't the ocean at all?" Murkfin paused for dramatic effect. "What if we stop living in this ocean and make the sky above into our new ocean — a new ocean full of possibilities, full of promise, full of... fish!"

"You really think there's fish up there in the sky?"

"Yes, Sully. Tasty fish. Fat, juicy fish. Fish who just wait around for sharks to bite. The sky is full of them."

"Wow, I never knew." Sully's face twisted in a different direction, trying to process this new information, information that was somehow easier to process than the idea that the ocean wasn't nice.

"Think about it, Sully. In a just world, there should be delicious fish for me to eat — plenty of them, in fact." Murkfin had never heard of theology but had begun to derive an ontological argument for the existence of perfect fish. If fish could exist in Murkfin's mind, then why not the sky?

"And yet," she continued, "I have been swimming the oceans for twenty years, and I have yet to find plenty of fish. And do you know why?"

"Are they hiding?"

"Why yes, Sully, in a manner of speaking, I suppose they are." She would have offered a patronizing smile if her face were capable. "But the best fish in the ocean could never hide from me in the ocean. No, they're hiding in the sky. The sky! It's the only explanation."

"Wow, I never knew." Sully's face relaxed as he gave up on processing the information and returned to his regular swimming.

"Now all we need is a way to swim into the sky and eat them."

Like most sharks, Murkfin had never built an airship. In fact, she had never built much of anything. Her body already included all the tools she needed for normal shark life — teeth, fins, gills, more teeth, nose, eyes, and even more teeth. You can't have too many teeth.

But if Murkfin had ever been an ordinary shark, she certainly wasn't one now. She was a shark with a mission. And so she devised a plan, a plan to build a flying machine. She just needed four elements:

1. A portable ocean. Murkfin knew enough about air to know that it was lacking something critical — water. She would have to bring the water with her. It took a week of searching, but Murkfin found a discarded shell from a giant clam big enough to hold her. And Sully. Sully could come, too. She needed someone to witness her triumph.

2. A lift mechanism. Murkfin had always considered birds to be fools for living outside the ocean, but in light of her new mission, she had to reconsider. Birds were fools, to be sure, but not for living in the sky — instead, they were fools for diving into the ocean to catch fish, rather than simply eating the fat, juicy sky fish that must live up above. Murkfin went to Seagull Rock, a favorite hangout for gulls and other birds, and told them of the wonderful sky fish that awaited if only they would come with her on the grand mission. Once the squawking died down, Murkfin had a flock of thirty-six shorebirds committed to her cause.

3. A harness to connect the portable ocean to the lift mechanism. It wouldn't do to have the birds simply grip the shell with their teeth. (Birds have teeth, right? Of course, they do. Everything does.) No, that would be a disaster — the minute they saw a juicy sky fish, they'd open their beaks and down would come Murkfin, clam shell and all. Instead, Murkfin told Sully to collect long, strong strands of kelp and craft them into eighteen ropes. Each rope had a tangled loop at each end, suitable for attaching to a bird's neck. Together, all the ropes formed a giant, hammock-like tangle under the clam shell, cradling it in a nest of kelp.

4. A steering device. Shorebirds are not known for their listening skills, no more than sharks are known for their loud voices. In order to control the contraption, Murkfin told Sully to gather thirty-six more strands of kelp, each with a tangle that could loop around a bird's foot. By tugging on different strands, Murkfin could slow the flapping of specific birds or groups of birds, causing the craft to bank or descend.

When the preparations were complete, Murkfin, Sully, and thirty-six shorebirds gathered at Seagull Rock to launch their expedition into the sky.

"Dear friends," Murkfin began. She used the term broadly, but any bird who would literally support her plan by carrying a shell was temporarily considered a friend. "Today, we voyage into the great sea above the sea. We leave behind us all disappointment and failure. We rise to greet a new era of prosperity. We ascend to claim what is ours."

Some of the birds had begun to squawk in excitement, or perhaps impatience, or perhaps simply because they were noisy birds with nothing better to do, so Murkfin wrapped up her speech quickly before her voice was drowned out by the cacophony. "We go to eat fish!"

"Fin, fin, hooray!" Sully cheered, even more enthusiastic than his normally chipper self.

The flock began flapping and took to the sky!

Or attempted to...

It was not a coordinated flock. There was no countdown. No starting squawk. No rhythmic flapping. No discipline. No shared direction. Each bird was a lone shark.

Thirty-six birds bobbed up and down in the air — each one ascending until they reached the end of their tether, then stalling and falling under the weight of the shell and its passengers. Flapping up, halting with a jerk, and sinking again. And again. And again. In the process, the kelp ropes became increasingly tangled as the birds' paths crisscrossed, until all the birds were wrapped up in one giant ball of flapping chaos.

The feathery sphere squawked and thrashed about, all bound together by ropes of kelp and unable to fly. The failed flying machine settled in the water, where its seventy-two wings thrashed and splashed like an Old Testament vision of God.

For once, Sully was speechless. So was Murkfin. The two ocean-fish watched as the ball continued struggling, only becoming more tangled with the effort. The kelp was strong — eighteen long ropes and thirty-six additional strands, wrapped around and around, crossing over each other like the lattice on top of a pie.

A pie filled with birds. Large birds. Juicy birds.

No, these were more than birds. These were fish, the long-lost fish of the sky. Murkfin had never heard of theology, but now she was a true believer. More than a believer — a prophet for the religion she had just invented, which no one else had heard of and Sully didn't understand. This is what the ocean had been missing all along. This was dream made real, the promise fulfilled — better yet, this was dinner!

Murkfin and Sully rested in the clamshell, waiting for the birds to exhaust themselves. When the thrashing finally died down, it was time for the sky fish to die as well. Murkfin swam over to claim her prize. She sank her teeth, her mighty serrated teeth, into feathers, flesh, and seaweed, swallowing it all. Using every tooth at once. Every tooth in her giant, hungry, great white mouth.

Each bite tasted like victory. She gorged until she could eat no more.

After the feast, Murkfin paused to reflect. "You know, Sully, I might have to revise my teachings. There are actually Five Fishy Flaws." Sully may or may not have been listening, but Murkfin didn't care.

"One, too difficult to catch.

"Two, too small to be worth the trouble.

"Three, too unpalatable to enjoy.

"Four, too friendly to kill.

"And number five, too many to eat. But that's the best kind of flaw."

Murkfin felt a satisfying gurgle in her belly as it slowly digested a tangled mass of bones, flesh, and feathers. She missed her delicious meal already. But there were plenty more fish in the sky.

Lobster's Lucky Day

By Willow Croft

The discovery had been an accidental one. Accidental, yet lucky. But then Harriet had always been lucky. On this fortuitous day, Harriet had been trying to work several lionfish spines free of her claws. She'd tried dragging her claws across the sand and even across the rock that protected her burrow but they still weren't coming out. She became so preoccupied with thinking about how to get the spines unwedged that she wasn't watching where she was going. She ran into something soft and squishy. The object moved, stirring up dust, and Harriet panicked. She'd run into a human.

As the foot lifted off the ground Harriet backed up as fast as her tail could take her. She scooted behind an old shoe and waited for the sand to settle. But it didn't settle. She poked her eyes out above the shoe just as the sand beneath her began to vibrate. Something heavy had fallen onto the ocean floor. She strained her eyes and made out a large shadowy mass in the swirling sand.

Should she move, or stay hidden? She wished she was home in her burrow or at least surrounded by her clan, but she had scavenged too far afield to make a run for it. And she didn't want to admit it, but she was afraid. She was glad her clan wasn't there; it wouldn't do for them to see their matriarch cowering behind an old shoe. Still, there wasn't a lobster alive that wasn't terrified of humans, even though there weren't many other lobsters who knew just how cruel humans could be. At least none that had lived to tell about it, and Harriet never told. She couldn't even bear to think about what had nearly happened to her.

The water began to clear, yet the shadowy mass remained. Was it a trap? Harriet's nervous system was still on fire, and she knew she wouldn't be able to relax until she investigated the large shape sprawled out in front of her. She inched forward, one set of claws at a time, and almost scuttled backwards again when a human foot became visible out of the gloom. She reached out with one shaky claw and touched the foot. Nothing happened. The human didn't move. As she crept around the foot, she saw that the lionfish spines from her claws were now embedded in the human's foot. She edged her way along the body until she reached the human's eyes. They were wide open, staring up through the ocean's water as if they could see the sky above.

The human was dead. Hungry fishes already hovered above the eyes, working up the courage to take the first nibble.

But how had the human died? She travelled back down to the human's foot and stared at the spines. Impossible. If lionfish venom could instantly kill humans, the greedy bastards would be bragging about it all throughout the ocean. Still, maybe she could try using spines again on another human. After all, lobsters like her needed all the help they could get.

After testing it again, and again instantly killing her prey, Harriet passed the word of her discovery along. The news flowed as fast as the current could carry it.

It was worth it to put up with the lionfishes' bragging, as they also went on the offensive against humans. And, because they were so aggressive and fearless, lionfish were now as plentiful dead as they were alive. Soon, every lobster in Harriet's clan carried lionfish spines in their claws. Though many of her clan still disappeared and were never heard from again, as time passed there were less and less lobster traps on the ocean floor. Even human divers armed with spears became an increasingly rare occurrence.

Harriet and her clan grew complacent, hunting further and

further from their burrows. She was feeding on the remnants of a fish when a shadow fell across her. Before she could call out a warning, she and her fellow lobsters were scooped up in a net. A tidal pull of water rushed past her as the net rose, pulling in a few small fish along the way. She tried to scrabble up the sides to the opening but it was too late. The net rose out of the water.

"Whatever you do, don't let go of your spines," she yelled out to her clan. "Lie still and wait for your chance." The lobsters obeyed her orders and quit thrashing around, but not so the fish. They were still panicking and for good reason. They didn't even have lionfish spines to protect them. It was up to her and her clan to save them all.

"Spines at the ready," she ordered. "And keep calm. Wait until you have a direct shot."

The lobsters huddled together, trying not to jab each other with their outstretched spines. It was white hot and dry out here on the surface, with light so bright Harriet could barely see.

"Wait until you're sure of your target," she repeated. Her voice sounded strange to her in the world above; a series of sharp, hissing clacks, rather than the firm, strong tone it had underneath the water. The fish grew more agitated, and the lobsters tried to shield their spines from flailing tails and fins.

The net came to rest against something hard, jarring Harriett's legs. She realized it was difficult to catch her breath up here, and she understood why the fish were panicking. Without water to flow over her gills, she, too, would die. She, the fish, and the rest of her clan. A smelly, dirty human hand removed the thrashing fish from the net. Harriet heard splashes as the fish hit the water. *We're next*, Harriet thought, and she suspected the fish hadn't been returned to the ocean.

"Ready the spines," she clacked. "Not all the spines into one hand. We need to space them out. These humans are as plentiful up here as the lionfish are in the ocean." *And just how do you know*, she waited for one of the other lobsters to call her on her statement, but nobody caught her slip-up. They were too busy watching and waiting to pay any attention to her. Except for one of the young lobsters.

"You got it, boss," Chad said, waving around his spines so eagerly he almost jabbed the lobster on his left.

A shadow loomed over them and the hand reached down into

the net again.

"Now," Harriet ordered. Chad eagerly jabbed all six of his spines into the human's hand. Relief washed over Harriet.

The human yelled, and the shadow disappeared.

Harriet was finding it harder to breathe, but she still sent a prayer to the Old One deep below. She could feel the vibration underneath her as the human walked off, and then everything was still except for the rocking of the boat.

"Time to go," Harriet rasped. One by one, the lobsters clumsily pulled themselves towards the open end of the boat where the ocean waited. "Chad, hurry up," she urged. She hardly had the breath left to talk.

"I can't," Chad wailed. "I'm stuck."

Harriet pulled herself closer to him. His tail was tangled up in the netting. She snipped away the netting as fast as she could. She felt vibration underneath her and she snapped the last strand. The spines hadn't worked. *Why hadn't they worked?*

"Go, Chad," she yelled. "Run for the water." Chad scooted towards the ocean, his carapace sliding and slipping as he scuttled away from her.

She watched him teeter on the edge of the boat. "Harriet, come on," Chad squeaked.

A shadow fell over her. "Now, Chad. Go now. That's an order." She turned away from him as he splashed down into the water. She raised her left claw that held the spikes. She braced herself as a hand reached down towards her.

Better make this one count, she thought, and steadied her claw as grasping fingers stretched out towards her.

Commander Romero stared down at the body on the deck of the boat. One of the fisherman's hands was bandaged, and the other had five spines protruding out of it.

"Another one, Commander?" Seaman Charles Hastings asked.

"Seems so," she answered.

"What's causing all these deaths, Commander?" Hastings pulled a net out from under the fisherman's body. *An illegal net,* Hastings realized with a mixture of excitement and dread. Something glinted in the net, and he peered closer. A lionfish spine. He held it up for the commander.

"Well, scientists say that lionfish have evolved... that their venom is more toxic now." She nodded at the net the young seaman held in his hands. "But this net's primarily used to catch lobsters. It's not usually used to catch fish like lionfish."

"Then how—"

"Maybe lobsters are evolving, too," Captain Romero said, trying to keep a straight face. "Arming themselves with lionfish spines."

"I see, sir." Hastings' eyes widened as he stared back down at the net.

She waited a couple of beats, then winked at him before bursting out laughing. "Kid, you got a lot to learn about the ocean. Lobsters don't even have a brain. Now get that net into our boat — it's evidence. We'll let the coroner do his job." She waved the coroner over.

Loose strands waved in the breeze as Hastings carried the net over to the Coast Guard cutter. He took a closer look at the net. The strands weren't frayed, they looked as if they'd been clipped straight through.

Suddenly he flashed back to a memory from his childhood.

Crying in a restaurant, begging his dad to rescue the lobster from the tank before it was eaten. His dad had refused, and Hastings had to watch the lobster frantically waving at him as his dad yanked him out of the restaurant. Once in the car, his dad spanked him and then yelled at him to stop crying. At home, he was sent to bed without supper. He dreamed on that long-ago night that the lobster had escaped with the fork he'd dropped into the tank and had made its way back into the ocean.

"What if..." he whispered, staring down at the spine he delicately cradled in his hand. "What if you are smarter than everybody thinks?"

There was one way to find out. He'd study marine biology in college. Find a way to protect them, in the way he hadn't been able to as a child. He tossed the spine overboard and clambered onto the cutter with the net.

The spine floated through the sparkling green water, shining and twisted until it hit the sandy ocean floor. A little ways away, a lobster named Harriet was teaching the latest batch of juvenile lobsters the best way to hold lionfish spines, to protect themselves against the horribly cruel humans that lived on the surface. Young lobsters that had been about the same age as she was when she discovered that humans ate lobsters. She'd been forced to watch as the greedy humans devoured her friends one by one. And they would have eaten her, too, if she hadn't hidden the fork the little boy had dropped in her tank. The fork that helped her prop open the tank lid and escape.

Even though that carapace had long ago moulted, she could still feel the itchy burn where she'd scraped her sides squeezing down a drainage pipe in the kitchen floor. She'd survived the long crawl back to the ocean. Survived to help other lobsters live. And if her luck continued to hold, she could outlive the last human. Even if the last human was the scared little boy that had saved her, all that time ago.

The Unshelled

By Mary E. Lowd

Salty air tickled Commander Wilker's long nose and whistled past his pointed ears. The light ocean breeze ruffled the long fur of his Collie mane. He placed a paw gently on the hull of his shuttle craft, parked on the small, sandy island in the middle of a yawning purple-blue sea. He was waiting for his copilot to join him, a local to this watery world.

Though he wouldn't mind if they were running late. The Collie dog had seldom been anywhere as peaceful as the surface of Kallendria 7. There was an entire, technologically advanced society on this world, but it was all beneath the waves. Up here, he could have been standing on a completely untouched, unpopulated world. Nothing as far as the eye could see except for rolling purple waves, deep blue sky, and the occasional silver sand island.

Cmdr. Wilker closed his eyes, letting the feel of the sand beneath his paws and the warmth of the orange sunlight on his fur sink into him. He loved chasing adventure down among the stars, but sometimes a dog just needed to feel his paws on solid earth, connecting him to the bulk of an entire world. On the starship Initiative, Cmdr. Wilker was among the stars, but he could feel the limits of the spaceship all around him. The air moved in small ways, suppressed by walls, ceilings, and filtrations systems.

Here, the air in his whiskers was part of currents that reached to the outer levels of the atmosphere and danced over mile after mile of rolling ocean. A planet was a smaller place than the cosmos, but sometimes it felt bigger.

Splish-splashing sounds broke Cmdr. Wilker's reverie, and he opened his eyes to see ivory claws crawling out of the wine-dark surf. Water streamed down the segmented legs as they emerged, ivory tips giving way to wide, armored legs, pearlescent and gleaming, dimpled with tiny spikes. Behind the first heavy pair of legs, six more delicate legs shuffled, all of them coming together at the base of a conical, twisting shell with the oily, rainbowed colors of abalone.

The crab-like creature stood nearly as tall as Cmdr. Wilker at the peak of its shell. Though their height changed significantly as the eight legs drew together or spread apart.

Cmdr. Wilker peered at the creature, trying to make out a recognizable face ... some part of it that he should look at while addressing it. Between the front talon-like legs, a gap in the shell revealed a squishy-looking collection of cilia or feelers, some of them tipped with eyes.

The collie could work with that — eye stalks counted as a face as far as he could tell. So, Cmdr. Wilker's own muzzle split in a grin, and he woofed, "You must be the Kallendrian emissary sent to join me on the rescue mission. I'm Commander Bill Wilker of the Tri-Galactic Navy starship *Initiative*. And this here trusty shuttlecraft is *The Little Bo-Peep*." He patted the shuttle's hull affectionately, and then he stuck his paw out toward the Kallendrian.

The Kallendrian's eyestalks lengthened, poking further out of the gap in their shell, seeming to examine the canine speaking to them. Then they extended one of their smaller legs from behind the larger talons and delicately took hold of Cmdr. Wilker's furry paw. With a burbly voice, they said, "I am Sydo. My people thank your people for the assistance you will render."

Cmdr. Wilker's grin widened even further. "It's our pleasure. Why don't we get started?" He gestured toward the open hatch on the *Bo-Peep* and waited while Sydo climbed aboard, one clacking, segmented leg after another. As the sunlight played over their pearlescent shell, Cmdr. Wilker saw intricate, pictorial carvings etched into the curves and crevices. He wondered what they meant as he followed the crab-like being aboard.

The *Bo-Peep* had two pilot's seats at the main controls up front, a small area in the middle where the pilots could rest or else a few passengers or minimal cargo could be carried, and access to the engine in the back. Cmdr. Wilker helped Sydo to adjust one of the pilot's seats, laying down its back so the crab could perch atop it. Then he took the remaining seat, fired up the engine, and launched them back into the sky.

"This should be a simple mission," Cmdr. Wilker barked. In fact, the mission was so simple — track down a missing Kallendrian vessel, using the shuttle's more advanced scanners — that he'd been sent alone. Usually, Cmdr. Wilker worked with a team, and he felt somewhat discombobulated without any other officers around to keep in order. "Why don't you tell me about your world? From what I saw, it was very beautiful."

"What?" Sydo exclaimed. "The surface?! It's nothing. Empty. Dead."

"Oh... well..." Cmdr. Wilker wasn't sure if he'd offended Sydo or just surprised them. "That is all I've had a chance to see. I'd love to see more."

So as they flew through thick purple-orange clouds of space dust surrounding Kallendria and the neighboring star-systems, Sydo told the eager collie dog about life under a purple-blue ocean — hatching from one of thousands of identical eggs as a mere squishy, tentacled youth, growing into their first crab shell, and earning the beautiful etchings that covered their current shell with different achievements and experiences.

In return, Cmdr. Wilker told Sydo about being a dog in the Tri-Galactic Navy, serving aboard a ship filled with other uplifted dogs and cats, along with the occasional alien exchange officer, such as Grawf the bear or Consul Eliana Tor the photosynthetic otter.

"I like the sound of her," Sydo said. "We have photosynthetic fish on my world. I had one as a pet for a while."

"I've been to Consul Tor's world," Cmdr. Wilker said. "Her people don't live under the ocean, but they do live at the edge of it. Instead of buildings, they have pools and slides."

Sydo had told Cmdr. Wilker about the buildings on their world

— grown out of living coral, trained on structures built out of whale bones. It sounded magnificent.

"She should come to the celebration party," Sydo said.

"Party?" Cmdr. Wilker liked the sound of that.

"When we bring the *Osmosotosa* home, there will be a big party to celebrate. You, of course, will be invited."

Cmdr. Wilker looked over at his crab-like copilot with a cheerful grin. He loved parties, and he loved the idea of visiting the civilization under the sea on Sydo's world. Besides, his captain would be very happy with him for securing an invitation. Forging friendly relationships with new species and new worlds was the driving force behind the existence of the Tri-Galactic Navy, and until now, when Kallendria needed help finding their missing vessel, the budding civilization of crabs had been very hesitant to interact with the wider society of space-faring planets in the triple galaxies.

"Well, this mission just keeps getting better and better!" Cmdr. Wilker barked. "I get to make a great new friend—" He knocked an elbow jovially against the hard shell on Sydo's closest pincer. "—and then I get to go to a party!"

The universe has a sense of timing, so of course, that was exactly the moment that the *Bo-Peep* hit a patch of turbulence, violently rocking the shuttle.

"What was that?" Sydo asked, drawing their segmented legs in closer, bracing for further quakes.

Cmdr. Wilker furiously studied the controls and readouts, finally announcing, "There's an unusual patch of magnetic waves in this area. The dust in this part of the Kalleh Nebula seems to be magnetically polarized. No wonder the *Osmosotosa* got lost. These waves are wreaking havoc on the *Bo-Peep's* scanners, and this is a fifth generation shuttlecraft, one of the most cutting edge technologies in the entire Tri-Galactic Navy."

The collie looked out the front viewscreen and saw that the space dust here was arranged in beautiful stripes of purple alternating with orange. Thus far, Cmdr. Wilker had been piloting the *Bo-Peep* along the *Osmosotosa's* planned flight path, scanning for any residual background radiation that could be signs of the vessel encountering problems that might have led to them leaving the path.

"Can you tell me more about the *Osmosotosa's* mission?" Cmdr.

Wilker asked. "If I knew what they were doing out here when they went missing, it might be easier to track them down."

"It's a science vessel," Sydo replied, matter-of-factly. "It was loaded with experiments — biology, chemistry, physics. Everything. There are all kinds of studies my people still need to do on the effects of space travel before we launch a fully fledged space fleet."

Cmdr. Wilker grinned again. He loved reading historical fiction about the time when dogs and cats were first launching spaceships from the gravitational confines of Earth, chasing after the mysterious humans who had uplifted them and then disappeared into the stars. There was nothing like a good piece of historical fiction for reminding him of the adventure and romance of space travel.

And the Kallendrians were living through that time period right now.

"Thank you," Cmdr. Wilker said. "That's helpful." Though, he wasn't sure it would help him find the *Osmosotosa*. But it did help him understand his copilot for this mission better. They were a member of such a young species.

As if punishing him for the arrogance of his thoughts regarding the relative youth of Kallendrian society, another wave of turbulence hit the shuttlecraft. This time the shuttle rocked hard enough to illicit a momentary flicker in the life support systems, including the artificial gravity. Cmdr. Wilker's stomach flipped nauseatingly before the gravity righted itself, and Sydo lost their perch on the chair beside him, rolling awkwardly to the floor.

"Are you okay?" Cmdr. Wilker asked once the systems were safely back on. He reached a paw toward one of Sydo's flailing limbs, but the crab got their legs under them before the collie could really help.

Then a thunderous crack rent the air inside the shuttle, and the front viewscreen went momentarily dark. Cmdr. Wilker turned his gaze back to the viewscreen in time to see a large, metallic-looking rock, cratered and pockmarked, flying away. It was nearly the size of the shuttle, and its glittery, reflective surface disguised it perfectly among the clouds of purple and orange space dust. Camouflage. They were lucky it hadn't damaged the shuttle.

Cmdr. Wilker got his paws back on the main control panel and ran a directional scan, aimed manually at the mysterious asteroid.

"It's magnetic," he said. Then he calibrated the scanners to detect fluctuations in the magnetic waves nearby and found the *Bo-Peep* was surrounded by similarly disguised asteroids. "There's an entire asteroid belt out here, and the magnetic waves in the region are interfering with our ability to detect them."

"I hope the *Osmosotosa* wasn't damaged..." Sydo burbled, mouth tentacles waggling frantically.

Before Cmdr. Wilker could reassure Sydo, the *Bo-Peep* took another blow from an asteroid, this time to the side. And this time, the inertial dampening shields didn't hold. The shuttle bent like a tin can, crunching inward at the middle. The life support flickered, causing waves of artificial gravity alternated with the natural zero-gee of space to dance across Cmdr. Wilker's stomach like tap dancing butterflies. Then it went out entirely, leaving the collie and crab alien floating helplessly in the dark. The only light came from the backlit control panels. The gentle circulation of air stopped, immediately stifling even though the shuttle held several hours worth of breathable air, even without the algae filtration systems running.

"This is not good," Cmdr. Wilker woofed. He immediately regretted the words. He should be putting up a strong front for Sydo — it was his responsibility to get the two of them out of here alive. He doggy-paddled through the air back to his pilot's seat at the controls. "Okay, I may have spoken too soon," he said. "The engines are running, so even with the life support and computer systems down, we can still fly our way out of here manually."

"What about finding the *Osmosotosa*?" Sydo asked. They'd managed to grip back onto their seat as well, clinging to it with sharp-tipped talons.

"We'll have to send someone else," Cmdr. Wilker said. "The scanners aren't online, and besides, with the life support systems out, we can't risk staying out here any longer than absolutely necessary. In fact, we're lucky we can fly out of here at all with the *Bo-Peep* crunched down the middle." He frowned and added to himself, "She's gonna steer awfully funny."

"No!" Sydo exclaimed, letting go of their seat. They floated in the zero gee, waving their talons expressively, as comfortably as if they'd grown up in outer space.

Cmdr. Wilker supposed, thinking about it, that Sydo had grown up in a form of quasi zero gee. An underwater society would be much better preparation for life in outer space than any surface dwelling society. Kallendrians would be used to floating.

"What do you mean, 'no'?" Cmdr. Wilker asked, trying to sound as patient as possible. "Us floating around in this deadly magnetic asteroid belt until we die won't help the *Osmosotosa*."

"Then let's fix the life support." Sydo crossed their heavy front pincers in a very judgmental way, as if Cmdr. Wilker must be a complete fool for not having considered the possibility of simply fixing the *Bo-Peep*.

Cmdr. Wilker almost laughed at the sight.

Except that their situation was deadly serious.

The collie waved a tired paw toward the crunched middle of the ship. "The life support systems that need to be repaired are in the back. Now I know that I'm a skinnier dog than I look — half of this bulk comes from my thick fur—" He slicked a paw along the front of his uniform. "—but I don't see myself being able to squeeze back there right now."

"Then tell me what to do," Sydo said, mouth tentacles waggling. "I'll do it."

This time Cmdr. Wilker did laugh. "What are you gonna do? Climb out of your shell? 'Cause there's no way in hell that shell's fitting through a space I can't squeeze through."

"Yes," Sydo said. "Exactly. Though... would you please look away?"

Cmdr. Wilker blinked, unable to summon any words at that moment.

"Please," Sydo reiterated. "It's taboo among my people to leave our shells in front of... well, anyone, really. But especially strangers."

Cmdr. Wilker felt unaccountably disheartened to be called a stranger by this alien who he'd only known a few hours. "I thought we were friends," he said. Still, he turned away, which was more difficult than usual due to the lack of gravity. When he turned back, Sydo's shell floated in the same space as where it had been before, but it had an eerie, empty quality. Like an abandoned house or a skeleton, decaying deep in the woods. Yet the only change was a hollow space where Sydo's face had been before and a few gaps at the many joints of the many legs.

The collie shuddered at the sight.

"Alright, I'm back here," Sydo said, their voice strangely cheerful. "Talk me through the repairs."

"First you need to pry off the cover of the access panel. If it's been bent out of shape, it might give you some trouble..."

"Got it," Sydo said. "Now what? There are a bunch of buttons and controls."

Cmdr. Wilker frowned, trying to remember the layout of the controls under the rear access panel in a standard design shuttle. It made him feel like he was back at the Tri-Galactic Academy, struggling to get the answers on a final exam. Except this time, he hadn't known he'd be taking a test, so he hadn't had the chance to stay up all night studying. "I'm sorry," he said, giving up. "I can't remember the layout. Can you describe what you're looking at for me?"

"Uh... sure... there's a round gray button, then a darker gray switch, then a row of three red lights..."

Sydo's voice burbled on and on, as Cmdr. Wilker struggled to visualize the words. But as soon as he figured one part out, he forgot the last part they'd described. Eventually, he exclaimed, "Dammit! I need to see it! I can't hold all of this in my head! I'd look up the schematics on the computer... but I won't be able to do that until you've fixed it."

After a long silence, Sydo said, "I think you'd be able to see the panel if you looked through the crunched space I crawled through to get here."

"But..." Cmdr. Wilker frowned more deeply. "There isn't anywhere for you to hide. I'd..." Now he felt embarrassed on Sydo's behalf; the Kallendrian had been so insistent that he not look at them without their shell on. "I'd see you without your shell."

There was an awkward pause before Sydo said, "I don't think we have a choice. It's okay. Just this once. But... don't tell anyone?"

"Are you sure?" Cmdr. Wilker asked.

"Yes."

The collie pushed himself off of the pilot's chair where he'd been hovering and floated over the crunched middle of the vessel. He peered through the gap and in the dim light from the various control panels, and he saw a ghostly white figure that, in spite of having too many tentacle-like limbs, looked almost cartoonishly like a sheep. The wavy, billowing shape of Sydo's squishy body could have easily been a cartoonists' take on a sheep's wool. Even a face composed of eyestalks and mouth cilia couldn't spoil the effect. Overall, they made Cmdr. Wilker think of the Earth mollusks called sea bunnies.

Sydo could have been a sea sheep.

They were adorable. Painfully adorable. And their sheep-like facade squeezed at Cmdr. Wilker's collie heart. Deep inside, beneath all the layers of uplift, evolution, and civilization, he was a shepherd, and Sydo was a sheep. He wanted to protect the Kallendrians more than ever now.

Working together, Sydo was able to follow Cmdr. Wilker's directions and repair the shuttlecraft's life support, get the computers back online, and run a safety check on the engines. When the air started circulating, filtrating through the algae scrubbers again, Cmdr. Wilker drew a deep breath of relief. He'd believed he could pilot them back to Kallendria before the air would run out, but it's an awful feeling floating in space, stale air growing staler by the minute. There's not much that can make you feel more alone or helpless than that.

When the full lights came back on, Cmdr. Wilker got a clearer, brighter view of Sydo without their shell, before he had a chance to turn away. Their fleshy skin was dimpled with tiny, short cilia, giving their wavy curves a rumpled effect that looked even more like a sheep's wool than they had in the dark.

Being a professional, though, Cmdr. Wilker knew better than to comment on Sydo's appearance. So, he waited quietly for them to crawl back through the crunched middle of the ship and into their shell, which had settled heavily on the second pilot's seat when the artificial gravity turned back on.

"You can look now," Sydo said.

Cmdr. Wilker nodded, glanced in Sydo's direction, and smiled. As best as he could, he used the exact same smile as he'd used when interacting with Sydo before. He didn't want to make them uncomfortable in any way. This shuttle crash would be a traumatizing ordeal for anyone; adding the necessity of breaking one of their society's most deeply held taboos must have made it so much worse.

"Alright, then," Cmdr. Wilker said. "Let's go find the *Osmosotosa!*"

After a few minutes of flying the *Bo-Peep* through the waves of purple and orange dust, assiduously dodging the magnetic asteroids, Cmdr. Wilker lost himself into the zone — he enjoyed piloting small vessels, and now that he knew what to look for, this flight was an enjoyable challenge. He began telling Sydo about the time he got into a shuttle race during his academy days, but the Kallendrian cut him off.

"You're not acting different toward me." The words were quiet, yet they carried the weight of surprise. And maybe, a little bit of wonder.

"Differently? Why should I act differently?" Cmdr. Wilker asked. He spared a glance for Sydo, but he really didn't know how to read their face — which, again, was mostly eyestalks and mouth cilia — or their demeanor. Perhaps with practice he could learn. For now, though, he would have to rely on words.

"You've seen me without my shell," Sydo explained.

"Ah." Cmdr. Willker shrugged. "You're the same person, with or without a shell."

Sydo said ponderously, "I don't feel the same."

"How so?" Cmdr. Wilker didn't want to press Sydo to talk about anything that made them uncomfortable, but he was intrigued. He'd never known a species who wore optional shells, almost like mechas.

"I feel... freer," Sydo said. "More like myself."

"With your shell on?" Cmdr. Wilker could understand that. Wearing a shell all the time, it would become a part of you. Besides, Sydo's body without the shell had looked soft and delicate. There's a freedom in feeling safe.

"No," Sydo countered. "I feel more like myself without it. My shell feels... heavy. Like a burden. Society expects me to carry it, and so I do. But I keep it as light as possible. No adornments."

"Adornments?" Cmdr. Wilker asked. "You mean like the etchings?"

"Sort of," Sydo said. "Most of my people decorate their shells much more extensively, gluing on rocks and gems. Clockwork gears, mechanical gadgets and doodads. Sometimes even the abandoned shells of smaller creatures. Our shells are supposedly expressions of our truest selves... but... I always felt like myself... my *true* self... was already inside. And the more I glued onto my shell, the deeper I was burying myself."

Cmdr. Wilker didn't know what to say. It sounded devastating to live in a society that shamed you for being yourself, and insisted that you hide yourself under layers of unwanted junk and trinkets, literally glued to your body. But he didn't want to say that. He didn't want to make it harder, when there was nothing he could do to help. So, he settled for saying, "That sounds hard."

"Yes," Sydo agreed solemnly.

The collie and the strange aquatic facsimile of a sheep were quiet for a moment, simply sharing each other's company and focusing on the *Bo-Peep's* flight. Then Sydo added, "But it feels easy being here with you."

Cmdr. Wilker could have burst with pride. He couldn't imagine a higher compliment. And from a sheep, no less! Well, something like a sheep.

Going out on a limb, Cmdr. Wilker decided to tell Sydo about his species' history as companion animals to the naked-skinned apes who had first developed a technological civilization on Earth, and specifically, about the history of herd dogs, how they'd been bred and developed for protecting and guiding sheep, cows, and other herd animals.

"That's a fascinating history," Sydo said. "My people don't have such a complicated past. We're more like the primates in your story, developing intelligence and society ourselves. Are most species in the Tri-Galactic Union more like your species? Uplifted by others?"

"Not so far," Cmdr. Wilker woofed. "Most of them evolved intelligence and society on their own. From scratch. But it's a big universe, and we've only explored a small fraction of it. So, who knows what else we'll find."

Amid the clusters of metallic, cratered asteroids scattered in front of the *Bo-Peep*, a sliver of shining luminescence appeared. Cmdr. Wilker steered the Bo-Peep closer, zooming around the various asteroids, and an entire pearlescent spacecraft came into view.

"Speaking of finding things!" Cmdr. Wilker whistled in appreciation. "That is one beautiful vessel."

The *Osmosotosa* curled and twisted like a seashell, and its surface gleamed with all the colors of an oil slick, picking up the slight scattered light in the cloud of space dust. It almost glowed.

"We grow the hulls for our ships organically," Sydo said. "They're very similar in composition to our own shells."

"That is so cool!" Cmdr. Wilker barked. "Anyway, business first... let's hail them." He sent a request for a video connection, and expected to see a Kallendrian or two appear on the shuttle's viewscreen shortly thereafter.

Instead, the screen stayed dark, showing the view of the ship itself in front of them. However, an audio channel opened, and a burbling voice said, "This is Captain Reinoo of the *Osmosotosa*. Can I help you?"

"Actually," Cmdr. Wilker woofed, "We're here to help you. I'm Commander Bill Wilker from the Tri-Galactic Navy. When your vessel was lost, the Kallendrian government asked for our help, so I'm here with Diplomat Sydo to do that. I take you must have sustained damage, since your video communications aren't working?"

There was a long pause. Long enough for Cmdr. Wilker to start feeling awkward and worried, so he filled the emptiness with more words. "Our shuttle sustained damage from these asteroids as well, but we got it running again. We can come aboard and help repair whatever damage the *Osmosotosa* has sustained as well..."

"That won't be necessary," Captain Reinoo burbled. "We've already... repaired most of the damage. If you could simply point us in the right direction, we should be good to go, and you can be on your way. No need for you to wait for us."

"My shuttle has advanced scanners," Cmdr. Wilker said. "And now that they're attuned to the magnetic waves of the asteroids here, we can help you navigate them. It's no trouble for us to guide you home."

Another long pause ensued. This time Cmdr. Wilker waited.

"Thank you," Captain Reinoo burbled. Though Cmdr. Wilker could have sworn the Kallendrian's voice sounded less thankful and more resentful. He really didn't have a good handle on Kallendrian emotional signaling yet. Ah well, there was still time to learn. "We will be ready momentarily."

Cmdr. Wilker waited until the *Osmosotosa's* engines had engaged, and then he turned the *Bo-Peep* around and began guiding them through the maze of magnetic rocks back toward Kallendria.

"The flight home should take a few hours, but that gives us more time to chat before the big party," Cmdr. Wilker said. "Overall, that was very easy!"

"It was strange," Sydo said.

Cmdr. Wilker glanced over at Sydo. Their mouth cilia were wiggling in a way that looked thoughtful or maybe nervous to the collie.

"Doesn't it seem coincidental that they'd finished their repairs just in time to follow us home?" Sydo continued. "And why didn't they turn on the viewscreen? What kind of damage could they have sustained that would leave them stranded out here, until exactly the time when we showed up, and left the video communications too difficult to repair?"

"Maybe repairing video communications was simply their lowest priority?" Cmdr. Wilker hazarded. "And in a universe this big, coincidences happen. For instance," he cleared his throat, nervously, "it turns out that, without your shell on, you actually look a lot like a sheep."

An awkward pause followed where Cmdr. Wilker regretted his indiscretion. He shouldn't have commented on Sydo's body. It was uncalled for, unprofessional, and completely out of line. He started to apologize, but Sydo cut him off, asking, "You mean, those Earth creatures you were telling me about? The ones that your breed of dog was developed to herd?"

"Yes." He felt very small and very sorry.

Then Sydo's mouth cilia wriggled and burbled, overflowing with infectious laughter. "That's delightful!" they said. "And hilarious."

Cmdr. Wilker grinned and laughed too. He was so relieved that he hadn't read their companionability wrong. It had been a risk, but he and Sydo had been getting along so well. He felt like they were friends, and friends risk telling each other truths, even when they're weird or a little awkward.

"That must be very strange for you," Sydo observed, thoughtfully.

"A little, yes," Cmdr. Wilker admitted. "Though, mostly, it was weird telling you about it. I didn't... you know, I didn't want to offend you by commenting on something I wasn't supposed to see."

Another long pause followed, but Cmdr. Wilker was getting used to the long pauses. He didn't mind them, not when he felt secure in his friendship with Sydo.

"Would you mind..." Sydo curled their mouth cilia and eyestalks, pulling them back into the gap in their shell, shyly. Then they emerged again, and continued: "Would you mind if I took my shell off again? Just until we get back to Kallendria."

"Not at all," Cmdr. Wilker replied. "Not if you don't mind. My people don't have any taboos regarding wearing or not wearing shells. Though... I suppose most of colleagues would find it pretty weird if I suddenly started wearing a shell."

The mecha-like shell next to Cmdr. Wilker clacked and rattled as Sydo squeezed out through the gap in the front, extruding themself in a squishy way that a creature with internal bones could never manage. The shell settled behind them on the floor of the shuttle, hauntingly empty again, and Sydo perched on the copilot's seat, looking absurdly happy, like only a cartoon character or undersea creature who's just shed their heavy shell can.

For the rest of the flight, Cmdr. Wilker and Sydo chatted even more naturally, feeling like they'd known each other forever and simply forgotten it for awhile, almost like a long history of past lives had come rushing back to them. The collie was naturally gifted at making friends, and Sydo felt freer and more like themself than they ever had before. It was the perfect recipe for opening their hearts and sharing deep secrets.

Then the purple, oceanic sphere of Kallendria came into view, and Sydo drew deathly quiet. Reluctantly, they began to climb back into their shell, but Cmdr. Wilker interrupted them, barking, "Wait— Do your people... Look, there's a thing my people do to express friendship sometimes. It's... called a hug." He spread his arms wide. "We wrap our arms around each other, and just hold each other, usually just for a few seconds. But it's nice. Would you like to try?"

Sydo's eyestalks and mouth cilia waggled in a disconcertingly alien way, but then they said, "Yes," and crawled toward the collie, three tentacles stretched wide in a way that mirrored his arms.

Furry limbs wrapped, gently, around a squishy, fleshy body, and Cmdr. Wilker felt Sydo's bumpy, ciliated tentacles wrap around his middle. All the way around him. For a beat, their embrace was as light as the fluttering touch of butterfly wings. Then Sydo seemed to sigh, and they squeezed tightly. Staying as careful of their squishy body as he could, Cmdr. Wilker squeezed them back. He felt content with Sydo in his arms; the firm, evenness of the pressure from their tentacles was calming, and he felt like he was protecting something infinitely precious — maybe a sheep, or maybe the delicate blooming friendship between a collie and a sheep. Maybe, even, the tender beginnings of a profound relationship between two societies.

Then Sydo's tentacles loosened, and Cmdr. Wilker let go too.

The funny caricature of a sheep twisted and distorted,

extruding into a shape that could squeeze back through the narrow gaps in their shell. Once Sydo had returned to their crab form, they said, "Thank you. That was nice. I will cherish the memory."

Cmdr. Wilker and Sydo parted ways, planning to see each other again at the party planned for celebrating the successful return of the *Osmosotosa* in several days' time. The collie flew his shuttlecraft back to the starship *Initiative* feeling pensive, and he spent much of the next few days distracted, pondering Sydo's predicament.

When the time for the party came, Cmdr. Wilker was invited to bring a guest, and so he asked Consul Eliana Tor, the ship's delegate from Cetazed to join him, just as he'd promised Sydo he would. He didn't talk about it — because that would be unprofessional — but Cmdr. Wilker had something of a crush on the green otter woman. She had empathic abilities, and could almost certainly read his feelings for her, which always left him feeling a little flustered around her. But flustered in a calm way? He liked being around her. There was something restful about not having to worry about whether he was showing his feelings too much or too little, because she could see right into his mind anyway.

Having an excuse to invite Consul Tor to a party with him was nice. And the idea of her meeting Sydo was even better. Cmdr. Wilker was sure they'd hit it off, and maybe, Consul Tor could help Sydo. See, the sly collie dog had a plan. If Sydo was unhappy among their own people, maybe they'd be happier as an exchange officer in the Tri-Galactic Navy — that way, Cmdr. Wilker could help his friend and also help forge an alliance between the Tri-Galactic Union and Kallendria at the same time!

"You're up to something," Consul Tor said to Cmdr. Wilker, as soon as she saw him in the corridor outside the teleporter chamber. The green otter saw right through him.

Cmdr. Wilker grinned. He liked the feeling of being seen through. It made him feel understood. Understandable. "I bet it really gets to you that you can tell I'm up to something... but not what it is."

The otteroid shrugged a grassy green shoulder. Unlike the regular officers of the Tri-Galactic Navy, she wore a skimpy lavender sundress, designed to leave as much of her photosynthetic fur revealed and able to soak up light as possible while maintaining Tri-Galactic Union ideas of modesty. "If it's something I'm meant to find out," she said, "I will."

The collie and otteroid entered the teleporter room together and stepped onto the teleporter pad, side by side. Cmdr. Wilker affixed a breathing mask to his long face. He was already wearing a special water-proof uniform. Consul Tor didn't need either the special uniform or breathing mask. Her sundress was already designed for being worn underwater as easily as in dry air, and the grassy blades of her fur could absorb enough of the gasses she'd need to survive from the water for a few hours. Usually that ability only supplemented her lungs, but it could take over for a while.

Quantum energy sparkled through their bodies — taking the collie and otteroid apart sub-atomic particle by sub-atomic particle, and then putting them back together the same way but deep under the oceans of Kallendria.

Cmdr. Wilker was a dog who spent a lot of time grinning, but his usual grin widened even further as he felt the lightness of floating and the gentle swirling of the watery currents against the long fur of his mane. Of course, his grin was hidden inside a breathing mask, but his eyes sparkled too, giving away the grin.

Cmdr. Wilker and Consul Tor had teleported into a small, simple chamber, with smooth rock walls. But the chamber looked out on a riotous scene: colors assaulted their eyes in complicated, constantly moving patterns, swaying and skittering. Bright pinks, iridescent greens, violent oranges, and gentle purples. Everything looked like it was alive — bulging tubes, puckering anemones, and crenulated corals. Small golden shapes flitted in every direction, like coins glittering as they tumbled to the bottom of a fountain. Even smaller shapes, tiny and white, drifted through the water like confetti or cherry blossoms blowing on the wind.

Looking at the chaotic, colorful scene, Cmdr. Wilker understood better why Sydo had been so confused to hear him call the surface of Kallendria beautiful. They were right — compared to this, the surface was dead. An empty space. And if this space was any indication, Kallendrians weren't used to spaces with any emptiness.

"Let's find my friend, Sydo," Cmdr. Wilker barked, and the breathing mask transmitted the sound into the surrounding water. A translator fob inside his ear picked up the sound and reversed the distortion caused by the thicker, aquatic atmosphere. Cmdr. Wilker loved technology. It made it possible for him to attend a party thrown by alien crab-sea-bunny people deep under the ocean, where he wouldn't normally be able to breathe, let alone communicate.

"Sounds like a plan," Consul Tor agreed. "Lead the way."

Cmdr. Wilker waved his arms through the water and kicked his legs behind him, flailing his way forward. His own awkwardness made him laugh. He'd done his share of recreational swimming, but generally, he was swimming along the surface of the water. Here, he didn't have anything so clear to guide him, and his body didn't seem to know what to do.

Consul Tor had no such trouble. She shot past him like a green arrow, rudder-like tail waving sinuously behind her. She turned around and looked back him, smiling and laughing as well. "Perhaps I'll lead then." She held out a paw, and once the collie had grabbed on, the otter swam forward again, pulling him after her.

Even though Cmdr. Wilker was much larger than Consul Tor, his weight was little concern in the water, and she easily led him around the large space, gracefully navigating between all the party-goers in their opalescent shells. Sydo had been right, again, and most of the Kallendrians sported much more complicated, fancily-decorated shells. It was easy to find Sydo, with their relatively plain shell, in the crowd.

Once they found Sydo, the collie, otteroid, and Kallendrian floated together in the colorful chaos. Sydo told them about the various fishes — including the small golden shapes, flitting about — that swam through the room, ready to be plucked from the water and eaten. There were triangular, tiger-striped ones and blue ones with draping fins. The small golden ones were particular delicacies, and Cmdr. Wilker risked popping a few under his breathing mask to give them a try. They were squishy on the outside, crunchy in the middle, and tasted strangely of mango. He liked them.

"Are the little squiggly white ones edible treats too?" Cmdr. Wilker asked, trying to point toward some of the miniscule bits of white drifting by like cherry blossoms.

"Oh, no!" Sydo exclaimed. "Those are our children, after they've hatched but before they're large enough for their first shells. Though, they are also edible. But mostly, we don't eat them; they don't taste very good. Still, it can be satisfying to munch a tentacle-full if you're in a bad mood and want to hurt someone. It's the way of life. Some don't survive."

Cmdr. Wilker stared levelly at Sydo, trying really hard to figure out if the Kallendrian was joking. But their face of eye-stalks and mouth-cilia gave him absolutely no clues to work with. "Are they joking?" he finally gave up and asked Consul Tor.

"They are not," the otteroid answered.

"You can read my emotions," Sydo stated in response.

"I can," she agreed.

Now it was their turn to stare levelly at each other — photosynthetic green otteroid and precious caricature of a sheep, hidden inside a heavy crab shell.

"And you can read the emotions of those around us?" Sydo asked, breaking the stand-off. Float off.

"Yes, I can read their emotions as well. On my own world, most of the people are telepaths and can communicate entirely by sharing thoughts. My abilities are weaker, but I can still pick up on emotions, especially strong ones."

"Are there any especially strong feelings at this party?" Sydo asked.

"Do you want to talk about your feelings?" Consul Tor countered.

Sydo's mouth-cilia wriggled in amusement. "I suppose not. I didn't realize my feelings are the strongest."

"Well..." Consul Tor looked about them, glancing at the various crab-like aliens in their heavy, complicatedly-decorated shells. She seemed unsure about whether she wanted to mention something.

"Is it the scientists from the *Osmosotosa*?" Sydo asked. As the three of them had floated together, a series of the scientists had come up to thank Cmdr. Wilker and Sydo for rescuing them.

"Yes," Consul Tor agreed. "There's something strange about their feelings. They're hiding something. Impatience. And resentment."

"Resentment?" Cmdr. Wilker asked, confused. "About being rescued?"

"I don't think they wanted to be rescued. Actually," she said, "I don't think they needed to be rescued at all."

Cmdr. Wilker's eyes narrowed, and he noticed that Sydo had gone deathly still. "What is it?" he asked.

"Does she know?" Sydo asked. "Our secret?"

"I promised I would tell no one." Cmdr. Wilker was hurt that

Sydo would doubt him. Doubt their friendship. But in fairness, they hadn't known each other very long. And Sydo lived in an entire society that rejected them and their true nature at a deep level. That would make it hard to trust. "She doesn't know."

Consul Tor stayed quiet — curious but quiet. She knew better than to ask about a secret, especially when the person who it belonged to sounded so raw and scared at the idea of it being shared.

"Then why did you bring an empath to the party?" Sydo asked.

"You said I should," Cmdr. Wilker answered.

Sydo didn't look convinced. Their mouth-cilia were all crisscrossed and tangled in an unhappy-looking way.

"Besides... I was hoping..." The collie steeled himself. This was where he needed to reveal his plan. "I was hoping she could convince you to become an exchange officer in the Tri-Galactic Navy, like she is. It would forge the connection between our people, and it would give you a chance... Well, I think you'd find living among the people of the Tri-Galactic Union... freeing, in some ways."

The silence that followed Cmdr. Wilker's pitch was so icy that he started to worry the water would freeze around them. The moment stretched on and on, as Cmdr. Wilker struggled inside, trying to figure out if there was something more he should say, or if he'd already said too much. He didn't know what had happened, how it had all gone wrong. He and Sydo had felt like such close friends, and now... It felt like he'd imagined the whole thing.

"Come on," Consul Tor said to Cmdr. Wilker, taking him by the paw. "We have a duty, as emissaries here, to interact with more people." She turned her attention to the crab, who'd gotten all clammed up, and said, "Thank you, Sydo, for spending so much time with us."

"It was nothing," Sydo said, and with a complicated twist of their armored legs, they turned and swam away.

Cmdr. Wilker felt pierced through the heart, run through by a serrated crab leg. He had thought his friendship with Sydo was a beginning, not something that would end so suddenly, so abruptly. But he docilely let Consul Tor pull him by the paw and swim away in the other direction.

They mingled and mixed with Kallendrians, exactly like the captain would want them to, exactly like good, responsible officers in the Tri-Galactic Navy should. But when the ebb and flow of the party — the currents and eddies of party-goers — led to a momentary lull for them, Cmdr. Wilker took control and awkwardly swam to a quiet cove, pulling Consul Tor along as he half-flailed and half-dogpaddled.

Once they were settled among the lavender and lilac shades of coral, Cmdr. Wilker looked around, to be sure they wouldn't be overheard, and said, "I don't understand what happened. Can you help me? I thought Sydo, and I were friends. I thought I could help them. But... everything went wrong."

"I can only tell you what I sensed," Consul Tor said, "but Sydo does have strong, friendly feelings toward you, and they felt very... conflicted... by everything that was said. But also, I get the sense that they aren't ready for something... something that friendship with you represents."

Cmdr. Wilker stared into the green otteroid's lilac eyes, nearly the exact same shade as the crenulated coral behind her. The grassy fur on her brow furrowed. She could sense that he was conflicted too; certainly she could. But he couldn't tell Sydo's secret, even to someone else who would keep it as carefully as him, someone else who would never use the secret to hurt them.

"You don't have to tell me the secret," Consul Tor said. It was like she could read his thoughts, not just his feelings. "I wouldn't want you to break a promise to a friend. And I don't need to know what it is to tell you that it's not at all unusual for species without telepathic or empathic powers to be threatened by those of us who have them—"

Cmdr. Wilker felt abashed, thinking of how many of his own crewmates and colleagues — other dogs and cats on the starship *Initiative* — must have reacted to Consul Tor in exactly that way when they met her. He hoped he hadn't been one of them. He didn't think he had been. He found her more fascinating than threatening. And yet, he couldn't be sure. He felt nearly certain that she must understand his feelings better by sensing them indirectly than he could through feeling them himself.

Some things are easier to see from far away.

"—and regardless of my empathic abilities, Sydo was never going to agree to your plan."

"They weren't?" Cmdr. Wilker asked in surprise. It had seemed like such a good plan. A perfect plan.

"They're far too attached to their home world."

"But they're so unhappy," Cmdr. Wilker objected.

Consul Tor shrugged. "Leaving your entire life behind isn't always the cure for unhappiness."

Cmdr. Wilker nodded. He had to admit that was true. He was still disappointed. And he wished there was something he could do for Sydo, some way to help them.

"There's one more thing I can tell you that might help," Consul Tor said, looking away from the collie, letting her gaze pass over the array of partying crabs.

"Really?" Cmdr. Wilker tried not get his hopes up, but he wasn't any good at it.

"You remember how Sydo was curious about the feelings of the crew of the *Osmosotosa*?"

Cmdr. Wilker nodded.

"Every one of them who talked to us was just as curious about Sydo."

"What does that mean?" Cmdr. Wilker asked, confused.

"I don't know," Consul Tor said. "But I got the strong sense that they wanted to help Sydo, much like you do. Perhaps, if you talked to one of them privately..."

"I could learn something."

Now Consul Tor nodded.

"I'll see what I can do."

The collie looked over the lay of the land in front of him — everything floating and swaying and moving, obscured by fish swimming by and decorative strands of something like kelp. He located a Kallendrian who he recognized as a crewmember of the *Osmosotosa*; in fact, he believed it was the captain.

Cmdr. Wilker remembered because he'd been particularly entranced by a piece of clockwork machinery that spiraled all the way around the captain's shell when they'd come over to thank him. Tiny green spheres, like marbles made from sea glass, tumbled endlessly around on narrow tracks, always moving. It was a beautiful, but very distracting piece of machinery to wear on your body at all times.

As he thought about it, Cmdr. Wilker realized that most of the crewmembers of the *Osmosotosa* who'd come to thank him had sported particularly ornate shells. He wondered if it had something to do with being scientists.

The collie swam like a drowning dog over toward Captain Reinoo. Other Kallendrians cleared a path around him, avoiding the spastic dog's flailing limbs. But he managed to catch Captain Reinoo's gaze, and the Kallendrian stared steadily at him with an array of eyestalks as he approached.

"The good Commander Wilker," Captain Reinoo said when the collie arrived, out of breath and feeling foolish at their side. "To what do I owe the honor?"

Now that Cmdr. Wilker was face to... uh... face-like collection of protuberances with Captain Reinoo, the collie wished he'd formulated more of a plan. Perhaps Consul Tor could have given him a list of questions to ask. And yet, Consul Tor hadn't been there when he'd connected with Sydo.

Cmdr. Wilker would have to befriend this alien crab on his own. It was harder, though, than it had been with Sydo, because now he was so frustrated with how Kallendrian society treated his friend.

"I wanted to ask you about the machinery on your shell," Cmdr. Wilker blurted out.

"Oh this?" Captain Reinoo's pincers and legs twisted about, pointing at the track the marbles continued to roll along. On the slightly shorter side of the conical, spiraling shell, there was an additional piece of machinery that moved the marbles back up to the top of the track, so they could begin rolling again. "It's fun, isn't it?"

"Extremely," Cmdr. Wilker agreed. Although, it kind of made him want to catch all the marbles and make them stop rolling. "But see, my copilot on the mission, Sydo, told me that the decorations on Kallendrian shells usually have special significance. Does this piece of machinery mean something? Perhaps about the endless cycle of life? I hope you don't mind my asking."

The Kallendrian floated in the water before the collie, waving their eyestalks methodically back and forth, sizing the alien dog up. "I could make up a story for you," Captain Reinoo said, "but no, not really."

"I'm surprised," Cmdr. Wilker said. "I was sure Sydo said—"

Captain Reinoo cut the collie dog off. "I could lie to you, but no one is listening to us. And I can easily explain that you've misunderstood me if you try to tell anyone what I've said. So, why bother?"

Cmdr. Wilker had no answer for that.

"Do you want to tell me what you really want to know?" Captain Reinoo asked.

Cmdr. Wilker did want to tell Captain Reinoo, but he didn't know how, without betraying Sydo's confidence.

"I see," Captain Reinoo said. "I've trusted you, but you won't trust me."

"It's a rather limited sort of trust," Cmdr. Wilker countered, "when it relies on your ability to malign me."

Captain Reinoo's mouth-cilia wriggled in what seemed like laughter.

Cmdr. Wilker tried a different tack. "Why weren't you happy to have us rescue you?"

Now Captain Reinoo's face parts curled up, tightening like tiny fists. "What makes you say this? We've all thanked you. Every one of my officers at the party tonight."

"My friend, the green one who came with me, has empathic powers," Cmdr. Wilker said. "She told me you weren't happy, and that you were hiding something."

"Come with me," Captain Reinoo said.

Cmdr. Wilker struggled to follow the Kallendrian, swimming through schools of alien fish and around other party-goers with dangerously flailing pincers and shells like antique store curios. He found himself wishing that Captain Reinoo would offer to let him hold onto the pointy end of one of their segmented legs, towing the collie along like Consul Tor had done. He'd never thought of himself as a bad swimmer before, but here, surrounded by aliens who lived their lives in the water, he felt really terrible at it.

Above average for a dog turned out to be less than passable for a crab.

With great relief, the collie swam under a broad yellow coral shaped like a small tree or gigantic toadstool, and found Captain Reinoo had settled, segmented legs crossed sternly. A veil of bubbles fizzed up from vents in the rocky floor beneath the yellow coral, effectively concealing them.

The captain crab looked very serious, worrisomely so, but from Cmdr. Wilker's perspective, the most important, most pertinent point was that they were holding still. He let his own hind paws touch the rocky floor beneath the coral and found a surprising amount of comfort in the simple sensation of pressure against the pads of his feet. The feeling anchored him, at least a little, in this strange underwater world.

"I don't know what kind of game you're playing," Captain Reinoo said, "but if you were to reveal our secret to the government, you'd be responsible — *personally* responsible — for the deaths of hundreds of people."

Well, that had escalated quickly. Cmdr. Wilker had no idea what Captain Reinoo was talking about, but Consul Tor had certainly been right about speaking to them privately. He was already learning a lot.

"I wouldn't want that," Cmdr. Wilker said, stiffly. "Obviously, I wouldn't want that."

"Good." Captain Reinoo's crossed legs relaxed slightly.

Cmdr. Wilker was tempted to say more, perhaps ask questions poking around the edges of what he didn't know, but Captain Reinoo had already revealed so much without his asking that reason told him keeping quiet was the best bet. Most likely, Captain Reinoo had severely overestimated how much Consul Tor had been able to read of their mind and the minds of the rest of the *Osmosotosa's* crew. Cmdr. Wilker hoped to take as much advantage of that fact as possible.

So he waited.

And Captain Reinoo said, "We were so close when you arrived. Almost there. Another day... Just one more day, and I'd be home now, instead of here."

"Home?" Cmdr. Wilker asked.

"Of course, I think of it as home," Captain Reinoo snapped, clacking the joints in several of their legs in time with the words. "I may not have been there yet, but it's my home. All of our homes. Why do you think you'd cause hundreds of deaths if you revealed our colony? The government wouldn't kill us. Those of us who couldn't face losing our home... couldn't face coming back... they'd take their own lives."

Cmdr. Wilker felt like everything just kept getting worse and worse as he listened to Captain Reinoo talk. And he couldn't stand hearing the crab reveal their darkest secrets, impelled by an implied lie.

Cmdr. Wilker lifted a paw and said, "Stop, please. I don't know anything. There's nothing I could reveal to your government, even if I wanted to, and even if I did want to... The policies of the Tri-

Galactic Union forbid any officer to interfere in an outside culture's policies."

Captain Reinoo's mouth-cilia wriggled in laughter again. Possibly bitter laughter, given the words that followed: "You've already done that. But then, I guess the question is: does the Colony of the Unshelled count as its own culture? Or are we nothing but a rebellious subset, troublesome rabble-rousers and rule-breakers, to you and your loft Tri-Galactic Union?"

From all the words Captain Reinoo had said, one phrase stood out to Cmdr. Wilker, as if it had been written in bubble letters, colored in with highlighter, and made to flash somehow: "The Colony of the Unshelled?"

"It's a temporary name," Captain Reinoo said.

All the pieces fell together inside the collie's head, and he worked through laying down the final pieces of the jigsaw by saying the words out loud: "The Osmosotosa didn't get lost. You were fleeing. From persecution. For not wanting to wear your shells... And the colony you were fleeing to... No one wears shells there. Ever."

"Well, I mean, sometimes a shell is useful if you're doing hard labor," Captain Reinoo said. "So, not never. But we don't live in them." Their mouth-cilia curled into a tangle, like ribbon on top of a present. A smile perhaps. And then the captain said, "I wish you could see what we look like without our shells. We're entirely different people."

"I know," Cmdr. Wilker said, reverently remembering the embrace that he and Sydo had shared. "I mean, I can imagine," he said, quickly, trying to cover his mistake. And then, he did imagine. He imagined the entire crowd of party-goers with their complicated, ornate shells... all bare. A whole crowd of squishy, tentacled, cloud creatures. A herd of cartoon sheep, under the sea. It was a lovely image. "I can understand why this colony must be so important to you. There were times in my people's past when some groups... were not treated well. I would never want to deny your people a freedom that they so desperately need."

"The freedom to be ourselves," Captain Reinoo agreed.

"Yes."

The Kallendrian looked mollified.

"May I ask, then," Cmdr. Wilker began, "why so many of your crew have such particularly ornate shells? If you all long to be freed of them?"

"Cover," Captain Reinoo answered. "Those with bare shells... plain ones, like Sydo's... they draw attention. Others wonder if there's something... wrong with them. If they're like us. And the costs for being caught can be high. It's still considered acceptable to lock a Kallendrian in their shell for months at a time, as a form of therapy. Those of us who know ourselves... that's why we work harder to hide than those who are still figuring themselves out. We know that isn't therapy. Only cruelty."

Cmdr. Wilker shuddered at the idea of Sydo being locked in their shell when they took so much obvious pleasure in abandoning it. To have that freedom removed as a possibility, even in private? Cmdr. Wilker could see how cruel that could be. He even wondered if it would qualify as a civil rights violation as far as the Tri-Galactic Union was concerned. They might not concern themselves with the internal workings of an isolated society on a barely space-faring world... but if it came to a conflict between Kallendria proper and the Colony of the Unshelled, it could easily become the deciding factor on the TGU's choice of policy.

Cmdr. Wilker explained thus to Captain Reinoo, but he couldn't leave it at that. He was still worried for Sydo.

"For a Kallendrian who was still figuring themself out..." Cmdr. Wilker knew he was treading on delicate ground, given that the only Kallendrian he'd interacted with closely for any sustained time was Sydo, and he didn't want to indirectly reveal their secret. But he had to ask. "Are there resources for them? Some way to find out about the colony?"

"We look for our own," Captain Reinoo said. "There are secret societies. When one of our kind is ready, others will find them. And the *Osmosotosa* won't be the last science vessel to get lost."

Somehow, Cmdr. Wilker imagined that if Captain Reinoo were a dog like him, they'd have put air quotes around "science vessel" and "lost."

"That's good," Cmdr. Wilker said. "If someone were to have a friend — someone who wasn't ready, someone who still hiding from themself, maybe — then they'd want to know..." His voice choked off.

"There will be help for them when they're ready." One of Captain Reinoo's armored legs grew eerily light, and then a tentacle extended, nakedly from one of its upper joints.

Cmdr. Wilker reached out a paw, and Captain Reinoo wrapped their bare tentacle around it. The moment was short. And then the tentacle withdrew, disappeared from sight, and filled the armored leg up again. The captain likely feared revealing himself, in case any other Kallendrian happened to blunder under their umbrella of yellow coral. But it was meaningful. Perhaps not as meaningful as the embrace with Sydo, but a sort of coda or reprise of that moment.

Cmdr. Wilker would have to trust Captain Reinoo to take care of the others in their society seeking an escape. The collie couldn't do that for them. And he would have to trust Sydo to find their own way to accepting themself and seeking out a better way to live.

Cmdr. Wilker couldn't do that for Sydo either, no matter how much he wanted to.

What he could do was say, "If you have a colony on another planet, then the Tri-Galactic Union might well accept it as a society in its own right. You could reach out to us for aid."

"I will keep that in mind," Captain Reinoo said. "We launch again in a month. Next time, if a Tri-Galactic Navy ship crosses our path before we reach the colony, perhaps we'll keep going."

"Why did you turn back? My shuttle wasn't equipped to stop a vessel of your size, even if we'd tried to."

"We couldn't risk anyone discovering and revealing the location of our colony."

"The Tri-Galactic Union would never reveal that information without the colony's consent."

"Perhaps," Captain Reinoo said. "I find you... strangely trustworthy. I will think about extending that trust to the rest of your people. But not yet. We can't take risks with a colony that's so young."

Cmdr. Wilker said, "I understand." But he didn't really. He couldn't. He could only imagine what it was like to have a shell, and then he had to imagine on top of that what it would be like to wish the shell gone and still be trapped in it. Extending those musings all the way to imagining what it would be like to live embroiled, enmeshed in the whirlpool of politics surrounding the simple question of whether it was okay to live without a shell... It was a tower of cards, too delicate to place any true weight on it.

He couldn't herd these sheep into formation, fixing their lives for them. Because he wasn't really a shepherd. And they weren't really sheep.

He was just an officer who had done his job, and they were an entire, complex society.

All he could do was try to empathize, offer what help they would accept, and appreciate how his life had been enriched by meeting these sea sheep who masqueraded as crabs to pass in their society.

Cmdr. Wilker did his best to enjoy the rest of the party, and when the time came, he sought out Sydo to say goodbye. He wished he could tell Sydo about the Colony of the Unshelled. He wanted to believe that Sydo would happily join the crew of the *Osmosotosa* and move to a place where they'd feel accepted and free to be themself. All their problems would be solved.

But Cmdr. Wilker could no more share Captain Reinoo's secret with Sydo than he could share Sydo's secret with Captain Reinoo. And he understood why each of them wasn't ready yet to directly trust the other.

He hoped that someday, they would be. And he hoped, when that day came, Sydo would reach out to him again.

The Ocean Is Not Wide Enough

By K.C. Shaw

Moonlight-on-Small-Waves dived, sending a steady stream of clicks ahead to see where she was going. The water was shallow here, barely four narwhal-lengths deep. She hunted along the sea floor and swallowed a cod whole, along with a few shrimp.

The winter ice was forming, thicker every day. Moonlight rose toward the surface well before she needed to, since she might have to swim some distance to find a breathing fissure. She was in luck, though. A seal's hole was not far away. It was small but she rose into it for a breath before sinking below the water again.

She recognized the seal, who was on her way back to the hole. Moonlight gave a whistled greeting. "Good hunting, Pebble?"

"Good enough," Pebble said. She jetted through the water and turned gracefully to arc toward the breathing hole. "I haven't seen you around lately. How's that calf of yours?"

Moonlight froze in the water, drifting with the current. Pebble surfaced at her breathing hole and dived again, looking at Moonlight quizzically.

"He's gone," Moonlight managed.

Pebble was instantly contrite, which somehow made it worse. "I didn't mean to open a wound," she said. "I lost last year's pup. It hurts but life goes on."

"Yes. Thank you." Moonlight turned and pushed her way through the water so forcefully she probably tumbled the poor seal over. She had to get away.

She swam for the edge of the ice, but that was a mistake. It was a sunny day and every narwhal within miles had gathered to splash around in the open water. She heard the chatter and whistled laughter long before they were in view.

She didn't want to talk to anyone. She couldn't pretend to be lighthearted to join them, and her gloomy presence would ruin the party atmosphere. She veered away to find a stretch of water to herself.

Maybe she was getting over her grief. After the shock of Pebble's innocent question had eased, she didn't feel too bad. Swimming fast always helped.

But when she slowed, she realized she was listening for her son's navigation clicks to keep track of him.

She dived, hoping that hunting would occupy her. She was in deeper water and felt the increased pressure as she approached the bottom.

She had found a good hunting ground, and for a little while her mind was still while she slurped up shrimp and the occasional squid. But when she surfaced for a breath, she listened for her son's breath too. When it didn't come, panic rose in her, followed by a wave of misery.

It had been a month since her calf died. If he had been killed by an orca or some other predator, it would have been terrible but understandable. But although he had seemed healthy, something inside her son went wrong. He had lost weight, lost energy. She hadn't known what to do.

The last day he said, "Mama, I'm cold." When she'd swum close beside him to share the warmth of her bulk, he was unmoving.

He never moved again. She pushed his body to the surface in case he was only unconscious, waited a full day and night for him to breathe before she could believe he was gone.

She had to stop thinking about him. Moonlight rose and took a breath, then submerged again — not a dive, but a gentle downward glide. She sank until the cheery sunlight faded to deep blue, then hung nearly motionless, only giving her tail a shallow pump now and then.

The only way she could quiet her mind these days was by listening. The water was full of sounds, most of them so ordinary and unimportant that she paid little attention to them. But now she concentrated on everything she heard.

The sound of ice was foremost, of course. It squeaked and creaked in an endless cacophony, occasionally punctuated by a crack caused by too much sunshine. The movement of water was quieter but just as constant: the distant crash of waves on shore, the susurration of sand. She could still hear the other narwhals in the distance, too far away to make out more than an occasional word, just a general happy chatter.

Moonlight concentrated on the smaller, fainter noises: the pattering of some small creature on the sea floor below her, the bloop of a bubble reaching the water's surface.

Her anxiety eased, replaced by peace. She would be all right.

Very faintly — so faint, in fact, that she thought at first she was imagining it — she heard a whale's song. The big whales weren't common here, although occasionally one came through and caused excitement. Moonlight had seen one feeding once, seen it gulp so much water into its massive mouth that the pleated skin stretched taut, then watched in wonder as it pushed the water out through baleen plates and swallowed whatever small creatures were left.

More often, all the narwhals knew of the big whales were their songs. The males sang long, deep, tender songs to call lovers from untold miles away, but occasionally Moonlight heard a more ordinary-sounding conversation. The big whales spoke a different language from the narwhals, belugas, and the other water folk from around the ice, though, and she never knew what such strange creatures had to talk about.

This song was different from the other big whale songs she had heard. It was just on the edge of hearing, less of a song than a melodic croak, as though sung by a whale who was not used to the activity. It was the same mournful tune over and over, unvaried.

She listened to it until she had to rise for another breath. The afternoon was wearing on. She should do some more hunting. But she sank again until the sound of the choppy waves at the surface didn't drown out the whale's faint, slow song.

She wished she could hear it better. Without thinking she started swimming toward it. But the big whales could travel farther in a single day than she would in her whole life. Their voices could travel even farther. This whale might be anywhere.

But... this wasn't an ordinary big whale's voice. It was different, so it might not be so far away. It couldn't hurt if she swam a little farther to try and hear it better.

She had to stop frequently to listen for the song, since she couldn't hear it over her own navigating clicks. When it stopped after an hour, she stopped too.

She was being ridiculous. She was in open ocean now, the sea floor too deep for a comfortable dive. She should go back to the ice and fill her belly, then sleep in the safety of territory she knew with other narwhals nearby.

Instead, Moonlight hung in the water, waiting for the song to resume. Maybe the whale had become bored with his melancholy tune. More likely he was gathering food.

The tune stayed in her memory, though. Narwhals weren't singers, but suddenly she wanted to try.

It took her considerable effort to modify a whistle until it sounded like song. She hadn't known how difficult singing was. She kept at it until she managed a wobbly rendition of the tune.

As though the big whale heard her small voice across the miles, he started singing again. Moonlight swam toward it.

She could go hungry one or two days to satisfy her curiosity.

Moonlight made up words of her own to fit the tune. When the big whale stopped singing, she stopped swimming and sang it herself. It was almost as though she was communicating with the big whale, although she knew he couldn't possibly hear her. Her voice was too high-pitched, too weak to carry far.

Eventually, long past nightfall, the big whale fell silent. *Sleeping,* Moonlight thought, and realized she was sleepy too.

She was far from shore. She had not seen or heard anything

nearby for hours. She slept.

The old dream returned. She hadn't had it for several nights, but it was sharp and terrible again. She was swimming along the surface, her son at her flank. Sunshine sparkled on the waves and she thought she would give him that name. Sunshine-on-Waves was a common whale name, but it suited her son perfectly. He laughed easily and played gentle little pranks.

As she swam in her dream, the light dimmed. The reassuring nudge of her calf against her flank was gone, had been gone for some time. She hadn't noticed when he fell behind.

She searched for him, but when she found him he was listless, weak, thin. "Mama, I'm cold."

She woke with a shudder and shot to the surface for a breath, although she didn't need one yet. A crescent moon shone amid a million stars. Tiny animals winked and flashed in the water like starlight, too small to eat. A big whale would engulf them in a mouthful of water and swallow them down.

Moonlight listened for the big whale's song, but he was still silent, probably still sleeping. She tried to sleep again too.

The next time she woke, it was to the same mournful tune. The water was pale with dawn as Moonlight rose for a breath.

To her surprise, she could make out words in the song now. She must be getting closer. It was definitely louder than before too.

The accent was strange, but the words were intelligible: *The ocean is not wide enough for my sorrow. The ocean is not wide enough for my sorrow.*

Moonlight floated quietly for a few minutes, listening. Then she swam toward it, much faster than before.

She swam all day. The song continued intermittently, sometimes for hours at a time, sometimes with long gaps of silence. Moonlight was lucky enough to find and eat a few small squid and a fish, and ignored her lingering hunger.

The song grew louder. She wondered if she would still be swimming toward it when winter turned to spring.

But toward evening, she found the whale.

She knew she was getting close because the song seemed to surround her now. It filled the water. Then her soft navigational clicking reflected something huge in the water ahead.

The song fell instantly silent. The whale had heard her too. She slowed, suddenly nervous.

The big whales were harmless... but was this a big whale? It didn't have the shape she remembered.

"*Go away!*"

The voice was so loud Moonlight backfinned to stop moving. It was like being shouted at by thunder. The water actually shivered.

She would not go away. She had come too far to see the singer. She was hungry, tired, and very far from home and family. She would not go away.

The silence continued. The big whale would not sing until she left, that was clear. But she wouldn't leave.

Hesitantly, she sang his own tune back to him in her tremulous whistle. "The ocean is not wide enough for my sorrow."

After another minute he said, "Who are you?"

"Moonlight-on-Small-Waves. Who are you?"

She heard him repeat her name clumsily, then change the pronunciation. "Oh. Moonlight-on-Small-Waves. I am Silent-While-Hunting. Go away."

It wasn't a demand this time, or not as much of one. Moonlight swam closer slowly, sending a spray of questioning clicks ahead of her to see what Silent-While-Hunting looked like.

He was enormous, nearly as long as a big whale but far more bulky. His massive head alone seemed larger than an iceberg. His jaw was slung underneath like a shark's mouth, but long and narrow; it was partially open and Moonlight saw sharp teeth, not baleen. He was big enough to swallow her whole.

He sent a similar burst of clicks toward her, his voice so strong that she felt every pulse. She wondered what he thought of her, a small plump whale with a round head.

She said, "I came to hear your song."

"The song is not for you." His harsh voice shivered the water again.

Moonlight said, "A song is for everyone who hears it."

"This song is for me alone." The anger in Silent-While-Hunting's voice faded, replaced with weariness. "You are too small, too young to understand."

Moonlight stopped and hung in the water again. If she came too close, he might leave. One pump of his great tail and he would be a mile away.

She sang again, the same tune but the words she had made for it:

My first calf, Sunshine-on-waves.
I am young too, I am a new mother.
I do things wrong, what did I do wrong?
"Mama, I'm cold." I'm cold inside too.
The ocean is not wide enough for my sorrow.
The ocean is not wide enough for my sorrow.

She fell silent and waited for his reply. She wanted him to understand. She needed someone to understand her grief.

Silent-While-Hunting sang the song back to her slowly, his deep voice a physical force in the water. Moonlight joined in and they sang together.

Finally he said kindly, "Go home to the ice, small whale."

"Come with me," Moonlight said.

He rose to the surface for a breath, so Moonlight did too. Stars were out in a deep blue sky. Their faint light silvered the water's surface.

Silent-While-Hunting turned and swam toward Moonlight. She braced herself, half-expecting the toothed jaw to close on her body.

Instead he passed her, his massive head like a mountain. He slowed and stopped, waiting for her.

She turned and caught up to him.

They swam toward the ice and home.

The Clamshell Baby

By Huskyteer

They rode towards the storm, leaving a trail of squid ink and a turbulent wake behind them.

There were four of them, and they called themselves the Hell's Anglerfish: Big Rig the bull elephant seal, Derrick the fur seal, and the two California sea lions, Oily and his kid brother Blep. Rig was the largest and the leader. He could swim and dive further than the others, and had brought back the biggest squid from the dark and dangerous depths, a fourteen-footer with blue running lights along its flanks.

Sometimes they raced each other on squidback along the seabed, kicking up sand and dodging rocks, sometimes they rumbled with their rivals, the Spider Crabs, or stole fish from a slower hunter, or bullied a killer whale until it left their territory. But today they were stormchasing.

Black clouds covered the sky and turned the sea from blue to murky grey, with bubbling foam where the waves smashed down to the heaving surface. With a bellow, Rig urged his squid towards the center of the storm.

"Keep going! Last one to the eye is a shrimp!"

Blep was nervous about speaking up; he was the newest member of the gang and had only recently completed the initiation. There were still scabs on his anglerfish tattoo — the sign every member had inscribed on their flipper using the ink from a squid he'd captured and broken to harness.

"Are you sure?" he asked. Only his brother Oily heard.

"Don't show me up, loser," he snarled, slapping his tail against his squid's flank so it bucked and plunged.

Blep patted his squid. It was on the small side, greyish in color, with a tendency to make sideways jerks that threw him off if he didn't hang on tight, but it was *his* squid. He'd dived for it and he'd got it.

"Hang in there, Squidney," he told it.

He followed the other three along the path of the storm, fighting the currents. Big Rig pointed his squid at the surface, the water growing wilder as they travelled upwards. Blep's squid got tangled in a clump of seaweed, and by the time he got free he could only just make out the blue lights of Rig's mount, far above. He leaned forward, streamlining his tubby body as best he could, and burst up above the water. Lightning like jagged pink coral branched down, turning the sky purple. Squidney wallowed and floundered in the churning water. High above him, Big Rig was riding the curl of an immense wave, his squid's tentacles thrashing at the center of a tunnel of foam.

Blep heard a roar and turned to see another wave bearing down on him. He wheeled his squid, paddling with his flippers to help Squidney along, and felt himself picked up by the rushing water. The waves parted to show him a circle of jagged rocks, before closing over them again. Then he was perched on the crest of the wave, foam arcing around him, rain hissing off his back and shoulders, travelling faster than he had ever moved before. He could not bellow as loudly and deeply as the big bull Rig, but he hugged his squid's sides and blared out his joy to the waves and the seabirds.

One moment he was surfing, the next the wave had sucked him under and spun him around. Blep closed his mouth and nostrils and turned his earflaps down to keep the water out. His squid was torn from under him, and he was battered by pebbles stirred up from the seabed. In the darkness he wasn't certain which way was up, and the tightness in his muscles told him to breathe.

Then his head broke the surface and he took a big gulp of air, then let it out with a honk. He had washed up close to the rocks, lapped now by a tame and friendly sea.

Big Rig, popping up like a huge cork, flung his head back. "What a ride!" he declared. "What. A. Ride!"

Derrick and Oily were okay too, Blep saw, and Squidney was swimming placidly round in circles. Turning the other squid loose to graze on small creatures, the Hell's Anglerfish heaved themselves up onto the rocks. Derrick the fur seal shook water from the thick mane of fur around his neck. The rain eased. Steam rose from their wet flanks.

"What was that?" Derrick pricked up his long earflaps.

They heard it again: a faint, plaintive squeak, almost drowned by the crashing waves. Derrick raised himself up, looked around, and pointed.

It looked like a clump of brown seaweed, then a pink mouth with tiny teeth appeared. Jammed up against the rocks, its head only just out of the water, a small sea otter was mewing for help. They lolloped over as quickly as they could.

"It's stuck," Blep said, nosing at it. One paw was caught in the shell of a clam, and the pup couldn't pull free. A chomp of Blep's teeth and the shell fell in two, the hinge snapped. The little otter grabbed at the contents, stuffed the clam into his mouth, and smacked his lips. He rolled over onto his back and floated.

"He's a little cutie," Derrick said, then stopped, looking anxiously at his leader.

Big Rig pushed his face close up to the otter pup, his trunk wobbling. "No," he said, baring his teeth. His mouth was big enough to snap off the baby's head in one bite. The pup looked solemnly back at him, then chuckled and reached for his whiskers. "He's a little Hell's Anglerfish."

They called the clam baby Littleneck, and from then on he went everywhere with them. Most of the time they hung out around the offshore drilling platform, where there were plenty of fish attracted by the trash the workers threw in the sea. Some of the trash was pretty tasty, too. They played hide and seek with the pup around the legs of the platform.

When it was time to ride, Littleneck came too, of course. The faster they rode, and the more stunts they pulled, the more the otter laughed and kicked his chubby legs. He liked it best with Rig, leaning against the bull seal's big belly astride the mantle of the squid, but they all took turns at carrying him.

"I don't want to take the baby," Oily complained. It was a squally morning before breakfast, and everyone was snappy. "It's not my turn. It's Blep's."

Derrick blinked his big, dark eyes. "Shall I tell Rig you don't want to?"

"That's all you ever do," Oily muttered. "Tell Rig. You snitch." He looked scared, though, and moved towards the baby otter.

Blep just knew his brother would be rough with the little guy. "I don't mind," he said. He waggled his hindquarters. Littleneck hopped on, and the sea lion bounced him up and down on his flippers.

"He'll throw up," Oily said, disgusted.

"Hey!" Rig wallowed into the sea and rounded up his squid. "Check it out!"

They heard a regular thudding in the sky, like the beat of waves on the shore, growing louder and closer. A dark speck took form; the tubular shape of a seagull, but without wings.

"What is it?" Blep asked. Oily rolled his eyes, but Blep noticed he didn't supply an answer.

"Whirlybird," Rig shouted, bobbing up and down in the water. "Come on! We're gonna race it!"

The other three splashed into the water behind him and mounted up. They hadn't a chance of beating the helicopter that carried workers to and from the oil rig, but they didn't care. They plunged towards the drilling platform, popping in and out of the water in a tangle of tentacles. Derrick was slapping at his squid with his tail, trying to keep pace with Rig. The squid's usual sand-brown color changed to a deep and angry red.

Directly above them, the whirlybird blocked the sun so a shadow fell across Blep's face. He squinted up at the dark shape hovering there, as the downdraft from two sets of rotor blades whipped a ring of spreading, choppy ripples around the Hell's Anglerfish. The noise pulsed in his ears. The bird rolled to one side so its occupants could get a better look at this startling example of pinniped behavior. Blep gazed back, raising himself out of the water for a better look.

"Dive, you fool!" Rig's belly smacked the water as he plunged down. Blep, blushing at the rebuke, dived deep and fast below the surface. The cool water soothed the hot flush in his skin.

That was only the start of a busy day for the Hell's Anglerfish. They romped through a colony of basking seals, splashing them with water and rolling the more unwary from their napping spots into the sea. They mixed themselves up with a pod of dolphins and put them off their graceful leaps and rolls until the pod drove the intruders away with snapping snouts and angry squeaks. Finally, they surrounded a small fishing-boat, diving around and under it until it capsized, and making off with the catch.

Now the setting sun was turning the upper layers of the water pink and pearl. They stopped off on a flat rock in the shallows above a bed of seagrass to graze the squid and let Littleneck practice his diving. He was starting to babble now, imitating the barks and honks of his funny family.

Big Rig scratched his stomach contentedly, blinking at his gang. He yawned and fell asleep.

Derrick lay spread out on the rocks with the sun warming his back, and gazed at his leader. No harm would come to Big Rig on Derrick's watch.

Blep lay down, eyes on Littleneck as the otter bobbed in the water. His brother lay down next to him, crowding him with his shoulder. Blep shuffled away. Oily flopped sideways until he was next to him again. Blep shuffled. Oily flopped.

"Go away, Oily. You smell like a rotting whale carcass."

"No, *you* do." He laid his neck over Blep's.

Blep struggled free, huffing. "Just leave me alone!" he growled. Oily slapped him with his flipper. He didn't mean to hurt, but he caught Blep's squid ink tattoo, still raw. Blep headbutted his brother so hard Oily slid along the rock, pebbles bruising his belly.

"I only let you join because Mum said I had to!" Oily hadn't meant to yell it so loudly. He looked over his shoulder. Rig and Derrick had heard his outburst and were staring at him.

Rig, who had been woken from his nap, glowered. "Use your underwater voice, for crying out loud," he growled.

Oily covered his face with his flipper and curled up his

163

hindquarters.

"That's not nice, Oily," Derrick said. "Blep passed the initiation fair and square."

The California sea lion gave an angry honk, dived off the rock, belly-flopped into the water, and swam very far away. Blep rubbed awkwardly at his gang tattoo, where the scab was itching, and turned his back on the others.

None of them saw the raid coming. Blep's squid rose from the seabed and gave an anxious wiggle, but Blep wasn't watching. He saw nothing until water splashed across his warm, dry fur.

"Oily..." he began, angrily. But his brother was nowhere in sight. Instead, a pack of six interlopers was circling them. They rode red devil squid, streamlined and shiny, with tangerine-flake bodywork. "Spider Crabs!" Blep squeaked, beating his flippers on the rock.

The rival gang was upon them, leaping out of the water and rolling the Hell's Anglerfish into the waves. Six Steller sea lions with red-brown coats, bigger than their California cousins Blep and Oily, bigger than Derrick the fur seal, almost as big as Big Rig himself.

"You snooze, you lose!" Pearl, the leader of the Spider Crabs, whooped. She put her flipper to her nose and waggled her finny fingers. The Hell's Anglerfish thrashed around in the water, spitting out seaweed and calling for their squid. The Spider Crabs, up on the rock, clapped and barked with laughter.

Big Rig hauled himself back up out of the sea, roaring with rage. But the elephant seal's bulk, and his hind flippers, built for swimming not for land, meant he could only flop along like a beached fish. The Spider Crabs swung their hind flippers forward and lolloped away, yelping with derision and triumph. Rig opened his mouth wide and bawled after them as they jumped back in the water, revved up their squid and zoomed off.

"Mount up! Get them!" Rig looked left and right, so fast he slapped himself in the face with his own trunk. "Ow! Grab Littleneck and let's go!"

"Rig. He's not here." Derrick trembled, and his squid went dead white.

"I think," Blep said, timidly, "I think the Spider Crabs took him."

"None of you was *watching* him?" Rig blared, rising up on his substantial rear and baring his fierce, blunt teeth.

Derrick's squid turned the grey color of the surrounding rocks. Derrick tried to hide behind it.

"He's not angry at you," Blep said. "He's angry at himself."

"Shut up, Blep!" Oily shoved him.

"And so are you," Blep said, but very quietly.

Big Rig flumped into the water, whistling up his squid. It rushed up in a swirl of bubbles, and spun as it ploughed through the water, Rig hanging on by his claws.

The chase was on.

Red devil squid are fast, but the Hell's Anglerfish were angry and desperate. Big Rig took the lead with Derrick on his right as wingman. Oily and Blep rode the slipstream behind, forming a staggered V shape.

The Spider Crabs would be heading for their hideout: the steel hulk of a destroyer wrecked long ago that jutted out of the water. Once they had reached it, the Spider Crabs could keep their enemies at bay by throwing rocks from the deck.

The six sea lions rode in a tight formation, their squid almost touching. Pearl's was the largest, its sides white with old scars where it had fought battles and escaped from fishing-nets.

"Split up! Derrick, Oily, maneuver number three!" Big Rig's underwater voice was squeaky, but it reached Blep's ears just fine.

"What do I do?" he called from the rear.

Rig looked over his shoulder. "Just stay out of trouble," he advised. Blep saw the ship ahead, coming up fast, and the first of the Spider Crabs propelling herself out of the water to the deck. He stroked Squidney's mantle in the spot the squid liked.

"Engage supercharger!" Derrick yelled. He tickled his squid under the chin. A jet of water shot from its siphon, and it powered forwards. He headed round to the right of the Steller sea lions, darting through the seaweed.

Oily steered round to the left. "Now! Smokescreen!" he called. Both squid released a cloud of ink that spread through the water, hiding the Hell's Anglerfish from sight. The four paddled carefully through the eerie murk. Rocks plopped into the water around them, but the big Stellers were firing blind. The Hell's Anglerfish swam to the other side of the ship and hauled themselves on board.

"We've got you surrounded," Big Rig called, shaking himself. The Spider Crabs, six to their four, did not look impressed by this.

Blep, boarding last, searched anxiously for Littleneck, and spotted him with his head buried in Pearl's shoulder. The big sea lion was cradling him in one flipper. Pearl looked at Blep, and then down at Blep's squid, wallowing low in the water.

"Is it sick or something?" she asked.

"I'm not sure," Blep admitted.

"Don't talk to her," Rig snapped. "You! Give that baby back right now!"

"Or what?" She plucked a small jellyfish from her flank, popped it into her mouth, and placed Littleneck on the deck. Spotting his friends, he waved cheerfully. Pearl's gang barked and clapped their flippers, and the otter did his best to copy them.

"Maybe your buddy would rather ride with us?" Pearl continued. "We're faster than you guys. We're *better*."

"Give him back!" Big Rig said again. "Littleneck's not a toy, or a trophy! He's a little baby sea otter!"

"Look who's talking." She chewed on her jellyfish and scooped up the otter. Littleneck struggled in her arms, reaching out for Rig. "You guys should be ashamed of yourselves. An oil rigs no place to bring up a kid. Ever bother trying to find out where his real family is?"

"*We're* his real family!" Derrick roared. He hugged his squid, which turned violent pink. Rig waved a flipper to shush him.

"Maybe you're right," Rig admitted. "I promise we'll take him to the sea otter colony and find out if anyone's missing a kid, okay? Just give him back. Please?"

Blep and Derrick looked at each other. Neither of them had ever heard Rig say "please" before, let alone admit that someone else was right.

"The Spider Crabs are the greatest!" Pearl jiggled Littleneck upside-down so he chuckled. "Say it!"

Rig's eyes were an angry red. "The Spider..."

"All of you together."

The elephant seal rounded on his gang. "You heard the lady! Loud as you can! On three! One... two..."

Their declaration was drowned by the noise of the whirlybird, returning from the drilling platform with the workers at the end of their shift. It was so low that Blep threw himself down with his flippers over his ears. The downdraught from the twin rotors ruffled his fur. Littleneck, lying on his back, slid across the deck, giggling. Before anyone could grab him, he was on the edge of an open hatch. His forepaws scrabbled for a grip before he dropped out of sight. There was silence for a second, then a faint *plop* from below.

Crowded together, the two gangs stared down into the black water.

"Littleneck!" Rig bawled. He tried to cram himself through the hatch, but got stuck at his shoulders and pulled back, huffing. "Littleneck!"

Nothing moved.

Blep noticed it first: a greenish glow that shimmered and rippled, making the square of water dance with light.

"What is it? Rig asked.

Pearl spat out the remains of her jellyfish. "Dunno. Never seen it before," she admitted. She backed away a little. Rig did the same.

Blep peered closer and made out tentacles.

"It's Squidney!" he hooted, and plunged nose first down the hatch.

The water he found himself in was warm and sluggish, tasting of iron and oil. He took a deep breath, closed his mouth and nostrils and dived. His squid rose to meet him, twirled in the water, and sank again into the underwater corridors. In the shallows it had been a dingy grey color, but here in the gloomy innards of the abandoned ship it shone with a luminescence that bounced off the walls, lighting Blep's way. Its flickering glow showed broken pipes, jagged and rusty, and dark, gaping hatchways.

"Good boy. Find the baby," Blep said. "Find Littleneck."

They dived lower. The stale water grew cold. Blep couldn't smell, but he strained his ears and caught a faint chirp. Littleneck's underwater voice. Which direction was it coming from?

Blep's little squid seemed to inflate and stretch itself out before shooting into a narrow corridor. Holding on to the slippery mantle, Blep hoped it knew where it was going. He also hoped it knew mammals had to breathe sometimes.

Passages branched off to either side. As they flashed past, Blep caught a glimpse of something moving. "Whoa there, Squidney! Back up!"

Unable to turn round in the confined space, Squidney reversed its siphon and swam back the way they had come, arms first. The side passage opened out into a dark space like a cave. Blep peered about in the shifting light from his squid. Pieces of human furniture, tables and chairs, were bolted to the floor, and there was a rock up against one wall.

A rock? Humans didn't sit on rocks.

He paddled Squidney forward and poked the rock with a flipper. It flushed red. As it uncurled Blep recognized the scarred flanks of Pearl's monster squid. It was holding Littleneck, one of its eight arms wound tightly around him. A huge eye stared at Blep, and the red devil made off in a rush of water and bubbles.

Whether it was scared by glowing Squidney or it wanted to carry the baby sea otter off and eat him, Blep didn't know and didn't care. He and his squid gave chase, swimming across the mess and out through a back door. The red devil flicked around a corner and down a twisting stairwell, heading further and lower into the ship. Blep could feel his muscles fizzing in protest at the lack of oxygen. How long could a baby sea otter hold its breath down here? How deep could its little body go before the pressure got too much?

Squidney's arms uncurled and streamed out behind it. Blep clung on, ducking and leaning as pipes and bulkheads came close to hitting him. They were gaining on the red devil as it struggled to squeeze itself through gaps and around corners that Blep's nimble little mount could manage easily.

Blep had never caught up with anyone before.

As he hurtled along behind, one of the red devil's feeding tentacles slapped his neck. He felt it tear the flesh with its hooked teeth. Blood floated from his wound, black in the dark water, and curled away behind him. Blep pushed on, slicing the water with his flippers to urge Squidney forward. The tentacle uncoiled towards him again, and this time he grabbed it in his teeth, just above the hooks. He was jerked from Squidney's back and reeled in towards the red devil's mouth, his jaws filled with writhing, rubbery anger.

He thought of the special spot under the mantle where his own squid liked to be tickled. He reached out his flipper and tickled the red devil. Its arms writhed in delight, and its grip on Littleneck loosened. Blep grabbed the baby and flipped away. When Squidney rose to meet him, he tumbled onto its back.

Littleneck pressed his head into the sea lion's chest, not wasting his breath with so much as a squeak hello. They had to get back to the surface, and quickly. Blep, holding the otter closely to him, could feel his brain going fuzzy. The edges of his vision darkened.

His instinct was to go up, but he wouldn't be able to get out the way he had got in; the hatch was too high. *Think.* Squidney had gotten into the ship somehow, underwater. That meant Blep and the baby could get out. He had to head down — down to where the ship rested on the seabed. Maybe there would be a hole where the hull had struck a rock.

He felt the flow of fresher water across his whiskers, and swung his squid towards it. A metal door had bent inwards slightly so that a gap showed at the top. Squidney wriggled from under him and oozed through. Blep pushed the baby otter through the gap. Squidney's phosphorescent glow disappeared, and he hoped the squid was taking Littleneck back to the surface. At least the little otter would be saved. And the others would see that Blep was just as tough as the rest of them, even though he was small.

Small. Tough.

Blep fitted one flipper into the gap, then the other. Then his head. Bracing himself against the ceiling, he pushed with all his sea lion bulk.

The metal scraped painfully across his stomach, but with a last wiggle of his hind flippers Blep swam out into clean salt water. Far above, light glittered on the surface of the sea. He pushed towards it, his flippers numb where his body had diverted blood to his brain to keep him conscious. When his head broke the surface in a foam of bubbles, he opened mouth and nostrils to gulp in the air. Pearl and Rig, with Littleneck already on his shoulders, helped Blep climb back up onto the sloping deck.

Oily lumbered towards him. The two brothers coiled their necks together, nuzzling.

"I thought I'd lost you," Oily gasped. "Don't tell Mum," he added.

"I won't!"

"It's settled, then." Big Rig shook himself so his trunk wobbled. Littleneck laughed. The sea otter was curled up against Rig's side, gnawing on a crab, as the five of them lazed on the wharf. "Tomorrow we set out to find this little guy's family. He's not a thing to be passed around. He's a person."

"Maybe we won't find them," Oily said hopefully. "Maybe they won't want him back. Maybe he'd rather stay with us."

"I thought you didn't like the baby," Blep muttered, looking out to the deeper water where his squid was going around in circles.

"I don't!" Oily said quickly. "But... I know *you* like him." He poked Blep with his snout.

"It's for his own good. Besides. He slows us down." Rig glared at Littleneck, who just laughed more.

"It's okay to be sad, Rig. Loving someone doesn't make you any less tough." Derrick reached out his brown flipper and placed it on top of Rig's. The elephant seal stared down at him and bared his teeth, but Derrick didn't take his flipper away. He looked up at his leader, and Big Rig's scowl gradually changed to a smile. He nuzzled the top of the fur seal's head.

"No, it doesn't, and I'll fight anyone who says it does!" Rig barked. "So let's give our newest recruit a day to remember before we go looking for his family. We want him to come back when he's bigger, and catch a squid and get a tattoo and ride with us, right?"

They whistled, and the four squid swam up. Blep leaned down to scratch his between its eyes.

"I've been thinking," he said. "Squidney's not a trophy either, and I don't think he's happy here with me. I think he wants to go back to the dark deeps, where he belongs."

The others looked at him.

"You know you can't be in the Hell's Anglerfish without a squid to ride," Big Rig rumbled.

"That's not true! You only need to *catch* one!" Oily nodded his head and drummed his flippers in his excitement. "Blep can ride with me — can't you, kid? There's room on here for two, and the baby too."

"Go on, Squidney," Blep whispered. "You're free!"

His small grey squid spun around in the water a few times before diving. They saw a green glow from the depths, which gradually faded as the squid swam away.

Blep climbed on to Oily's squid behind his brother, Littleneck sitting between them.

"Okay!" Big Rig threw his head back, and his trunk flopped to the side. He looked proudly at his gang. "Let's ride!"

The Singer of the Seas

By Su Haddrell

Navin waited beneath the anemone canopy and braced herself. The Shirras were raiding again, but this time they were ready for it. The Vanguard had been summoned and Navin, the swiftest and deadliest of the Wresh warriors, was at their forefront. She dipped her head and let her spines feel for the subtle changes in water temperature and direction that indicated movement.

There...

She beat her tail hard, swinging out from the canopy into the open water and the face of her startled enemy. He was young. His face mottled with a flicker of color and he hovered before her, tentacles undulating with agitation beneath him. Navin grinned at his fear. She sang and clicked through the deep, calling the Vanguard to her aid. Raising her long knife, she pressed forward, eager to fight and impatient for the taste of Shirras blood in the water. She sensed the Wresh appearing around her. Their presence was a pulse through the water, reassuring her, urging her on. Navin could feel the Shirras signaling to each other, heavy vibrations that caused the fan of her tail to twitch with unease.

The song of her Wresh brethren amplified. There were more of the Shirras than the small Vanguard had anticipated, but they seemed young and inexperienced in the face of the ancient warrior line. Navin had prepared for such threats her entire life and the call of war sang through her blood as thick as algae on coral.

The Shirras counter-attacked and Navin reacted instinctively, calling out a barrage of clicks and whistles to each unit, ordering their repositioning and advancement on the raiders. The fight was swift and brutal.

The Shirras carried tridents tipped with shock hooks. Their tactic was to sweep in close, wrap their tentacles around Wresh tails, and force a close quarters fight. The barbs on their tridents could easily knock out an unwary creature and the Vanguard knew to stay well clear if possible.

The Wresh retaliated with a combination of bone spears and long knives, using their powerful tails to dart in and out of the pack of raiders, attempting to gash their limbs. Navin sang with the joy of it and her bloodlust boosted her troop into a frenzy. The Shirras soon retreated, their deep vibrating calls signaling defeat and fear as they pulled themselves away and back into the dark waters. The Wresh roared their victory into the deep.

Rikasha glanced sideways at the two guards escorting them into the Wresh Conclave and his feelers twitched with anxiety. Branesh didn't seem concerned, but years of experience told him that the Shirras Consul was carefully maintaining an air of professional civility.

The stress of the situation would hit him later on when he had time to sit and mull over the meeting. For now, they just needed to get through this audience successfully. Rikasha felt the water vibrate slightly against his thick old tentacles.

The Wresh escorts were as tense as he, although he sensed it was more of a fight response than fear. He squeezed his old webbed fingers tighter around his trident.

The Wresh Conclave rose up in front of them, a great winding polyp of woven carbonate that towered over the reef, fanning out like a fungus at its head. The trunk of it was busy with dens and caves that tunneled through the giant coral. As they reached the top, the Conclave opened out into a huge arched dome, patterned with a rainbow of delicate branches and swirls and beautifully lit with cleverly placed phosphorous lichen. Rikasha once again found himself impressed with Wresh artistry. The Shirras were a functional species that were more focused on farming sea-grass and protecting their young.

Whilst Rikasha had always agreed with the necessity of their darkened caverns, looking around the Conclave gave him a longing for color that surprised him. Few things felt new and interesting at his age. The Wresh Magister greeted them with a warm warble and gestured for them to settle comfortably. The two guards were dismissed and almost instantly, Rikasha felt the tension leave the water.

"Thank you for granting us an audience, Magister Deposk," Branesh began, gesturing formally. The mass of tendrils across his head were smoothed back and his facial colors flickered with soft browns to indicate placidity. He settled into a hollow and folded his tentacles beneath him.

Rikasha followed suit, placing his trident before him. The journey to the Wresh city had been tiring and he was eager to rest. Not for the first time, he wondered why Branesh had asked him along. He was an old warrior, wizened in the ways of ambush and defense, but the waters had begun to chill his limbs and he felt the pull of the deep calling him.

The Magister offered them refreshments, a leafy plate containing sweet fruits. Both Shirras accepted the offering only out of politeness, but when the fragrant kernels burst in his mouth, Rikasha instantly wished for a thousand more.

Magister Deposk smiled as though expecting the reaction and settled himself back into a hollow framed by an ornate lattice of woven fronds. He was large, even by Wresh standards. His chest and belly sagged towards his tail and his arms were flabby sacks of pale skin that rippled unpleasantly when he moved. His tail was almost entirely golden, a sign of maturity, and it shimmered beneath the glowing lichen. His head spines were short and Rikasha wondered if he were able to sense anything at all in the waters.

The Wresh were lazy, he realised. Cultured and creative, yes, but lethargic and arrogant. Their ancient Vanguard was all that truly protected them from the potential horrors of the deep. The tactical advantage of this realization was not lost on Rikasha but it soon turned into pity. The Shirras were on the verge of annihilation, and if it came to pass, then soon after the beautifully created cities of the Wresh would be nothing but white bone. He pursed his lips and waited for the negotiation to begin.

"Your request for an audience surprised me," the Magister trilled. "I confess, I agreed to it out of curiosity more than diplomacy." His tone was arrogant and Rikasha's feelers bristled. He bunched his hands into fists. If Branesh took offence, he didn't show it.

"Hopefully, curiosity will lead to diplomacy, Magister," the politician replied, letting a calm vibration enter his voice. The Magister twitched the fan of his tail in agreement.

"What do the Shirras require of the Wresh?" Deposk asked. Rikasha sensed the tension in the water, as though the Magister were deliberately provoking the Consul into an aggressive response.

"We seek a truce between our two species to enable the defeat of a greater evil," Branesh said. The Magister raised his eyebrows and leaned back, gesturing for the Consul to continue.

"My people are under attack by a great beast. It slips through our trenches during the dark tides, attacking and feasting on our brethren. It is fast and tough. As you are aware, our species are slow breeders and our young rarely make it to maturity. The protection of our clutches are our greatest priority. However, the stress of these attacks is deeply affecting our females. Fewer and fewer broods are now being produced. The beast will soon devour us all."

The Magister popped a fruit into his mouth and blinked at the two Shirras as though he were listening them tell a hatchling tale. He seemed unconcerned with the Consul's account.

"This beast does not appear to stop your raiding parties," the Magister warbled mildly. "Our Vanguard drew blood against one such group this very tide."

Branesh was slow to reply. "There has been much... debate... between our people. They bicker and fight among themselves as though the problem doesn't exist." The Consul whistled coolly. "I am not here on their say so," he said after a reluctant pause.

Rikasha rippled with surprise and tried not to show his reaction in his colours. If the other Shirras found out that the Consul had come here without their knowledge, then it would only intensify the internal fighting.

"The younger Shirras form raiding parties on your city to prove their worth," Branesh continued. "Traditionally our people were ambush fighters and not raiders. We have lost many of our oldest warriors due to the ongoing attacks and so many of them now are inexperienced. I come here seeking your aid in stopping the beast as I believe we no longer have the capability to do so ourselves."

Navin was just stirring in her den when the messenger fish came to summon her for a private audience with the Magister. She was both unnerved and excited by the prospect, having no true idea as to why she had been requested. She mulled over the earlier skirmish as she pulled on her best plate armor. The attack had been successfully overcome and none of her brethren had been injured - she knew she had behaved with discipline. If she were to be admonished for some transgression – or better still, praised for her command - then she would have been called in front of the Guardian. The Guardian administered justice and commanded troops when necessary, but was nearing an age where he would no longer be able to venture into the deep. It was generally accepted that he preferred the warmer waters of the Wresh Conclave to leading the Vanguard into battle, so the Magister had no reason to request a private audience for Navin specifically. Unless something was wrong with the Guardian himself and it was time...

Navin's tail fan fluttered anxiously as she pushed her way up to the Conclave. Yellow anemones swayed gently as she passed by and a school of wrasse darted shyly back into their depths. Crabs skittered up the side of the tower, their pink and white shells patterning the coral like tiny colored lights. The waters grew warm as she floated higher up and she felt the great jets from inside the tower surging the liquid around and into the canopy itself. She entered the woven Conclave and gave an involuntary hiss of agitation.

Two Shirras were settled calmly before the Magister as though their presence in Wresh territory were a completely normal occurrence.

The skin of one was dappled like sand colored marble and he had large dark eyes and a mouth that was wide and appeasing.

Navin knew a politician when she saw one and her spines prickled at the serene patience he radiated.

The other Shirras looked almost dead on his tentacles. His coloring was a thunderous grey and his head tendrils flicked listlessly. He slumped slightly, as though holding his gaunt frame up were an effort in itself. He was old but a glance at his trident indicated he was warrior nonetheless and not one to be trifled with. His eyes were small and quick and he took in everything around him with shrewd regard.

Navin realised she had instinctively moved into an attack position and quickly reasserted herself, turning to the Magister and bowing. Magister Deposk smiled expansively.

"This is Navin, the commander of our Vanguard," he chirped with pride. Navin's spines crawled. She didn't enjoy being the subject of ego, paraded about to prove her worth to the abyss-damned Shirras.

"You require use of my skills, Magister?" she asked, trying to keep the tone of her clicks neutral. The overweight Wresh clapped his hands together.

"I do!" he said. "I have consented to a treaty with the Shirras. Until such time as this has been finalized, they require your aid."

Navin growled. Every instinct in her body told her to beat her tail, raise her spear and shed Shirras blood. A treaty with them! After the amount of young they had destroyed, they were only fit for Old Shadow himself. She looked back at Magister Deposk, intent on launching into a raging tirade but hesitated when she sensed his dangerous low rumble. The Magister had made a decision. The Guardian had likely been informed already and regardless of his approval, Navin was required to fulfil her duty.

Duty had always been foremost and serving the Wresh was her true obligation. The thought calmed her enough to notice that the Magister was flicking his tail fan and had changed the tone of his rumble slightly. Navin's eyes widened and her spines rippled with surprise. They communicated covertly between one another for some seconds and suddenly Navin understood the full reason for her summons.

"What do the Shirras require of me?" she asked.

"The Shirras are being terrorized by a shark," Deposk said, unable to keep the mocking tone from his warble. Navin kept her expression neutral.

"With respect, sharks are a myth," she said. "They have never been seen in these territories. Sharks are tales told by travelers."

The younger Shirras spoke up. "The beast is tough and quick. It is described as having rows of teeth that are sharper than razorshells. It passes through the water without any vibration; you can never sense it coming."

Navin raised her eyebrows. "I've heard those stories too. A hunter that steals its prey away to devour it in a frenzy of blood and entrails. Some say it's even invisible! Have you actually seen it?" she asked.

The politician shifted uncomfortably. "Not personally." he trilled.

"I have." The old warrior rose up on his tentacles, a smooth sinuous movement that belied his elderly appearance. He picked up the trident before him and stood proud, clutching the weapon with gnarled fingers. "I've seen the darkness that flits through the water without a ripple. It is fast and silent. It hunts my brethren and disappears without a trace. But I have seen it. I have watched it from my den. It is as legend described. It is a *shark*."

Navin watched the old warrior shrewdly.

"And how did you survive whilst watching from your den? Why did he not feast on your old bones?"

"You would do well to aid us in our request," the warrior replied, ignoring her question. "If the Shirras are lost, then the Wresh will be next."

Navin felt a tremor of excitement shiver through to her tail fan. "I am eager to take on this task and destroy the beast for both our peoples," she trilled, feeling slightly foolish as she did so.

Magister Deposk clapped his hands together again in pleasure and she tipped her head respectfully to him.

"The Shirras should accompany me," she added in an attempt to sound magnanimous. "They would do well to retain their honor in killing the beast."

"Rikasha will accompany you," the politician shirras said. The warrior Shirras turned to him in protest, and his clicks of indignation reverberating shrilly.

"What would you have me...?" the old warrior, Rikasha, started. The Shirras raised his hands.

"Our peoples honor cannot be tarnished," he said. "We agree to treaty, and humbly accept the aid of the Wresh, but our people will not. I do this for the good of our brethren, but we must retain our honor if this is to be accomplished at all." The Shirras' tone brooked no argument.

They left the Wresh city under the cover of a dark tide. Rikasha was pleased to finally be in cooler waters, away from the realm of politics and negotiation. He feared that he would always associate bright colors and warm water with tense arguments and the uncomfortable sensation of not belonging. He was fuming at Branesh who had all but tricked him into the ridiculous quest under the guise of honor, knowing that honor would be the very thing that trapped him there.

If they failed their crusade, then an elderly warrior had died an honorable death. If they succeeded, then he would influence the other warriors for tides to come. He stewed silently and sensed the Wresh, Navin, doing the same at his side. Neither were particularly enthralled with one another's company and it occurred to Rikasha that this in itself was common ground.

He rumbled quietly to himself, letting his tentacles beneath him flick with irritation. If there were to be common ground between the two species, then there were worse places to start.

Navin was headstrong and fierce. Her tail was dappled with blue and gold, pearly and iridescent as it flickered through the deep. She held her spines up proudly and her armor was a thing of beauty, sculpted from the secretions of hunja corals, a rare but almost indestructible material.

Rikasha looked down at his old chest plate, scuffed and beaten but still strong, and wondered if he could stand up to the ancient beast at all.

They travelled deeper into darker waters, past hollows and rock formations that were unrecognizable to Rikasha. The coral trees reached high up into the waters, and brown algae began to grow thickly beneath them. Curved sponges scattered themselves across the rocks, forming nurseries for myriads of tiny colored fish. Sea urchins clung to the jagged crusts, spikes of bright red and orange that stabbed at the dark.

The Wresh had some knowledge of the creature they hunted, maps and stories that had been etched into clam shells and stored over many tides. The songs were all tales of exploration and daring, of great heroes setting out to bring back new materials or encountering strange and terrifying monsters. Their research identified a cave system some distance out from the territories that would perhaps be a suitable lair for the beast to retreat to, and maybe to raise young. Rikasha looked across to Navin, who thrummed with nervous tension.

"Your people are very proud of you," he said conversationally. Navin twitched in surprise, lost in her own thoughts.

"Of course," she clicked irritably. "I am the best fighter."

"My people take pride in learning about our enemy. You win your battles with ease and must be a clever warrior," he continued.

Navin stopped and spun to glare at him. Her teeth flashed at him, sharp and white in the gloom. "Do not seek to befriend me with fine words, Shirras."

Rikasha mottled with color and calmed himself. "I do not seek friendship, only an ally against a greater foe," he replied.

Navin was nervous. A thousand tides of training had prepared her for this and still she was as twitchy as a young whelp. She couldn't help it. She had always known the Guardian would have to accept the call of the deep, she just hadn't realised it would be so *soon*.

It had been foretold that he would step down, but the moment had finally arrived when Navin was obligated to take his place, and she had suddenly come to the realization that she was to be more than just a warrior. She would be a general. A protector. She would become the Singer of the Seas.

The responsibility tightened around her like seaweed wrapping around her tail. She clutched her spear tightly and beat slowly through the dark water, all but forgetting the Shirras at her side until he spoke.

He was attempting to charm her with compliments, and again there was the temptation to take her long knife and slit his throat. She remembered her duty to the Magister, the Wresh, and the Old Shadow himself. Allies indeed. Navin glanced over to the old warrior and rippled her spines with reluctant assent.

"You are right," she warbled to Rikasha. "We have a greater

enemy than one another." She sensed the Shirras relax slightly.

"I confess; I know little of the creature to plan an attack," he said. "Your folk seem to have much lore on it. Do you have any suggestions?"

Navin couldn't decide if Rikasha was trying to ingratiate himself to her, but chose to ignore it. "The beast is quick, so we have to be cunning," she replied. "Your shock trident will be enough to distract it whilst my long knife will make the killing blow. We can use a combination of ambush and speed," she finished, devising a strategy without realizing she was doing so.

Rikasha nodded with approval. "Using both of our methods will make us a formidable team," he rumbled.

Navin did not reply.

Rikasha was wary. He had never travelled so far from his den, and the tremors in the water felt alien to him. Every temperature change made his tentacles tighten.

They passed through a thick forest of kelp. The fronds grew up around them, long flat belts of brown that waved with the rhythm of the tide. The waters were relatively calm and Navin could sense the movement of many creatures beneath her, hastening for cover as they swam by.

The gorge deepened beneath them they moved into murky waters, a cavern system of volcanic rocks that were dimpled and rough with age. They navigated carefully, looking down at the darkened caves beneath them - easy shelter for predators.

Rikasha kept glancing into the dark cracks in the bedrock, waiting with apprehension for a sudden ambush or the snap of a heavy jaw. They swam deeper into the murk, gliding down into the fathoms, where the silence became oppressive and the darkness felt claustrophobic. Rikasha swore he saw the bodies of other creatures scattered against the crags, pale remnants of bone and fin, left behind to warn other explorers.

Something caught his eye and he looked back. A black shape glided behind them.

Rikasha twisted around. He switched his shock trident into his other hand and pumped his tentacles against the water. The shape moved again, a curving blackness that was there one second and gone the next.

There was no sound, no vibration in the water, no change in temperature or any indication that the dark shape was even out there, but Rikasha could still somehow sense it. A prickle in his tendrils that was more instinct than knowledge.

He remembered hiding in the back of his den, shivering like a coward whilst his brethren were slaughtered by blackness ahead of him. The memory flared bright and hot, a twisted knot of shame and anger and fear.

Navin hovered beside him, searching the darkness, beating her tail slowly and keeping her long knife at the ready. Rikasha wondered how she stayed so calm.

Between them they scanned the caverns, and then, with a low whistle of communication between them, they descend further, taking shelter beneath the cover of a jutting precipice. Rikasha controlled his colors, focusing into a camouflaging mosaic of greys and blacks.

The shadow passed overhead, lower this time, an elliptical void that slowly advanced on its prey. It seemed to be circling, maneuvering carefully until it was ready to strike.

Rikasha tensed. Every fibre of his old body strained to sense where the predator was. A silhouette appeared directly ahead of them. It grew bigger, approaching as fast as a marlin chasing tuna.

Suddenly all Rikasha could see was the shark - a blunt nose and a wide mouth that opened to reveal a black maw of serrated teeth. So many teeth, fast approaching and terrifyingly sharp. Rikasha froze with fear. Navin began to sing.

Navin sang a soft clear whistle that formed gently into melody and then into chant. She moved out from beneath the shelter, warbling rhythmically, pumping her tail slowly and clutching her long knife before her.

The shark hesitated. A tremor of relief shivered through the Wresh, but she kept singing, letting the song of her ancestors hum though her from her spines to her tail fan. She poured her heart into the song, focusing every thought, every feeling into the long whistles as she had been taught her entire life.

It was the culmination of her training and the final test of her skills. A single trill out of sync, or whistle off key would break the ancient spell.

The shark closed its mouth. It was the first time she had ever seen it in real life and it was as magnificent as the Guardian had described. Its ridged skin was a deep blue-grey that curved smoothly into a thick strong tail and blade-like fins.

Navin edged forward, singing continuously until she aligned herself alongside the great creature. The shark began to move slowly from side to side, waving its massive tail and keeping itself moving, but no longer pushing forward. Navin moved with it and her voice carried through the nebulous deep. She watched the black pit of the shark's eye. It blinked slowly. Its fins changed position, dipping slightly. Navin stopped singing.

Rikasha stayed beneath the canopy and watched the Wresh, his colors flickering with shock and his tentacles churned the water beneath him. He drew up his trident and made ready to attack.

"I wouldn't do that," Navin said to him. She poised calmly next to the shark and lowered her blade. Rikasha finally understood.

"You knew about it all along," he said, needing her to admit it. He sensed his final moments in the deep drawing closer.

"Old Shadow is our ancestral heritage," Navin trilled with pride. "His blood spawned the Wresh many millions of tides ago. He protects us and watches over our territories."

"This was never about saving our people," Rikasha growled at her. "This was a rite of passage for you." He suddenly felt stupid. Telling the young warrior that he had figured out what was going on didn't change the situation. It wouldn't save his life. A surge of anger fired through him.

"You are my sacrifice," the Wresh told him. "Your death will create the bond between Old Shadow and I. Together we will continue the work that my predecessor started and we will wipe your wretched species from existence."

Rikasha's thoughts raced. The beast was under Wresh control, but it was a predator nonetheless. It had no loyalties, only instinct.

Navin seemed to sense his thoughts and signaled the old shark with a sharp whistle. It opened its mouth, skimming forward with barely a surge. Rikasha reacted without thinking, drawing his trident up and thrusting forward, sending a shock of electricity into the creature's nose.

The shark jerked his head upwards and flipped out with its heavy tail. It circled briefly overhead and then turned to torpedo downwards, but Rikasha was ready for it. He thrust forward from beneath the cave, undulating his tentacles furiously and rising up to meet the beast head on.

Behind him he heard Navin whistle, a shriek that cut through the water like a missile. Old Shadow hesitated in its path and for the first time, Rikasha sensed something from the shark. It was confused. The Shirras leapt on the advantage, pressing forward and jabbing his trident against the blunt of shark's snout. There was a low crack and Old Shadow veered off again.

The beast weaved to and fro in the darkness above them, endlessly circling as though it were dazed. Navin gave a cry of frustration. She beat her tail and raised her blade, coming up to attack Rikasha directly.

The old warrior sensed the movement in the water and grinned manically, turning to meet her. The Wresh had failed her assignment and had lost her temper. He let her come to him, remaining calm and almost motionless in the water. He watched her swing the long knife and as she did so, he spun in close, a whirl within the water.

Thick tentacles wrapped themselves around her torso, pinning her arms to her sides, and restraining the thumping golden tail. The Shirras grabbed her throat and held the barbs of his trident to her chin. Navin wrestled against him helplessly. Above them, Old Shadow turned once more.

"Your people slaughtered my brethren," he hissed at her. "The beast is no longer within your control."

He felt the call of the deep, a cold ripple of death that sang painfully through him. Only vengeance mattered now. Old Shadow began to race down towards them. The great mouth opened and the white needles glowed against black. Navin wriggled, but the attempt was useless. The Shirras held her as tight as a whelk against rock.

"My death will be honorable and will save the lives of my brethren," Rikasha growled with pleasure. "Yours will be worthless."

The silhouette moved without a ripple. The shark plummeted

towards them and all they could see were the broken points of thousands of pale teeth.

Navin gaped, opening her mouth to cry, to scream, to sing, but no sound emerged with the shirras' tight grip on her throat. There was only silence. The darkness filled their vision and the abyss engulfed them.

Old Shadow circled the caves for a while after feeding, enjoying the aftertaste of meat and blood. The frenzy had not lasted long. The remnants of his feast slowly sank to the bottom of the ocean where other fish would pick at it, whittling away at the flesh and fin until nothing remained.

The shark felt his head clear as though a restraint of vibration had been released. The tailed creature that had controlled him had been young, different from the one that had come previously. It had tasted strong and had been far more filling than the others he had been forced to hunt. Old Shadow swam into the kelp forest and the direction of the Wresh city. It was time to hunt for a richer food source.

Courage under Pressure

By Daniel R. Robichaud

All my life, I only wanted to prove myself to myself as well as to everyone else. This was true ever since I was a little squid, roaming about the mighty Pacific. Growing larger and bolder with every passing year, I ultimately grew large enough to tangle with and devour whales. Demonstrable courage was my goal, and the best kind was that arising under pressure.

So, imagine my surprise when I encountered such an opportunity under the strangest circumstances. Sudden pressure fluctuations blasted my concentration and sent me spinning without direction. I was little more than a confused baby squid, all right, my tentacles all in a tizzy. My pod, too, went nuts. It was a terrifying thing, having the water we were so comfortable in pounded so mercilessly. This was worse than any booming thunderstorm.

Yes, I know about thunderstorms. When I was newborn and easily terrified, I dreaded those events. But as I grew, I sought out efforts to test my character, and I eventually ventured up to the surface of my watery world during one of those terrible displays so

I might behold the mighty lights and sounds high overhead. It was all a marvel and a terror, that experience, for at the time it was senseless. Years later, I found the sense of it. A mermaid calling herself Circe explained what thunderstorms were, she getting her information from a land walker who studied the tortoises in the Galapagos Islands.

But on this day I'm talking about, in what your calendar would call the year of your Lord 1868, but which we call Tuesday, I found myself not underneath a pounding, flashing display but in the midst of one. The pod I traveled with were frightened to their guts, of course, and since I longed to understand and test myself, I rose to see what was occurring.

Small canisters descended from the surface. They burst before too long. Man things. Charges that exploded in the depths. Were they hunting my pod? Were they seeing the blubber and blood of the great whales, as I'd heard was a favored process in the distant Atlantic?

No. It turned out these miserable contraptions were seeking out a fellow swimmer in the depths, but one who could not communicate by means other than hums and groans. I mistook the poor little thing as some simpleton in need of help. He did not look like good eating, but I wasn't about to let some rude surface riding vessel ruin a fellow sea denizen's day. I swam up and up, dodging those little canisters when I could, and taking the brunt of their concussive forces when I could not. They stung when they did not tickle.

Finally, I found the source of them. A man craft whose sails were full up with wind circled around this spot of sea, doing its damnedest to ruin that poor simpleton's life. Well, I reached up and patted the hull to send it on its way, but it and its man crew proved even more simple that their humming and groaning prey, which swam below me. They threw more stinging charges upon me. No fool, I threw as many of them back as I could. It was an object lesson to those little manlings, a taste of what they were giving to the sea. Having seen how far they've gone since that day, I'd say more of them could use such a lesson.

Well, their craft ended up ablaze — which Circe tells me is a bad thing — and they then chose to hobble homeward. At the time, I assumed they would sink, but I later learned it must've survived, since Circe later met a man who claimed there was a drawing of me in some famous news source or other. Apparently, even a giant squid can know fame in the surface world it rarely visits.

I then descended to find my pod and let them know they were safe.

Before I met up with them, I encountered the simpleton, who was still humming and groaning. Being far younger and prouder at the time, I passed along its starboard side and said, "You are free, little moron. Go about your life and try not to attract such troubles, again. There might not be a strong lad like me to end them."

It either did not understand or ignored me outright.

I tried once more to be polite: "I have helped you. You can calm yourself now. Stop flitting about like an idiot. The menace is gone."

It bit me. Well. I was young and proud, as I have said before, though I am older and perhaps wiser now, these many years later. When bitten, I tended to fight back. Courage makes one blind to peril, you see. I cannot say I am particularly proud of my actions anymore, but I admit I was acting from a place of concussion-reddened flesh, irritated tentacles, and stung pride. Surely no court in the land would convict me of the course of action I then took.

I wrapped the simpleton in my arms and battered my tentacles against its body, and finally tried to shake some sense into its broken, cuttlefish-sized brain. For such a grand creature, it should have had more wisdom, no? I've known jellyfish who are more charming and witty!

The blasted thing then blazed hot as a thousand electric eels, and I realized to my horror that I could not control my limbs. The muscles were all frozen in place. I could not crush, I could not batter, but I also could not release. I was paralyzed!

The simpleton tried to free itself from my grip. To be honest, I would have been only too happy to let it go. Unfortunately, as I said, my body refused to act.

Seconds passed, and I realized that I was once again regaining some control. I was mere seconds away from regaining enough command of my own body to push off that thing when, blast its eyes, that scalding sensation coursed through me one more time, locking me in place once again.

When the little shapes emerged from it, like the remoras that ride and clean Great White Sharks, I realized the truth. This simpleton was no living creature like myself at all. It was yet another man craft, a submersible sort that was unknown at the time but has become more predominant in the decades since.

Those little men swam out in their bulky apparatuses and jabbed and poked. I was an easy target, stunned as I was. When I regained enough control of my limbs to swat at them, I shamefully admit I did so with zeal. Youthful pride was struck, after all. I shooed some away, grabbed the most ornately garbed of them, and tried to crush him to goo.

That seemed to be going well until someone lanced my eye with a harpoon.

By then, I realized my pod was speeding away and this brought me back to a clearer state of mind. I am not proud of going berserk, but that was the one battle that revealed to me the honest state of my angers and my self-destructive behavior. It would be years before I bested those impulses, of course.

I left the strange little vessel and its man crew to their business and spirited after my pod as quickly as I could propel myself.

Time heals all tentacles. At least it did mine, after that little encounter. My wounded eye sadly remained forever murky. It is not completely blind, but it grants me little more than cloudy impressions of the world I swim through. I wish it were not so, but the excesses of youth leave their scars.

When I caught up to that pod, they were aghast at the situation and awed by my response. They never beheld such courage, first against the man craft on the surface and then against the strange intruder into our depths. I wish I could say I was honorable and did not ply that respect to surround myself with several prospective mates when I broadcast my spermatozoa, but as I say, I was young. Foolish. Proud. And, yes, hurt. Physically, sure, but emotionally worst of all. Spiritually.

Courage alone, it seems, was not all I held it up to be. Soon after I took to heart about my desires to prove myself. I recognized my own anger, as I said. I still struggle with rages, but not quite as hotly as before.

So, there you have it. The submersible man craft and I parted as honored enemies, equals on the field of battle. It was clearly a draw. I understand there's a rumor flitted about at the time and continues to this day that this man craft... Circe tells me it was called a Nautilus though it looks nothing like any nautilus I ever saw. Anyway, Circe tells me the story has it that the Nautilus and its fearsome Captain bested me in that little battle, but I am here to tell you that I braved its every effort to repel me and only after we were both weary from useless tentacular fisticuffs and only after my frightened pod was clear did I decide to swim away, alive and whole thank you kindly.

Whatever else you might have heard from that Nemo, Captain of the poorly named Nautilus, or his braggartly crew, I did not die. You might weigh everything else said about him and his miracle submersible against a grain of salt to see what, if anything, has weight. I suspect you will find all those rumors and legends are little more than gross exaggerations conceived by fevered brains and bruised egos.

Apologies for catching and holding your ship a little too tightly. The leaks should be easy to stopper, yes? Your companions seem to be doing just fine.

And now, my story complete, I return to the open sea. Farewell!

The Promise and the Price

By Frances Pauli

Ever since he was a fry, Martin struggled with the promise.

His school swam in the basin at the center of a ring coral. The stony tips of its distant spires flirted with the ocean surface, but for sardines like Martin, they were only an out-of-reach shadow. He swam in the sand, belly down, under the protection of the larger schools and completely at their mercy.

The morning dawned, a slowly building glow that tinted the water pale green. It improved visibility enough that the school, which had been drifting, began to stir and move with purpose toward the clouds of crustaceans floating near the surface. Martin swam groggily upwards, sandwiched between his sister and his best friend, Carl, until the warmer water began to stir his thoughts just as the light had awoken his body.

"Hey, Martin, there's your buddy," Carl whispered and threshed his tail to increase speed. "Let's keep our mouths shut today, okay?"

Martin opened his mouth as wide as it would stretch, matching pace with Carl but looking outward, toward the herders and his personal, over-sized bully. Kane's familiar outline swam just off the school's edge, circling with the other large fish, but somehow always ending up wherever Martin was.

"Close your mouth, idiot." Gen, Martin's sister, flicked her caudal fin and knocked him hard enough that he bumped into Carl.

His mouth snapped shut on impact, but he was tempted to gape again. The mere sight of Kane sent a rebellious shiver down his spine, and his scales tingled with a mixture of fear and fury. "He's not looking, jeeze."

"Doesn't mean he won't. Your lip has gotten us into trouble three times already this week. I'm hungry today. Keep it shut."

She flicked her tail again, and Martin flinched, stuttered in his forward swim and listed into Carl. Gen shot ahead of them, leaving a trail of bubbles in her wake.

"She's in a bad mood," Carl said. The sigh in his voice was ever-present when it came to Martin's sister. Despite his friend's every effort, Martin doubted Gen would ever think of him as more than her brother's goofy buddy. He felt bad for Carl, but then, he felt bad for anyone Gen *did* pay attention to as well.

"She's probably just hungry. Always gets cranky when her belly's empty."

"Hurry up, shrimp." The grating vibration of Kane's voice assaulted anyone in hearing range.

Martin flipped his tail obediently, speeding up in answer to the order and grinding his bony lips together in an effort not to smart back. *Not today, Kane.* Martin focused on Gen's bubbles and his empty belly. *You're not winning today.*

The big fish eased closer to the school. Martin caught the flash of Kane's scales, dark and spotted. The bully's body was easily six times his size, taller and rounder and with fins that stretched spiny sails into the water. Kane's big mouth hung open more often than not, and his eyes rolled when he talked, as if they were too large to lay flat against his head.

"Easy," Carl whispered.

Martin swam straight up, following the school. As the water warmed and brightened, the sardines spread their ranks, leaving more space between fish in preparation for feeding. The flash of silver echoed forward and back, and to the left. To Martin's right stretched open water marred only by the continued presence of

Kane.

Martin angled his fins and tilted more sharply toward the surface, ignoring the bigger fish's presence. Why Kane had attached himself to Martin specifically he couldn't have guessed. Gen blamed his mouth, his refusal to shut up and obey their protectors. Carl knew better than to venture a theory.

In Martin's opinion, it had been a random selection. Years ago, when they were all still fry, still swimming together in the nursery ponds, Kane had picked Martin out from the crowd and made him a personal project.

Martin cringed. He didn't need to remember Kane's taunting. The big fish took great pleasure in reminding him every single morning.

They reached the surface before he'd thought of a reason to trade places with Carl. Just below the silver sheet that marked the end of the world, a thick layer of krill drifted. The sardine school assembled below was ravenous and ready to feed.

"Another day greets us!" A deep voice echoed from the leader of Kane's school. The rest of the big fish chanted in response, repeating the ritual words from all sides.

"Another day." Their chorus made the water vibrate.

"We renew the pact," the herder's voice boomed. "We make the promise."

"Protection." From all around, the big fish chanted. "Loyalty, and obedience."

The cloud of krill shifted, and Martin fixed his gaze on them. His belly was empty as a bubble, but he longed to resist just the same, to turn away and race for the distant coral. The silence after the chant stretched, and as he did every morning, Martin prayed no one would speak.

A voice from his own school killed his hopes. It shouted, soft as a whisper compared to the big fish's declaration. "We make the promise."

Martin flicked his tail irritably, but the others echoed the first speaker. One voice after the other joined in until the entire school chanted the word, "Promise. Promise, promise."

"Then sing!" The big fish shouted over the entire school.

Martin glanced sideways, couldn't resist the urge, and found Kane watching. Two enormous eyes fixed on him alone, waiting for his humiliation.

"Small is bad," the sardines sang.

Martin mumbled as the words caught in his throat.

"Big is good."

They began again, and Martin stilled his fins, drifting closer to Carl.

"Small is bad. Big is good." Carl chanted obediently, just as Gen would, as they all did every morning before being allowed to dine. The price of the big fish's protection was nothing short of humiliation, and it burned beneath Martin's scales like a tear in the ocean floor.

"I can't hear you, shrimp." Kane eased closer. "What was that?"

"Martin," Carl whispered and angled his body away, leveraging his tail to put distance between them.

"Say it, shrimp." Kane swam so near that the eddies from his fins battered at Martin's sides. "Sing for me."

"Small is... bad," Martin coughed up.

"And?"

Every morning. Martin ground his lips tight and remembered the nursery ponds, remembered how he'd felt shame every time he grew even a little, how he'd compared his body to the other fish, praying to stay small forever, to never be big like Kane. He heard the bully's taunts even now, even though the words had changed.

Big is strong and small is food.

"Say it!" Kane barely moved his tail, but he shot forward, looming in Martin's face with an open mouth easily large enough to swim inside. "Say it, shrimp."

"Big. Is. Good," Martin spat.

The rest of the school chanted together, would sing the words until the herders decided to let them eat. They might as well have not been there. Martin and Kane stared at one another, the dark giant and the silver dwarf in a battle of wills that always ended the same way.

"Again," Kane ordered.

"Small is bad," Martin said.

Once, he'd switched the words round, possessed by a sudden bravery that Gen called suicidal. Kane had spun his body far faster than he'd guessed possible and whacked him so hard with his giant tail that Martin awoke on the seafloor long after the school had finished their meal.

He sighed at the memory. "Bad is good."

The school finished, letting the chant die naturally, and drifting at the current's whim while the big fish digested their homage. Martin watched Kane, unable to relax with Kane's attention focused entirely on him.

They held position, nose to nose, until the lead herder released them.

"Eat!"

The order shook the sardines from their fugue. The school surged upward, mouths open and gills wide. The krill cloud swirled, and the sardines darted in and out, filling their bellies while their minds emptied of everything that had just happened.

Martin floated away, using the tiniest movements of his fins to open the gap between Kane and himself. The bigger fish watched him go, silent and staring, but by the time Martin felt safe enough to angle upwards, the meal had thinned. He had to race for the last few mouthfuls and ended up nearly as hungry as he'd begun the day.

The herders drifted farther out now that they'd renewed the promise. Even Kane became a far away shadow, an indistinguishable figure as the big fish swam for the ring coral to begin whatever they spent their day doing.

Martin eyed the surface hungrily. He drifted in the warm water long after it was safe. Long after Carl and Gen sank back down to the sand. They'd always made the promise. As far as he knew, the herders had always protected them. It did no good to argue, to resist, to antagonize Kane.

But no matter how he tried to swallow that truth, Martin couldn't forget the nursery taunt. He couldn't forget. Maybe the big fish were stronger, and maybe they kept the sardines safe. But Martin would never believe they were good.

"You're getting skinny." Carl tagged along beside him, pointing his nose toward the sand as they skimmed over it. "You gotta stay away from him."

"Tell *him* that." Martin rooted through the sand, blew out and dislodged the grains, clouding the water. They'd been searching for most of the day, and so far, hadn't dug up anything edible.

Carl poked his nose through the detritus. "Find anything?"

"No."

"Me neither." Carl sighed and went back to his own search. His fins relaxed, and he rocked softly from one side to the other.

"Don't you ever get sick of it?" Martin asked.

"Of course I do."

"So?"

"So what? What am I gonna do about it?" Carl curled his body away. "What are *you* gonna do about it? Or anybody? It's just the way things are."

"That's stupid," Martin said.

"We were born sardines, Martin. There's no changing that."

"I don't think it has to be like this." Martin huffed at the sand again, even though he'd smelled nothing at all. "What if we could be more? What if we could be anything we wanted?"

"Anything?" Finally, a note of interest crept into Carl's voice.

"Yeah." Martin brightened, imagining swimming to the coral spires and beyond. "If you could be anything, Carl, what would you be?"

"Gen's mate."

"I'm serious." Martin sighed and threshed his tail, churning a wall of bubbles behind them. "I don't want to live like this forever."

Carl opened his mouth to reply, but a swirl of current over their heads announced Gen's arrival. She sank into view facing them both.

"Well, if you don't start eating you won't have to worry about that."

"I eat." Martin eyed her silver scales and tried to calculate how long she'd been above them, and if she'd heard Carl's confession or not. "But the herders—"

"Want us all assembled in the basin," Gen announced. "They've got something to say to everyone."

"W-what do you think it is?" Carl apparently shared Martin's suspicion. His voice trembled, and he tilted his head down so that he didn't quite have to look at Gen.

"Gather with the rest of us and find out." She leaned to one side, showed a flash of silver scales, and then shot off as quickly as she'd appeared.

Carl just stared after her.

"Come on," Martin said, propelling himself into Gen's wake. "Let's see what the bastards want."

"But the krill are as plentiful as ever." One of the sardines near the front of the school raised his voice enough to be heard over the muttering.

They gathered in a clump before the line of herders, in a place where the sand was smooth and the sunlight turned the basin golden. Martin swam between Gen and Carl, but the irritation of the crowd had set them all milling back and forth, silver flashes against the yellow backdrop.

"They may seem plentiful," the lead herder explained in a voice dripping with patronization, "to a small fish who can't see the larger picture. But we monitor the floats quite carefully, and they're definitely waning."

A murmur spread through the sardine school. Martin eased forward, slipping his body between the two fish in front of him and wedging them apart. Carl and Gen closed the gap, whispering something he couldn't make out.

All the big fish had gathered behind their leader, so Kane was hard to pick out. Martin searched for his tormentor among the dark bodies, certain something horrible was about to happen. How could they have let the Krill floats diminish? It wasn't as if the sardines were gorging themselves during their brief, daily feed.

"The only logical solution is to separate into smaller schools." The leader of the big fish swung his body from side to side, leisurely surveying the sardines with absolute unconcern. "We'll spread them out, send a few schools nearer to the reef or beyond to feed."

Beyond the reef. Martin twisted, trying to catch sight of those distant shadows while a soft excitement spread beneath his scales. The reef had always been the farthest thing in his universe, and the idea of reaching it thrilled him. He shivered and swam forward. What might lie beyond those spires? Danger, yes, but what else?

All they knew was what the herders told them, and Martin suffered a sudden suspicion, a feeling that there was more to fear inside the coral than could ever wait outside it.

"Taking volunteers, of course." The big fish kept speaking, even when the crowd's mumbles washed over his words, drowning them.

Martin worked his way closer, forgetting Carl and Gen, seeking only to get near enough to hear. His heart fluttered, and his head filled with possibilities. To swim beyond the coral might mean anything, but in Martin's fantasies, it could only lead to freedom.

"The first group will leave today. We'll need thirty volunteers."

"What if no one wants to go?" someone in the sardine school shouted.

Martin pushed with his tail, shoved with his body, and worked his way closer, almost to the very front of the school. He would volunteer. He had to. But when he finally broke through the final line of sardines, Martin spread his fins wide and stopped short.

Kane waited just beside his leader. He hovered in the other fish's shadow with a triumphant expression, a haughty delight painted all over his scales.

"I can't see why you wouldn't," the leader continued. "But if no one swims forward, we'll be forced to choose volunteers for each new school."

As he said it, Kane picked Martin out of the crowd. Somehow, the bully always knew where he'd be. When their eyes met, the delight in his expression magnified. Martin had seen that look too many times not to know what it meant. He had a special torture in mind, a new torment there would be no avoiding.

"Isn't it dangerous to go beyond the reef?" the fish to Martin's left called out.

"It is." The lead herder rocked his body thoughtfully. "And we're taking that fully under consideration. Of course, we'll be there to protect you as always. Our first sub-school will be led by Kane. I'll let him tell you about it before we get to volunteering."

Kane moved forward. The light emphasized his spots, illuminated the translucent skin between his fin ribs. His eyes rolled and then fixed on Martin, as if they were the only two fish present.

"We're moving outside the reef," he said. "Just past the wall."

Martin's excitement shriveled. Outside the wall twisted now from adventurous to insidious. Beyond the reef, no one would be watching. Kane would be in charge and in a smaller school what chance would there be to hide? As surely as Martin knew this sub-division would be his doom, he was certain that he had no choice in the matter.

"You'll be the first to try this." It was as if Kane spoke to him directly. "And I'm looking forward to our future outside the coral."

The weight of Martin's doom settled over him. If he said

nothing, Kane would find a way to make him go. He'd choose Martin, or worse, pick Carl or Gen to punish him. But if he volunteered, Kane would likely leave them be. He'd want Martin on his own, without supporters of any kind. Without witnesses.

A thread of hope whispered in the back of his thoughts. Maybe Kane would get his thirty volunteers. Maybe his school would fill before his net could ensnare Martin.

"All right then." The lead herder brushed past Kane, scanning the crowd with an encouraging smile. "Who would like to join Kane?"

Martin held his gills tight. He floated, still as a stone, while the school flashed and shifted and said absolutely nothing.

"Oh, come now," the big fish cajoled. "There has to be one brave fish among you?"

No one spoke. Martin listened for a whisper, a single voice among the school, but nothing broke that awful silence. He watched Kane's face, his huge eyes and fat, gaping lips. There was no hope for him, no path except the one Kane had already decided upon.

But if Martin had to go forward at Kane's whim, he'd much rather do it of his own accord. He'd much rather not be forced. His tail moved, half a swipe and just enough to scoot him from the crowd. He angled his nose up, toward the silver surface and the glow of sunlight. Up, away from the victorious smirk plastered to Kane's face.

Martin gazed for the last time at his home and spoke, loud and with only a tiny tremble. "I volunteer."

"He was going to pick me anyway." Martin paced, skimming his belly just above the sand and flicking his frustration free with each beat of his tail. "You two should have kept quiet."

"How were we supposed to know that?" Carl huffed and scooted half his length away.

"You're insane." Gen pushed forward, keeping closer to Carl than usual. "You're going to need us with you."

"I had no choice." Martin stopped, spun to face them, and held his fins wide to steady his body. "If I hadn't volunteered, Kane would have picked me."

"Of course he would have." Gen agreed. "And then he would

have picked us."

"No." Martin blew a frustrated trail of bubbles that rose quickly over their heads. "He wants me alone. You guys would have been safe."

"Or we would have been picked for a different school," Gen said. "At least this way we're all together."

Martin couldn't summon an argument against that. Nor did he fail to notice the way Gen swam close at Carl's side, the narrowing gap between them. She'd definitely heard Carl earlier, and if nothing else could have drawn her to him, apparently knowing he'd pick her over anything else in the ocean had done the trick.

He sighed, blowing a wash of bubbles toward them both. They'd been instructed to assemble near the nursery ponds, and Martin had no intention of showing up last. He might be forced to endure Kane's attention, but there was no sense in giving the big fish extra fodder to use against him.

They swam out. The conversation faded into an uncomfortable silence. Martin led them, but only by half a length, not willing to forego the comfort of his usual bookends and secretly grateful to have them with him still. He looked back once, back to the smooth basin and its golden sand. Then he pointed his nose outward, toward the coral ring, and didn't turn again.

The nursery ponds lay between the basin and the coral. Martin had never swam beyond them. Rock and rubble had been arranged into low walls around the fry schools, walls that had seemed so much taller when he'd lived inside them. They found the growing cluster of volunteers beside an empty pen, just merging into the group before Kane appeared to collect them.

"Are we all here?" Their new leader swam a circle around them, forcing their ranks tighter. "Line up so I can count your worthless tails."

The mini-school shifted, spreading out into a line. As they assembled, two latecomers swam through the nursery to join them. Kane drifted down the row, examining each sardine as he went, but when he reached Martin, he used his fins to halt his progress.

The big fish hovered in front of him, eyes tilting from his skull. He lingered just long enough to let Martin stand out, and then he swam on, saying nothing until he reached the end of the line. Once there, he waved his tail hard enough to knock the closest sardines off kilter and shouted.

"Small is bad!"

A murmur whispered through the group. To Martin's right, Carl whispered, "Don't."

Kane turned and worked his way back along the line, slower this time, sliding past each sardine and casting them into shadow. "Small is bad," he repeated. "But you can't help it, can you? Not your fault."

He reached Martin and this time continued past without hesitation.

"Can't help being born weaker. And yet, we can't go forgetting it either, can we?"

One of the sardines farther down the line spoke out, overly eager to please their new protector. His voice squeaked into a range that put an ache in Martin's scales.

"Big is good."

Kane moved so fast that his current tumbled the line. Fish scattered, whether they meant to or not, as the big fish swung his tail around. There was a smacking sound, a hard impact that echoed outward, and the unfortunate sardine who'd spoken out of turn fluttered to the ocean bottom. His scales flashed as he wafted down and then vanished as the sand stirred and covered him.

"We will remember to speak only when told," Kane shouted. "Now follow and repeat the promise until I tell you otherwise."

He turned his nose toward the far coral and swished his tail, launching his body away from the nursery ponds. The new school followed, tentatively, huddled together, and when Kane's call echoed back to them, they took up the chant without hesitation.

"Small is bad. Big is good."

Martin chanted with them. Gen and Carl squeezed in at his sides, and they swam together over the place where the other fish had fallen. The sand settled, only half covering the immobile sardine. Martin prayed he still breathed, that the poor guy would come back to his senses, preferably long after they'd moved on.

Twenty-nine now, and all doomed to live under Kane's temper. They swam and sang, watching the sand pass beneath them, and Martin's anxiety spread outward. Carl and Gen would not be immune to his bully's wrath. He couldn't take it all for them. The proof of that lay half-buried in the ocean bottom behind them. Without the herding leader to keep him in check, Kane could do anything, and that kind of power was not likely to manifest softly in a fish like Kane.

Martin lifted his gaze. Ahead of them, the spawning grounds filled the remaining space before the coral. He'd never swam here, was still too young to think about spawning. Yet, he'd always assumed he'd see the beds eventually, that he'd have been making this trip with someone special.

The sands grew coarser as they neared the ring, and divots cratered the bottom, surrounded by deeper piles. Beneath some of these, eggs incubated. New fry would be born, wiggling free to gather in the ponds, to eat their first meals, and to hear for the first time the chant that would brand them as inferior forever.

He spat the words, let them slip from his tongue muddled and full of his impotent rage. What crime had they committed, simply by being born? Martin flipped his tail and fixed his gaze on the black towers, looming now, growing into twisty spires pocked with darker holes. What made Kane's kind believe they were so much better than his?

"Small is bad." Martin glared at the coral, at his future. "Big is good."

The school sang with him, chanting obediently while Kane's voice echoed in Martin's memory. He shivered, flashing silver as he swam.

Big is strong and small is food.

"Stay away from the walls." Kane led them to a trench, a wide passageway cut into the coral ring. "Don't get close to those holes, or you'll regret it."

The new school huddled together, just outside the gap in the wall, while the big fish explained the dangers of the next part of their journey.

Martin fixed his eyes on the coral. Despite his dread, the ring had always felt like a beacon to him. Standing in its shadow only proved how massive, how amazing and unreal the coral spires seemed. Their bulging surfaces were, indeed, riddled with holes. Tunnels bored through the structure, and narrow cracks broke between them, making the wall a maze of crevasses and dark pits.

Even as Kane warned against them, a tugging in his gut eased Martin to the edge of the school. He tried to see inside the nearest divot, but the shadows fell too dark and too near the color of the coral itself.

"Move." Kane ordered.

The school flashed silver. If he'd meant to terrify them, the job was easily done. They swam after the big fish while the coral towered over them. The trench lay in darkness, and the walls blocked out any view of the ocean, of the wide spaces Martin was used to. He felt them closing in, and he imagined ugly eyes peering from the divots, long tentacles reaching for the unwary fish.

The sardines shifted, swimming single-file in the very center of the passage. Carl and Gen fell behind, and the entire school hushed in case the coral heard their chattering and awoke. Martin's scales felt prickly, as if something unseen watched him. His eyes scanned the walls to either side, searching for danger but finding only black coral and blacker holes.

When Kane finally shot from the trench into open water, the sardine school hurried after him. They spread out as they exited, flowing from the coral walls and into a mob again. Even with Kane at their head, Martin felt relief wash through him. He breathed and angled his fins to look upon the open ocean for the first time.

The familiar glow of shallow water beckoned overhead. The bright ripples of the surface shimmered. On this side of the coral ring, the floor dropped swiftly. The water darkened, losing the sun's touch and fading into deep blue, green, and inky black.

He could see only half the distance he was used to, as if a dim curtain had been pulled across the world. For all the width and depth of the water, it bore no features. No rocky border broke that swath of color. No far coral marked the end of the world.

"Follow me." Kane said, and even his bellowing seemed small against the backdrop of endless water.

He led them down the slope until the ocean greened. They followed the base of the ring coral, swam near to outside of the ring rather than venturing into the deeps. The water grew colder as they descended. Visibility narrowed until they had the solid fact of the coral on their left, and only a dark ambiguity to the right.

Kane swam with confidence, though Martin caught him glancing to the right often enough to believe the dangers of the open ocean were nothing to ignore.

The coral curved. The sardines followed their leader. Martin squeezed between Gen and Carl and tried to imagine something good at the end of the journey. He tried. Already, he'd seen more of the world than any sardine from inside the ring. But when they rounded the next lump of reef, their destination unfolded.

And Martin's heart sank.

"What's that?" Carl whispered.

"Are those what I think they are?" Gen's voice trembled.

"Yes." Martin had no doubt at all. He'd known Kane meant him no good before they'd even flicked a fin. Now the proof lay on the ocean bed before them.

A long shelf protruded from the base of the coral. It stretched away out of sight, and it was lined with huge, netted pens. Each enclosure was smaller than a nursery pond, completely covered in a mesh of fibers, and packed solid with flashing sardines.

Martin spread his fins and looked up to the surface, the sun, and the tide of bubbles lifting from each cage.

"Yes," he repeated. "It's a prison."

The entire school was herded into an empty cage. At least five big fish joined Kane, hovering all around the sardines. Martin followed Gen, his guts twisting as his sister swam through the square opening in the pen's front wall.

His tail swung from one side to the other, but his pectoral fins balked, tilted, and rocked his body upwards.

"Keep moving." Kane's voice shouted from the rear of the school.

Carl's nose rammed into Martin's tail as he was shoved from behind. Martin scooted closer to the opening, but panic froze his fins. If he went into that pen, he felt certain he would never come out again. Martin twisted to the left and found a big fish there, close in and making a solid wall of his body. They'd formed a blockade, holding the sardines in position, and there was no break in that barrier.

The school surged. Kane's order rang out again. Martin was shoved from behind, bracketed to the sides and above, and forced forward through the doorway. Sardines filed in behind him. Gen nudged him to one side, and the three of them huddled there together, watching the big fish push the netting across the opening and secure it in place with a few bits of broken coral.

The trap had closed. Martin's heart raced. The sardines in the pen beside theirs milled in a slow circle, eyeing the newcomers as they passed. Their voices whispered, a tide of speculation hissing through the netting. Over the top of that sound, Kane's voice rang out.

"Repeat the promise."

Martin's new school murmured, confused and disoriented. They'd spread out as much as possible inside the pen, but fin still brushed fin. Tails couldn't flip without hitting one another. A voice near the center dared to speak, forgetting the lesson they'd learned before heading out.

"Why are we caged?"

Martin braced himself, tensed as if the blow might fall on him. Instead of attacking, however, Kane laughed. His fellows echoed him, and the sea filled with their deep rumble.

"The nets are for our protection." The next school over chanted. "The nets keep us safe."

Martin eyed the mesh walls. He tilted as much as he could and examined the netting over their heads. Nothing about the cell suggested it meant to keep someone out. The open ocean might hold danger, but the only thing he really feared already knew how to open the cage door.

The big fish eased away into the depths, vanishing one by one until only Kane remained outside their pen. His bony lips curved into a smile, and his deadly tail swung slowly from one side to the other.

"Now," he shouted. "Repeat the promise."

There were no krill overhead, and even if there had been, the caged fish could not have reached them. Would they be let out to feed? Or left to starve until...

"Say it!"

From the cage next to them, the chant rose. "Small is bad. Big is good." It echoed down the line of pens, carried by hundreds of sardine voices. A few of the stunned fish in Martin's cage picked it up, but though most of them remained silent, the song carried over them, louder and louder, while Kane grinned from beyond the netting.

"Small is bad. Big is good."

Martin opened and closed his mouth soundlessly. He met Carl's terrified gaze, Gen's furious expression, and he turned away. His fins spun him in a slow circle. Net to all sides. Sand below, open sea to the front and, at their backs, a wall of coral that stretched up so high its dark fingers played with the surface.

Everywhere he looked, there was no hope, no exit, and no way out.

"Time to eat." Kane appeared at the front of their cage the following morning. He pushed a fat bladder in front of him, larger than Martin and swollen as if it might burst at the seams. The sardines huddled together, squeezing closer even though they were nearly always in contact.

Martin's scales itched. He hadn't slept well. Each time his body drifted off, someone touched him inadvertently and startled him awake again. The entire school looked sluggish and disoriented, if not terrified out of their wits, and on top of their own worries, the schools in the pens to either side whispered constantly.

As if there would never be quiet again.

When Kane delivered his swollen cargo to the base of their cage, the sardines tightened ranks, keeping away from the front mesh. More fins rubbed against Martin's body. Even if it had only been Carl and Gen, it would have felt too invasive.

"Who will sing the promise today?" Kane called to them. "I need a volunteer."

The sardine school shifted and tightened. Martin felt Carl's entire body against his right side, a stranger's on his left. He felt the nervous electricity zinging through the school, and he felt the moment when it broke, when one fish near the front swam forward.

Before the brave soul could open its mouth, however, Kane shouted again.

"Martin! I think you'll do today."

Martin tightened his fins to his sides.

"You there, back up and give *Martin* some room to come forward."

The school fell silent. Not even Gen dared to whisper to him, to remind him that all their fates rested on his scales. Martin pushed with his tail, and the school parted to let him through. He swam to the front, to Kane, and he steeled himself as he went.

It would do no good to hesitate, to disobey, to spit the words right into the bully's face. Kane expected exactly that. His smug expression told Martin he wanted a fight, that he'd every intention of provoking one.

Martin spread his fins. He halted before Kane and, without urging of any kind, sang the promise, clearly and as politely as he could. "Small is bad. Big is good."

Kane flinched and gaped at him, mouth falling even wider than usual. He'd expected a fight, yes, but he'd wanted it too badly. Martin found disappointing him almost pleasant.

"Say it again," Kane snarled.

"Small is bad. Big is good." Martin sang it loud and clear, as if he believed it, as he'd never sang it before. With each word, he saw Kane's face darken, until the big fish looked purple at the edges.

"Stop." Kane interrupted his fourth refrain, and Martin fell obediently silent.

The bastard had expected him to balk, had picked him, perhaps, just so he'd have someone to battle. Refusing his fight felt as good as sparring with him ever had. It felt like a win, like he'd stolen something Kane valued even more than intimidation.

"You will eat today," Kane announced it as if there had been some doubt. "And after..."

His gaze fixed on Martin again, and his eyes turned black and flat as the coral overhead. Martin's tail twitched, shifting him a fraction out of line, a smidge away from that gaze. Kane's eyes followed him.

"After, I will return to select one of you for *special duty*." He flipped his tail, turning his body to the side. His nose jabbed at the bladder he'd brought, and a slit in the side of the thing opened. A pink cloud released into the water, wafting into their pen as Kane pumped the bag.

The sardine school surged forward, toward the smell and sight of the krill, but they pulled up together as the tiny bodies fluttered toward the sand, limp and lifeless.

A whisper spread through their ranks. The word hissed between them. *Dead.* Kane emptied the bladder of its cargo with a final poke and a deep laugh. He nudged the empty bladder away and swam for the deep still chuckling at their expense.

The dead krill settled on the ocean floor.

"If you wait too long, the sand will have them." A fish from the next pen called in a less than friendly tone.

The sardine school shivered once, all together, and then shifted forward, noses down, sucking at the bodies and the sand both.

Martin had lost his appetite. With the school pressing forward, he found space near the back of the pen, space to sit and not be touched for a few breaths. He floated, pointing up toward the black towers and the silver surface. When Carl and Gen found him, he had to suppress a shiver as they closed ranks again, as the water filled with the constant motion of the school.

"He's going to pick you," Gen said.

"Of course he is." Martin eased back further, let the rear wall press a grid against his body. "So what?"

"What's special duty?" Carl asked.

They stared at one another while the school milled and the water inside the pen rocked them softly from one side to the other.

"It can't be good," Gen said. "Nothing here is good."

"I guess I'll find out," Martin said. He spread his fins and rolled his eyes up. How awful could it be? He could imagine a lot of ugly scenarios but speculating on them would do him no good. "When I get back, I'll tell you all about it."

From the pen beside theirs came a crackling sound, shivering through the mesh and into their space. The laugh felt thin and sharp both. It irritated Martin's scales, putting a twitch into his lateral line.

"What?" Gen spun to the barrier and the other school of sardines.

The strange fish pressed close to the wall, wide-eyed and thin of body. They watched through the mesh, and something had certainly amused them.

"What is it?" Gen demanded.

Martin didn't need to hear the answer. The mob's posture had already told him he was doomed. Still, when the school echoed his suspicions, it was as if a chill current washed over them all.

"No one comes back from special duty," they promised. "No one returns."

Martin waited at the front of the school. If Kane meant to finish him today, there was no point in waiting. There was nowhere to hide inside the pen, but once outside, Martin guessed his only salvation would be the void in front of them.

If he could make it that far, maybe he'd just swim away into the depths and wait for a *different* fish to end him.

Gen and Carl waited right behind him, huddled together and surrounded by the rest of the school. When Kane's shadow separated from the darker water, Martin heard his sister whimper, heard Carl whisper something for her alone.

He wanted to believe they'd be alright, that Kane would vent his ire on Martin only, but the pen said otherwise. The condition of the other sardines, the ones who'd been here much longer, suggested no one made it out of this place.

Martin stared at the square door and tried to believe he wasn't about to die.

Kane swam straight for them. The sardines all pressed to the rear of their cages. The big fish reached the square door and spread his fins wide.

"Special duty," he called. "One volunteer."

"Me," Martin said.

"I don't think so." Kane looked past him, shifted his weight, and tilted to one side "Let's see, who do we need?"

"Me." Martin surged forward, panic coursing through his body. Kane looked far too pleased, far too puffed up not to have something horrible in mind. "I volunteer."

"I think that little guy behind you." Kane grinned and waved his fins. "Carl, isn't it? Come on up, Carl."

"No!" Martin shifted sideways, using his body to block any path to the door. "I said I'd go."

"And *I* said, I want Carl," Kane growled it, sending a wash of bubbles toward the surface. "Now move aside."

"No." Martin drifted closer to the door.

Kane pressed his bony lips right up to the mesh and snarled. "Get back."

"Come in here and make me." Martin's body went cold. He stared until the big fish filled his whole vision, until nothing existed but Kane and his evil. He spoke without thinking, as if the words had always been inside him and only needed the final push to spill over. "You're a coward and a bully, Kane, and this is between us."

"I'll take you both," Kane said. He pried the door open and let it drop. "Get out here."

"Stay where you are, Carl." Martin aimed for the opening and tensed his body. Would Kane kill him here, in front of the school? If so, there'd be no hope for Carl, for Gen and the others. Maybe, there never had been.

Kane eased his body away from the opening. His eyes tilted, gleaming like dark bubbles. Martin imagined popping one. He imagined living another day but flicked his fins and shot forward through the open square.

"Now Carl," Kane ordered.

"Don't." Martin felt like a fry beside the huge body of Kane, dwarfed and impotent. Rage still gripped him, spilling over and pooling around the larger fish, focusing on Kane and his years of abuse. Out of one eye, he saw Carl easing from the school. He heard Gen sobbing.

Kane laughed again, and Martin spun on one fin. He drifted close to the mammoth spotted face, and he struck, smacking his tail broadside against Kane's cheek. The impact echoed into the deep. The schools froze, stunned and gaping. For a breath nothing moved.

Then Kane roared and spread his fins.

Martin bolted. He hadn't meant to survive the rebellion, but when Kane lunged, the sardine flipped his tail as fast as it would shift. He swam away from the pen, blind with panic, and he felt the big fish following, right on his tail. He imagined the hige mouth stretching open, the snap, and the swallow.

Other pens passed on his left. The open ocean lay to his right, but the depths hid more of Kane's kind. Martin swam along the nets, around the coral ring, until the pens stopped and only the black spires continued.

"There's nowhere to go," Kane snarled, close behind him but huffing with the effort of the chase.

Martin felt fatigue dragging at his fins, too. He wouldn't win this race, but he didn't mean to let Kane win either. With a flick and a shift of his body, he rocketed to the left, toward the coral wall. The spires loomed, dark and ominous. Martin chose a large pit and dove straight for it.

"Stop!"

Martin flinched but didn't slow. Inside the coral, something surely would eat him, but at least it would not be Kane. He swept into the hole he'd picked, let the black wall swallow him. Inside, he found a pocket of space, a cave like a round bubble with more holes leading off it.

The coral rattled as Kane slammed into the opening. Martin

turned about and came face to face with familiar, bony lips.

"Get out here," Kane ordered.

Martin searched the holes for any sign of tentacles.

"I won't hurt you." The big fish lied. "If you come out, I can protect you."

"From what?" Martin poked his nose into a larger pocket, found nothing but coral walls and more space, more holes leading deeper into the ring. "There's nothing in here."

Something in the silence that followed told Martin the truth. The coral was not their enemy. All the monsters he needed to worry about were *outside* it's knobby walls.

"You're breaking the promise," Kane argued, and desperation painted his words an ugly, trembling tone. "You need us."

Martin peered into a maze of tunnels. The coral was threaded through with holes, with pockets and pits. But it felt dead and empty. How could they have been so stupid? "There's nothing in here."

He repeated it mostly for himself, but Kane roared in fury and beat his head into the opening again, as if he might chip his way into the hiding place. Even if he had, Martin counted six exits too small for even one of Kane's fins to fit inside.

"The promise," Kane growled. "Small is bad."

Martin swam to a tiny hole, pressed his eye against a tiny pock in the outer wall, and watched Kane battering his frustration against the coral.

"Big is good. Small is bad. Big is good." The bully chanted, mad with frustration.

The deeps stretched away behind him. The nets were back to the right, but Martin thought he could easily reach them without leaving the coral at all. He could find his way inside this maze. He could reach the others, and he could free them.

"Small is bad, big is good." Kane chanted at the empty pocket.

Martin looked away, stared out into the watery void, and caught sight of a shadow looming. It was larger than Kane by six times, fat and dark and made of hunger.

"Say it." Kane's voice turned frantic. He screamed, far too loudly for a fish exposed to the deep.

"Stop," Martin warned. "Be quiet, fool."

"Small is bad." Kane howled. "Big is good."

By the time a new voice took up the chant, it was far too late.

Martin watched the horror dawning on his bully's face. He watched the giant shadow's smile spread into a wall of teeth.

"Big is strong," the shark sang. "Small is food."

Martin turned away before the end. He still heard the snapping and the crunch, would never forget it. While the shark finished dining, he worked his way deeper into the coral, where only the smallest fish might fit. Only a short dash away from the pens. It would be easy enough to dig beneath the nets when the big fish weren't watching. Martin swam and planned, filling the coral in his mind with his friends, his school, and all his kind.

Once he freed the others, they'd have the whole of the ring to themselves. The coral walls would guard them, would keep them safe, where the larger fish could not reach. As it turned out, that had been the danger all along. The promise meant to keep them *from* safety, not to protect them. To Kane's kind, the coral was dangerous indeed.

For the sardines, it was salvation.

As Martin navigated the tunnels, working his way back to Gen and Carl, he planned. He saw each coral chamber filled with families, and he saw the net pens empty, the large fish moving on, looking for easier food. Except for Kane, of course.

No matter how big you were, there was always someone bigger, and here beside the deep, *inside* the coral ring, it was very good to be small.

Luigi's Song

By Jude-Marie Green

Saturday night in Southern California. On the beach. Near the pier. The famous one you've seen in movies all your life. I'm sitting on this damp mound of sand, perched a few feet above the surf line, waiting for the grunion to bring me a gift. From Luigi. Luigi's a whale.

So what if I'm just about 18 and I don't have a boyfriend? My best friend's a whale. I watch the waves and imagine a night dive, which I can't do as my regular dive partner's busy.

"Alone again, naturally," I almost sing. I never sing. Not even karaoke. Look, my name's Daisy. How's that for lame? I hate it but I guess I don't have much in the way of imagination cuz I can't think of anything I'd rather be called. You ever see that movie with Barbra Streisand, *On a Clear Day You can See Forever*? The main character is psychic, talks to plants, has been reincarnated and sings really corny Broadway numbers, and her name is Daisy, too.

I guess 'Daisy' suits me well enough. I don't sing, but that psychic thing? Well, here's the story.

When I'm nine my 'rents take me to an aquarium. That's like a zoo for fish. A habitrail for humans snakes under some enormous tanks full of swimming and floating creatures. We walk underneath the killer whale exhibit.

I hear them talking to me.

"What is your name?"

I hear this, sounding distant and vibraty.

At first I think the 'rents are messing with my head, cuz 'rents like to do stuff like that. Santa Claus, the Easter Bunny, Mr. Ed. Talking Whales, not a big leap, if you get my drift. I play along.

"Daisy. What's yours?"

The 'rents jump a little.

Mom says, "What's our what?"

I grin at her and wait for the game to continue.

"We're the whale," that voice says again. I'm staring at my 'rents and their lips don't move, except to form skinny frowns. I'm surprised, but I hold it in pretty well, as least I think I do.

I look up and above me are a couple big black and white bullet-shaped hulks. The nameplate says killer whales. They twirl around and seem to be looking right at me.

I whisper, quiet as I can, "I can't talk right now; will you be here later?"

Though I guess that's kinda stupid, cuz, where could they go?

Some happy humming, but no words. I'm grinning like a kid with a secret cuz I'm a kid with a secret and a plan.

Now that I'm older, I wonder that I accepted so easy the idea that the fish could talk to me. Or actually that I could understand them, cuz fish talk to everybody, all the time. Noisy little souls. It's just us, we don't hear them. Except me. I hear 'em fine in my head.

The 'rents haul me along through the rest of the displays in the aquarium. We see flat sole, snaky eels and stringy coral. Now and again I say something like, "How are you today?" but no one answers, at least none of the fish. Once an old lady in a pink hat turns around and says back to me, "I'm fine today, young lady. How are you?"

My 'rents can't believe how sweet I'm being; not that I'm not usually, just usually I'm a lot less outgoing. They worry about that at night when they think I can't hear 'em discussing me. Maybe I should make an effort to be more out-going all the time. I'm scoring points.

I use the points when we sit down in the fishy themed restaurant for lunch.

"Can I - I mean *may* I go to the bathroom please?"

One big hard-and-fast rule of parenting is, 'Don't let the kids go anywhere alone.' They're afraid of rapists or something, maybe just the evening news. But we're sitting right next to the restrooms. They exchange glances, Mom worried, Dad startled, but they agree in that silent parental way of theirs.

"Okay, go ahead," Dad says.

"Come right back," Mom adds. She watches me until I push open the bathroom door and go through.

As I expect, they aren't watching for me to come back out right away. I wait for an older woman to leave and I slip out behind her. The 'rents don't see me return to the aquarium.

They find me about an hour later; that is, the security dude finds me. He uses the black walkie-talkie thing on his shoulder to call in the code that I've been found safe and sound, talking to myself.

Of course I'm not talking to myself. I'm chatting with the killer whale kids.

See, these killer whales grew up here. They aren't whales, by the way, they're kinda like dolphins; and they call themselves The One Tribe. Their mothers told 'em the stories of The One Tribe, about chasing seals and eating penguins and fighting battles with other dolphins. The One Tribe seems violent to me. PG at least. The moms told 'em how they'd rather die than live cut off from the world below, the world of the ocean. So the moms died. But the kids stayed and they like it here.

"Heaven," they call it, this aquarium.

But they're forgetting the stories their moms told 'em and they're happy to tell me; a new audience, right? I promise to come back when I can.

My mom grabs me up in a hug. When she finally lets go, I say, "Mom, don't die."

"What? What do you mean?" She's about to cry, I can tell.

Dad smiles in that fakey parent way and says, "Are you worried we'll leave you alone for running away and scaring us?"

I grab him into a hug, too, and wonder if he can talk himself into dying, like the killer whales' parents did.

And they, the killer whales, the orcas, are happy to be here. I stop talking while the adults buzz around me, crying and thanking and apologizing and everything.

I'm thinking on what the orcas told me.

Show and Tell in school on Monday and I talk about my trip to the Aquarium.

Some kid from the back row says, "My mom says aquariums are bad because the whales are kidnapped from the ocean and put into a prison and 'sploited for our fun." He sticks his tongue out at me so I have to respond.

"Nuh-uh, the orcas told me they like being in the aquarium. It's clean. And they get lots of food." At least I try to say that. But the kids laugh and the teacher claps her hands to shut them up and I don't even know what's going on. I look at the teacher and say, "What?"

"Now, Daisy," she says, super-tolerant voice, "I'm sure that animals did not talk to you. You must mean your parents told you the aquarium is a good place. Whales don't speak."

I see where this is going so I agree with her and sit down soon as I can. The kids only tease me for a day or two, call me nuts and invite me to the loony bin, before my mistake is forgotten.

I twig pretty fast that I better not tell anyone else about this, this talent, skill, whatever it was. I never try to share this power of mine, though sometimes it's lonely. Eight years I've kept the secret. But I'm not stupid. No loony bin for me, thank you.

Though I feel pretty silly sitting here on wet sand waiting for the grunion. The night is one like Persian poets would wax lyrical about, scented breezes, crash of waves, the fat full moon luminous above.

I read *The Rubaiyat of Omar Khayyam* one summer, while waiting for Luigi to return. Those Persians had sand, and I have oceans, but it's the same vast expanse that casual people assume is empty.

I sit here on the sand and wait for the flood of silver bodies. I've done this before, years ago, as a little kid: the midnight run of grunion, tiny fish washed ashore to spawn, laying eggs and spewing sperm before the next wave washes them off to sea again. I remember the creatures thick on the ground, us kids capturing a fleeting few: look ma, no hooks. Then we'd toss them back into the waves as soon as we were bored. Did I hear them back then? I don't remember. Probably whatever I heard I ignored. Little kids are so accepting.

Tonight I see a few silversides flash, a few dozen perhaps, not the waves of fish I expect. That I remember.

Grunion are small fish with simple minds. They're thinking about spawning. I sure hate bothering them during sex. Still, they're supposed to have the thing for me.

Luigi's gift.

So I talk to them, in Human-speak, which they understand perfectly well even if they don't want to hold a conversation with me right now.

"Do you have it? Where is it? What is it?"

They respond, group voice, annoyed and distracted. For some reason I'm thinking about tiny condoms (hey, I'm a teenager, it's only natural), not about the floating glass globes that the grunion bring with them and deposit like fist-sized eggs on the wet sand, their little bodies pushing the floats above the surf line.

I step carefully around the silver bodies; no one wants their sex lives disturbed, right? A stack of globes, a bunch, lots. Maybe two dozen. I only expected one.

The first time I saw one of these floats was the first time I met Luigi. Had to do with a high school project, learning to scuba dive so I could participate in Clean The Ocean Day.

Extra credit, yeah, and a fun way to see the good looking guys wear swim trunks and show off their buff bods. Of course they look at me too, I hope. Yeah, I'm pretty sure. I look pretty good in a bikini. But mostly I want to get in the water and see if I could still talk to whales.

See, even though I live in SoCal, I'd rather go to the mall than the beach. No one goes in the water. Eww. Every rainy season the news is full of overflowing sewage treatment plants, high bacteria counts and beach closures. Surfers get this rash caused by the dirty water. The surf foam is yellow and brown, not white and blue/green. I don't want anything to do with that.

But I miss using my 'special ability.' Everyone has a special ability, right? Mine's talking to whales. I mean, hearing them. But I'm not going to the beach, nuh uh. And the killer whales at the aquarium bore me; I got sick of their constant happy blathering years ago. But down in the ocean, if I could check out the whales in the ocean, I'm sure I'd hear something new.

So anyway. Scuba. The 'rents won't let me learn when I'm a kid 'cause they say it's a dangerous hobby. All that stuff about nitrogen narcosis and depth gauges and air pressure. It's expensive too, but I don't think the 'rents care about that. Still, til I'm 16, I can't do it without their permission, and I can't get their permission. Instead, they take me whale watching.

Whale watching season in SoCal is February through April, half-off the ticket price if you don't see any whales, but we always see some. I'm never close enough to talk to the creatures but I hear what they sing. They are happy. Gloriously free and happy, especially when they breach: jump outta the water into the air and fly into heaven.

That's what their songs say. "Heaven."

Now, these aren't aquarium whales performing circus acts for bits of cut-up fish. These are California Gray Whales, huge creatures, thirty feet long, full of barnacles and riddled with scars.

I'm in love.

I want to talk to them. So when the opportunity comes up to learn scuba through school, and I'm 16, and the 'rents can't raise enough objections, I sign up for the class.

The instructors are a little dopey. What can you expect from people who live in the water all the time? The instructor in charge was once a Navy SEAL. Of course I know what that is. I watch the movies. He's a little pudgy, old and still has the shaved head like in his Navy SEAL photos which are tacked all over the walls in his office. The other instructors, a beach-bunny type girl with a tan and a guy with dreads, also strike me as bubbly playacting types, beach types, not serious.

They're dead serious about the training and equipment, though.

After the class gets certified, we do the Clean The Ocean thing. OMG. I don't see much in the way of fish, but plenty of garbage floating in the water, on the sandy bottom and entangled in the seaweed stuff growing everywhere. Plastic, mostly, but other stuff too. Soggy cigarette boxes. Broken beer bottles. I grab as much of the crap as I can and stick it into my net sack. I have thirty minutes of air but I fill the sack in ten minutes.

So I get the extra credit and a close-up view of the ocean bottom.

How can I describe the bottom? It's green. Everything is green or gray; except some of the fish. And the trash. Sunlight flashes through the water, refracting off suspended particles and sparkling down on us like dust motes dancing in a partially lit, shadow-filled room. Like that, but wet.

And it's full of fish. Don't chase the fish. Don't touch the fish, either. But sometimes they'll come up and nibble; on my fingers, the bare parts of my legs and my cheeks once. Feels like the most fabulously delicate kisses.

I hang out at the dive office so much, looking for a dive partner, that Dreads starts going out with me most weekends. He's not my boyfriend, don't even think it. He and Sedna, the girl I thought was a beach bunny but she's actually kinda cool; anyway, they have a thing going.

But I like to dive all the time, and Sedna works, and Dreads (okay, his name is 'Charlie' but I call him 'Dreads' and he likes it) has the time.

Round about December Dreads says, "The gray whales are migrating, let's go out and see them."

I love this idea.

Dreads almost backs out, he was busy he said, but I whine until he gives in. "All right, no problem, geez. I've never known anyone so intense about the diving."

Hey. That is a pretty cool compliment, isn't it?

So we're in the water, we're dive partners and aren't too far from each other ever. Still I'm surprised when he grabs my shoulder and points. I follow where he's pointing and yeah, there they are.

Gray whales. Enormous humpy creatures, barnacles on their skin and small fish darting around them. I laugh. They are beautiful.

Dreads is trying to pull me up, away, but I make a slashing motion with my hand, diver speak for no, not yet.

Not yet. The whales are talking.

My tank is near exhausted, a good five minutes past what I should have used, when I decide to go up. Dreads is near hysterics and wants to skip the safety stop, dangerous, but I'm not worried, I'm almost giddy.

The whales tell stories to each other. And me, cuz I'm listening in. I hear part of an epic poem about migrating to the other great ocean. A couple start a call and response song about courtship so blunt that I'd blush except it's so sweet. Someone sings a quiet song comparing the perfect water long ago to the hard to tolerate water nowadays. The others shush him, ignore him.

I'm ashamed. But I'm also curious.

Are they so different from me, these creatures? Aside from being huge and ocean dwelling?

I climb on board and shed my gear. Dreads is ready to yell at me but I say, "Hush, they're breaching over there."

The whole pod, maybe six creatures, danced around the boat. They sing happy. I yell back at them, "You're beautiful!"

They sing, "We're beautiful!"

I yell, "You're beautiful!"

One particular whale swims close to the boat and snorts up at me.

"Come swim with us," he says. In whale.

"Okay," I say in human. "I'll be right down."

I take about five minutes to pull on my fresh tanks, rebreather, mask, and I take the giant step. Dreads is a few moments behind me, grousing about crazy women, and he's upset that I jump before he's ready: always take a partner, right? But the whale will be my partner.

I'm bobbing in the water and the creature is startled that I'm in there with him and he skims away, but he floats back again soon.

"Swim with me," he says.

"That's what I'm doing," I say. The whale flails then speaks to me again.

"You understand me?"

"Well duh," I say. "I'm speaking to you, aren't I?"

And so that's how I meet Luigi. That's as close as I can get to pronouncing his name. Also, I kinda like the idea of a pizza-making whale.

We talk for a while, exchanging stories. He says whales don't avoid people as much any more cuz people don't kill them so much any more. He says he can sing the names of his family killed by people. He says people took the bodies but couldn't take the songs.

He sounds kinda angry when he says this so I say in a big hurry, "Yeah, I bet the spirits all go to heaven, huh?"

And so he asks me about heaven.

And he asks where bad spirits go.

I tell him about hell. What I know of it, anyway. Fire and brimstone - which is only sulfur, after all - and eternal torment.

"So heaven's the sky? And hell is beneath the bottom?" Luigi considered this for a moment, then said, "I've lived between heaven and hell all my life! I live in the ocean!"

We both laugh a little. I tell him that heaven and hell are ideas, not real places.

He thinks about all this, his big eyes rolling at me. He says there is no heaven or hell for his family; there's just being alive and being remembered.

My tank alarm goes off and I realize I have to leave; only have thirty minutes of air, right? And only two dives today, I can't do more. As I make my way back up to the boat, Luigi tells me that his pod is finding the warmth south of here. He says they'll be back in four months. He says he hopes to see me again.

He gives me something, an irregular shaped bit of stone that he coughs up out of his mouth. Eww. Bigger than my fist. I stick it in my net bag and swim slowly away.

I don't tell Dreads that a whale gave me a gift. Who'd believe it? Remember, I'm trying to stay out of the loony bin.

When I get home I put the stone, a roly-poly bumpy thing of yellow glass, white sand, red shells and all colors of plastic, on my bookshelf. I figure it'll be safe there.

It sure looks like a float, one of those glass balls that fishermen put under their nets. I think for a while on where the float came from and I figure if the whale made it, there's only one way. Glass needs heat, right? Sometimes when an earthquake hits a fissure opens in the ocean floor. Not the end of the world or anything, just some magma flowing into the water.

That must be where he made this float.

Just so's you know, earthquakes are a California given. No place on Earth is immune to seismic activity, I read that in some geology book, but somehow only us Californians accept the shaking with a smile. What's the big deal? Not like you can predict one beforehand or avoid it during. Grin and bear it, that's my motto.

I didn't know the float was hollow. I suppose a scientist would have figured it out somehow, but I felt the weight of mine and assumed solidness. Maybe if it had sloshed or something, but nope. I found out my float was hollow during an earthquake.

Four in the morning is a rotten time to wake up, especially if the bed is swaying and the ground is moaning and the dumb cat is running around like he's on fire and the bookcase is tilting over.

I know better than to try and stop a falling piece of furniture.

The books plop out, cascading onto the floor. My trophies fall over and land on the books. The globe slides off the shelf and shatters.

Mind you, the earthquake itself only lasts a few seconds. The bookshelf falls for longer than that. The house is in utter silence so I hear the words with utter clarity.

It's music, a song. It takes a moment for me to understand I'm hearing words, English, human. I don't have a head for lyrics and I don't have time to write the words down, but I remember. They're sad. The tune is sad, the words mournful.

My 'rents are waking up and moving around and yell from across the house if I'm okay. Of course I am. But I'm confused.

I gather up the bits of float; it broke into thick chunks, maybe five pieces. The glassy bits outside are brilliant yellow, sun yellow, daffodil yellow. The insides are mother-of-pearl cream colored, iridescent if you look at it just right. I stroke the inside surface, thinking maybe I'd hear the words again; but no. Nothing but the smooth soft insides.

You can bet that I had Dreads on the water for the entire rest of whale watching season. I talk with every pod I see passing, tell them my name, ask after Luigi. I see maybe 100 whales that season. None of them want to converse with me, but they all talk. And sing. And I get another couple floats.

They use the trash we humans throw at 'em, our manna into their desert, empty coke bottles and plastic grocery bags and pantyhose and diapers, and somehow transform them into the shining shell-encrusted floats, using fire and water and I don't know what kind of tools, or maybe just their flippers and fins.

Somehow they get their songs inside. Their prayers.

Towards the end of whale watching season, in late March, I see Luigi again. This time he's headed north.

Luigi says he's sick. He wants to go to heaven, he says.

I've long since gotten past all my 'rents' mythologies (I like that word better than 'lies,' don't you?) and I know all this praying won't do a damned thing for Luigi; but I like this church, St. Francis by the Sea, all stained glass windows and copper ceiling ribs greened by the ocean mist. The quiet in here almost quiets my insides.

I pray to St. Francis to help my friend Luigi. I even put some coins in the collection plate, and light a candle — one of the yellow votives, cuz Luigi likes yellow.

Hard to wait through another year for another whale watching season, so I find out as much about whales as I can, and I read poetry, and I learn some stuff about making glass. I figure I could sell these whale floats for a fortune, if I could convince a dealer that they were made by whales. Once again though, I'd prefer to remain unmedicated.

I do smash open one more float. The words are someone's story. The voice is not Luigi's; it's different, and sad, and young.

I can't figure out how they're getting voices into the floats and it's making me crazy. Some kind of tool? Imagining a whale using a recording device - talking into a microphone - is even weirder than imagining them making the globes in the first place.

Of course there's always magic. Luigi in a wizard's hat and tapping a float with a magic wand while chanting a spell - well, geez. Come on.

And then there's the possibility I'm imagining it. Maybe the voices aren't real. Maybe they never have been.

But they sound real to me.

I see Luigi at the beginning of November and he doesn't want to play. He says he's tired; he wants to speak with me again when he returns from the warmth during March's full moon. He says he has a gift for me.

Other pods, other whales, pass the word. Wait on the night of the full moon, wait for the grunion, wait for the gift. I tell myself I'm imagining sadness in the songs, melancholy when they say Luigi's name.

Now I have the grunion gifts piled at my feet. Some are yellow, Luigi's art work, but I see many colors embedded in the floats. So many. Why so many?

I don't know if I've mentioned that I can't understand all the creatures from the sea. For some reason, dolphins and I don't communicate well; but there's a dolphin breaching the night surf, a few feet away from me, and he's not swimming away. He doesn't articulate well, but he manages to get his message across.

"Luigi is near," he sings... or something that sounds like Luigi's name, "going to heaven, going to heaven, going now." The dolphin ducks under the waves then comes back up. "Going now, going now, going." The dolphin ducks under and stays away.

California Gray Whales are big. I shouldn't have any trouble seeing him under this brilliant moonlight, even though it's way late at night. Early morning, even. I look north along the beach and nothing. I look south and see spume. I toss the globes into my net bag and run.

The waves crash in and slide out, crash in and slide out, crash in and bring Luigi with them. He surges onto the beach with help from the tide.

I scream.

"No! Luigi! No! No, go back, go back, you can't." But he can. And he does.

I sink to my knees beside him. He's huge, of course, but somehow he looks smaller here, shrunken somehow, than he ever looked underwater. I rub my hand across his flukes, I know he can feel me. He speaks very quietly.

Some tribe or another of American Indians would chant a song before they died, if they knew they were about to die or if they were going into a fierce battle, and the song would be all about their lives and happiness and desires. Their autobiographies, with feelings.

That's what Luigi tells me. Between the stanzas about his pod and his friends. How he loves to swim with certain fish and hates the smell of others. He says the same chorus over and over again. After the second time I join in.

"I live between heaven above and hell below."

I sing it in his language and he doesn't correct my pronunciation. Tears flow from my cheeks onto his skin, but he probably can't feel them. Hot salt water isn't much different from cold salt water, right? At least I hope he can't. His song is mostly happy.

Whale rescue shows up, a half-dozen people from a network that phones them when a whale beaches. They try to push me away from Luigi but I'm not going anywhere. Every time I lose contact with his skin he flails and they back away. After a few times they leave me be. But they still try to push Luigi into the water. They work at it for hours and I have to admire their energy.

He's not going.

Luigi is breathing hard, trying to sing his last song. I hear his lyrics, he's a master poet, and I want to sing with him, but I can't form his words correctly. I get the sense, though.

Heaven isn't what he expected. The weight of the world pressing down on him, the cold eyes of humans.

I'm such a failure. I feel that failure like gravity feels to Luigi.

"I can't help you," I say to him in English. In Human-speak.

He knows. He breaths something that sounds like forgiveness.

With the sun, the inevitable news van pulls up. Some pretty woman in a tan polyester suit and high heels staggers across the sand to Luigi. A skinny guy with a professional grade video camera follows her. He points his camera at us when Luigi coughs up his last breath, delivers one last float to me. Dies.

The reporter is here to talk to the rescuers about the dead, pretend to care about Luigi; that'll last until her next assignment. She begins to poke the microphone in my face but I turn away. I look pretty dramatic, I bet, with all the tears on my face. I hate this.

And I have a better idea.

I select a green globe from the pile at my feet. I wind up my pitching arm: good hard underhand pitch. The impact rocks that van and scars the white paint job. Even from this far away I can hear the message released from the globe.

I throw another.

Another.

"Listen to that, you bastards!" I'm screaming. Tears and snot and sweat, all in the open on my face. "Listen to that!"

The woman stands shocked and slack-jawed but the guy with the camera is watching. He's got the camera on his shoulder, switching from focus on me to follow the pitch and focus on the van where the float explodes.

The camera jerks on his shoulder when he realizes what he's hearing. I grab a yellow globe; one of Luigi's. My pitching arm aches now but I cock it back as well as I can.

"That's for Luigi!"

The camera guy nods. He records the whole thing.

I fall to my knees on the soft hot sand, the clean combed sand, next to the few remaining floats. I can wait to hear these messages.

For now, I'm just glad that someone else is gonna hear Luigi's songs.

How Manta Ray Was Created

By Mark Slauter

The Oramaic is a fictional culture that thrived from approximately 2100 BC to 1300 BC. Their territory covered Tropical and Sub-Tropical zones.

The god, Tatnikatl, was known as the Father of Animals. He took care of all creatures and maintained peace in the animal kingdom. With no physical body of his own, he was free to assume any form he chose, from the tiny ant to the large whale.

One day, when Tatnikatl had slipped into the body of Cownose ray, a young boy disobeyed his father by sneaking out and taking a fishing boat onto the water at night. The boy wanted to prove he was old enough and strong enough to fish independently and help feed the village.

Throughout the night, he cast his net without catching any fish. He saw ripples on the water at daybreak and knew there was a school of fish heading toward him. He cast the net several times without success. As the school's last few rays passed, he threw the net one more time and brought up a single ray, but did not know it was Tatnikatl. Knowing that rays were challenging to catch and that the Shaman used the tails, he cut it off and threw Tatnikatl's body in the water.

The boy was so excited that he jumped out of the boat before landing it safely on the beach and stepped on a venomous urchin. He did not go far before falling, unable to move. The village fishermen found him when they arrived for the day's work.

Having lost his tail, Tatnikatl was trapped. The ray's body sank to the ocean's bottom as the blood ran from it, killing Tatnikatl. His soul moved toward the lower realm, Yolcayo. Finding his way to the Dead House, Tatnikatl's soul was eaten by Lamcoatzin, who would determine if the soul would stay in Yolcayo or be allowed into paradise through her twin brother Micoatchi. Without knowing this was a god, she decided it was a good soul and gave it to Micoatchi.

Canichi, the twins' mother, knew of Tatnikatl's plight. Without asking the goddess of Yolcayo, Anliquitzchan, for permission, Canichi swallowed the soul and left the Yolcayo.

"Mother," asked Micoatchi, "why do you stop this soul from entering paradise?"

"The body of this soul was cruelly killed by a boy who disobeyed his father. The boy's ignorance is unjust cause for the soul not to live a full life." She did not tell the twins whose soul it was.

Locating the Cownose ray body on the ocean floor, she took it to a secret underwater cave along the coast. Using materials from the ocean, she kept the body shape and made it ten times larger to create manta ray. Wading into the water, she breathed Tatnikatl's soul into it.

"Thank you, sister Canichi for making me whole again."

"I cannot make you whole because the boy stole your tail. See that the tail I give you is short and round, not long and whip-like."

"That is fine. I can still shapeshift and watch over the animals."

"This is untrue. As you cannot be made whole, you are no longer Tatnikatl. You are now Catatotlo, Ocean Bird, and can only change form into other sea creatures."

"What of the boy?", asked Catatotlo.

"He lies dying in the Shaman's house."

"His ignorance should not be the cause of his death. Spare him."

"As you request, it will be done. However, because of what the boy did, you will care for the ugly sea creatures and apply justice to those humans who act maliciously toward others."

In her dog form, Canichi entered the Shaman's house to find the boy covered by a blanket and lying upon a table. The Shaman went down on his knees in prayer to her.

"Rise, Shaman. I am here to heal this boy and task you with his training in the art of medicine." She removed the blanket and, placing a paw upon the blackened foot, drew out the urchin venom.

When the child awoke, Canichi said, "I spare your life at the request of the one you killed. You will learn the art of healing from the Shaman. For as long as you seek out and care for sick and injured sea creatures, you will have a full life. If you fail in this charge, your life will cease."

The boy grew into manhood and taught many others the art of healing. While he did not fear death, he knew Canichi had given him a great gift. He lived for more than one hundred years.

Colored in Sepia

By S. Park

Sepia waved his mantle fins gently, hovering in place in front of his mirror and flashing a series of colors and patterns across his skin. Every chromatophore and iridophore seemed to be in working order.

Excellent.

He was going to have the time of his life at the light-club tonight.

He snatched up his carryall and curled an arm around it, tucking it up against his body securely.

Then, with a sigh of water out his siphon, he put on female blotches, slipping back into the old pattern, back to the person he'd once thought of as his "real" self before realizing that Coral was the lie, and Sepia the true cuttlefish.

Someday maybe he'd be brave enough to openly swim out his door in male stripes and let all the neighbors see, but today wasn't that day.

With a jet of his siphon and a vigorous waving of his fins he rushed out the door, pausing only to flip a tentacle and shut the rounded portal behind him, before hurrying up and over the little patch of suburbia where his modest home stood. It wasn't in a great neighborhood, being on the deep side of town. He was headed deeper still, though. The club was on the very edge of the Great Deeps, where it was a little dangerous, even in this modern age, and where it was dark down near the sea floor even when the sun was up.

It was night now, and glow-globes bobbed at the ends of their chains in a mild current, shedding a cool greenish light over the city below and the waterways above. Other cuttlefish swam around him, coming and going on their evening business, but the water wasn't crowded, and grew less so as he went deeper.

When he reached the twilight zone, where a mere hint of light would fall during the day, he glanced around and, finding no one nearby, swiftly shifted his pattern from classically feminine to classically masculine.

He knew on close examination he wouldn't quite pass, but in the light-club nobody would be paying attention anyway.

Sepia swam on, sinking down towards the ocean floor. There were glow-globes here too, but ahead he saw a different glow, a beam of white light reaching up into the water.

The club was a large, plain, windowless building that had probably once been a warehouse. It was marked out by the searchlight atop it, and by the rainbow of small, shifting lights that circled the front door.

Sepia swam up to the door, which stood open. The water around him pulsed with a muffled beat. The music inside was no doubt deafeningly loud. That was all part of the fun, of course.

"Welcome to The Lighthouse," flashed the bouncer, the color-words flickering on his skin.

"Thanks," replied Sepia. He uncurled the arm holding his carryall and presented proof of adult age along with an armful of shells to pay the entry fee to the bouncer, then swam in through the circular portal.

There was an entry area separating the dance room with its light and noise from everything else. The portal to the dance room lay to one side, while a second door led to the bar on the other. Sepia would visit that eventually, but for now he tucked the carryall up against his body again and swam into a world of flashing lights and pounding beats, feeling the music as much as hearing it as the song vibrated the water all around him. His chromatophores were already twitching in anticipation, the stripes of his masculine pattern pulsing in time to the music.

Inside, the cavernous space was full of light and sound, tactile as much as audible, with hundreds of lights flashing patterns and swirls and beams of color across the darkened walls, and across the cuttlefish floating inside. Everyone in the room was light-dancing, pulsing colors across their bodies in time to the music, seeking to match the lights that fell on them. The truly excellent dancers turned the mingling of their own colors and the colored lights into gorgeous art, while the mere amateurs simply tried to match what swirling colors fell on them. The novices lagged behind, failing to properly anticipate what light would swing across them next.

There were patterns to it, and ways to keep pace with the light show, and after coming here for more than a year, Sepia fell into those patterns easily. He kept his masculine stripes, but pulsed and shifted their shades to match each beam that touched his body. He wasn't creative enough to make a true show of it, but it was fun dancing all the same. He'd loved it even as a rank newbie who had no idea how to properly keep up with the light show.

Now he was good enough at it to let his skin take care of itself, partially, and look around the room, seeing the other cuttlefish hovering here and there. He enjoyed watching the expert light-dancers. People-watching in general was always interesting.

Cuttlefish hovered in the water, mantle fins rippling, all around him. Most were alone, though the crowd was dense enough that a body-length between each was as much as one might expect. He could reach out a tentacle and touch the nearest 'fish to him. Some were in twos or threes, though, tentacles touching, even intertwined, as they danced together. He saw three of them near him, the classic trio of masculine male, large and imposing, wearing a clear male pattern even as his colors danced, female, small and demure, in a female pattern, and a feminine male, visibly male since he had arms and tentacles unfurled, but in a female pattern.

They danced in near unison, colors moving across from one to the next in beautiful harmony.

Sepia blew a sigh out his siphon, paddling his fins faster to keep him in place against the jet of water. He was, frankly, jealous of the trio. He would love to have a classic relationship like that, to live together with a pair of supportive lovers and maybe even to jointly fertilize some eggs with a larger male. But of course that could never be. His masculine pattern was a lie, he had no sperm in any of his arms to present to a female, and while males in female colors had an accepted place in society, especially in trios like the one he watched with envy, females in male colors had no such place.

He'd been told more than once that he was unnatural, that he was betraying his femalehood, that he was tainting the beauty of his eggs by not wanting to lay any.

He didn't believe those things, exactly, but seeing them across another's skin was always hard. Hate writ in bright colors, searing his eyes with almost physical pain, was among the worst of his memories.

Sepia pushed that aside. Here at the club 'fish were more accepting. He'd never seen any words like that here. He could wear his male pattern and dance its colors across the spectrum without anyone judging.

He danced on, watching the light show, and the other dancers, enjoying the experts, and curling his tentacles in gentle amusement at the newcomers. Eventually, though, his skin began to feel tired. His chromatophores and iridophores had gotten quite a workout. Perhaps it was time to go have a little mind-altering relaxation.

He swam through the foyer and into the bar, a smaller room than the dance room, but still spacious enough. A bartender floated in front of ranks of bottles and drinking bladders. Sepia had heard that you could get pufferfish here, if you knew how to ask, and maybe even jellyfish venom, but simple alcohol was all he wanted right now.

The bartender served up a kelp spirit cocktail, and Sepia took it in one arm, holding the bladder and putting the attached straw to his beak. The biting, salty taste flowed into him, and he sighed, exhaling a long stream of water through his siphon. This was the life.

"Coral? Is that you?"

The name was like a punch to the mantle, and as he saw the source of the query his guts sank. It was Orchid, one of his oldest friends, but one that he hadn't spoken to recently, and who thus had no idea that he'd started to think of himself as Sepia and not Coral.

Oh hell.

"Coral?" The color rippled quizzically across Orchid's body.

"Yes." Sepia projected a flicker of the old color-name for a moment, assenting to that other self, even while something cringed and withered inside him.

"But..." Uncertainty wavered across Orchid's skin. "Why are you wearing male patterns?"

He hesitated, then settled on saying, "If males can wear female patterns, why can't females wear male ones?"

Orchid's arms quirked in puzzlement. "Well, I guess no reason you can't, but feminine males are traditional! I mean, Umber and I have been hoping to find a feminine third for ages. I've never even heard of a masculine female before, though."

"Well... I am, alright? Why not? Why can't I be!" Sepia was aware that his colors were growing strident, flashing over his whole body in stark bands, but it was hard to hold himself back. This was his place! This was where he could be himself! Merely seeing the color of Coral spoken here felt like a violation, like something sacred had been profaned.

"Hey, it's okay. You can be whatever you like. I don't mind." Orchid flashed soothing colors and waved her arms in a cheerful pattern. "I just hadn't seen such a thing before, that's all. So are you like a feminine male, female, but liking male things, or...?" Her colors signaled curiosity, and Sepia relaxed a little bit.

"Not quite. Feminine males are still males. I... I don't know. It's hard to explain. I wish I was a feminine male! I feel like that would be perfect for me. Or even a masculine male! Though I'm awfully small for that. But any masculinity I can find, I want to hold onto with every arm and tentacle, you know?"

Orchid gave an amused little flick of her tentacles. "I don't know! I'm just a female. But I think I see what you're saying. You wish you'd been hatched out male, one way or another."

"Yes."

"So... What else does that mean?" Orchid's patterns were still calm, curious, and Sepia managed to calm his own colors.

"Well... It means I'd like it if you called me Sepia, not Coral, for one thing."

"Oh! I see. Coral is a very pretty color, but... It's not very 'you' is it?" Orchid's arms and tentacles all curled up warmly.

Sepia managed to flash amusement and curled his own arms. "It never was. It is a pretty color, but Sepia is a better color for me."

"Orchid is perfect for me! But sure, I'll call you Sepia. It's a very nice color. A soft ink color." Her arms were still curled.

Sepia, seeing his color-name on her skin, felt a thrill go through him. He'd been so afraid when he'd seen her, but she didn't seem upset at all, and now she was using his proper color-name. He didn't have a color to express how good that felt.

"So, I just finished my drink. If you're done with yours, Sepia, would you like to dance?" asked Orchid.

Sepia couldn't keep himself from flashing a wave of surprise over his skin, but he followed it with delight. "Yes, I would." He drained the last of his drink bladder and tossed it into a trash net hung beside the bar, still rippling with pleased colors as he did.

They swam together into the dance room, immediately embraced by a flood of sound and color. They couldn't speak, the lights flashing over them obscured their colors too much, but that was okay. Sepia wasn't here to talk, he was here to dance. He and Orchid hovered side by side, flashing their colors in time to the lights that swirled around them. Sepia found himself watching Orchid as much as the light show, though. She was a very good dancer. Her colors were crisp and strong, and she had the trick of anticipating the sweep of a light beam, so that she danced with the light rather than a beat behind.

Without really meaning to, Sepia found himself following Orchid more than the room's lights. He turned towards her, mirroring her colors. She flashed brief pleasure, just visible in the chaos of light as a contrast to the color she should be dancing, and turned towards him as well.

They danced together, their colors becoming more and more in sync, guided by the light show, but attuned to each other as much as to the room. Sepia had never been terribly good at partnered dancing, but just now it seemed to come naturally, the colors flowing with hardly a thought.

When the song ended, in the brief period of dim quiet before the next began, Orchid reached out and brushed one of her tentacles along Sepia's. "That was fun. You're a good dancer."

Sepia colored all over with embarrassed pleasure, and dared to reach back, twining his tentacle with Orchid's. "Thank you. You're really good too. Better than I am."

Orchid flashed amusement, but then the next song started and the lights muffled whatever else she might have wanted to say. She kept his tentacle in hers, though, as they danced together to the next song.

They synchronized again, which made Sepia want to turn every kind of happy color there was. He settled for merely squeezing Orchid's tentacle as they danced. She squeezed back warmly.

When the song ended, Orchid waved her free tentacle towards the exit. "I am enjoying the dancing, but perhaps we could go spend some more private time together?"

Sepia managed to only flash shock for an instant before getting his colors under control. "Ah. Private, er, intimacy would be very nice, but I thought you and Umber had an exclusive bond?"

"Well, we're bonded, but not exclusively. I think I mentioned we'd been hoping to find a feminine male third? Well, we—"

The next song began, drowning out what she'd been saying, and Orchid gestured again towards the door. Sepia bobbed all his arms in a colorless agreement and let her tow him out of the dance room, and then out of the club entirely.

Away from the lights, Orchid could speak again, and she immediately picked up where she'd left off, though she was still also swimming, tugging Sepia gently along with her towards the city and shallower water.

"We're honestly open to any third that either of us likes. Ideally it'd be somefish we both like, of course, but that doesn't always work out. We've each had a few little intimacy flings. So far none of them have gone anywhere. But we have talked a lot about a proper triad, maybe somefish else to fertilize some eggs? Or even somefish else to lay some, though that's less traditional." She flashed amusement and added, "We're not always traditional people, but I gather neither are you!"

Sepia flashed surprise, only just managing to keep the color mild, and not bright, outright shock. "Are you saying you want me to be your third?"

Amusement again from Orchid, brightly blotched across her skin. "Not right away. But things could go that way, especially since I know you at least get along with Umber."

"Sure, he's always been a friend." Sepia flashed cautious agreement and bobbed his arms as well as he swam alongside Orchid. They had been since their school days. Still, the idea of intimate touching, of the bonding that sometimes even led to mating when the season came, was suddenly intimidating. He *felt* he was male, from his cuttlebone to his skin, but he could only put on male patterns, he couldn't summon up an arm full of sperm to mate with.

But then Orchid had only said maybe someday. For now... For now a little intimacy would be very nice. It had been a long time since he'd so much as touched tentacles, as they were now, let alone caressed arms.

So he let warm agreement color his skin, and was happy to see the pleased color that crossed Orchid's skin in return.

He'd been dismayed when Orchid had turned up at the bar, but now he was glad. She'd been so immediately accepting of his very much non-traditional self. Maybe things would work out for them to bond, or maybe they wouldn't. Maybe he'd get along with Umber as an intimate partner or maybe he wouldn't. Maybe his lack of sperm arm would be a problem. There were a lot of "maybes" ahead of him.

Sepia found himself thinking, though, that among those maybes was one that said maybe he could dare to leave home in his male colors next time. Maybe he could dare all sorts of things.

About the Authors

LOUIS EVANS

Louis Evans is a writer living and working in NYC. Lordly and mighty and portly is he. Reports of his delicious flesh have been exaggerated by his many hungry enemies. His fiction has appeared in *Nature: Futures, Analog Science Fiction and Fact, Interzone,* and elsewhere; he is online at *evanslouis.com* and tweets @louisevanswrite

ALLISON THAI

Allison is a Vietnamese-American writer based in Texas. She has anthro fiction published in ROAR, Infurno, Arcana - Tarot, Symbol of a Nation, and Wolf Warriors. Some of her non-anthro fiction stories are featured on Tor.com and Locus recommended reading lists. When she isn't writing about dysfunctional families, talking animals, and cultures real and imagined, she's studying medicine and caring for axolotls: her favorite critters and the closest thing she has to Pokemon.

KOJI A. DAE

Koji A. Dae is a queer American writer living in Bulgaria. She has work published in Daily Science Fiction, Bards & Sages Quarterly, and several anthologies. When not writing, she cares for her kids, dances the blues, and experiments with hair color. You can find out more about her at *kojiadae.ink.*

GUSTAVO BONDONI

Gustavo Bondoni is an Argentine writer with over two hundred stories published in fourteen countries, in seven languages. His latest book is Ice Station: Death (2019). He has also published three science fiction novels: Incursion (2017), Outside (2017) and Siege (2016) and an ebook novella entitled Branch. His short fiction is collected in Off the Beaten Path (2019) Tenth Orbit and Other Faraway Places (2010) and Virtuoso and Other Stories (2011).

In 2019, Gustavo was awarded second place in the Jim Baen Memorial Contest and in 2018 he received a Judges Commendation (and second place) in The James White Award.   He was also a 2019 finalist in the Writers of the Future Contest.
His website is at *www.gustavobondoni.com*

JAMES L. STEELE

James L. Steele is slowly becoming a stereotypical writer due to his low-paying job he tries to forget about by following his true passion of becoming a wine snob and occasionally writing a novel. And he does it with pride.

He has been printed in numerous anthologies and publications. His Archeons series has been released through KTM Publishing. Visit his blog at *DaydreamingInText.blogspot.com*

NENEKIRI BOOKWYRM

Nenekiri Bookwyrm is a dragon that loves writing and making games. He's also been known to paint and play the ukulele on occasion. This particular story would not exist without his roommate, who listened to a cavalcade of possible ideas and helped him settle on a krill. He's been published in *Reclamation Project: Year One, Boldly Going Forward,* and has two stories featured on the *Voice of Dog* podcast. You can find more of his writing and other projects on *www.nenekiri.com.* He'd like to say, from the deepest depths of the ocean: "Curl up with a good book and be kind to yourself."

KARY M. JOMB

Kary M. Jomb is a shadow mage who accidentally summoned a wormhole and fell into a twisted, sideways dimension where the animals talk, robots walk among us, and fairies hide in the flowers. She loves daffodils, sparkling water, and dark chocolate. She likes writing in coffee shops but doesn't drink coffee. Kary lives on the side of a hill in a liberal college town in the Pacific Northwest. She wants to thank Mary E. Lowd for her help with this story.

KITTARA FOXWORTHY

At about six years of age, Kittara first saw Disney's Robin Hood; from that point on she was always pretending to be a Fox. At Halloween, she wanted to have a red tail and ears, but her mother talked her into being a cat instead since fox ears and tail were harder to find and more expensive. She found the furry fandom in 1998 through a friend and realized for the first time that she wasn't alone. Kittara has been writing short stories and poems since she was about fourteen however in late 2010-early 2011, writing became her favorite hobby. Since then she's had a few short stories published in various anthologies. She was born in Canada but now lives in Texas with her husband, three dogs and four cats.

DANIEL LOWD

Daniel Lowd likes dogs, unicycles, and researching artificial intelligence. By day, he is a computer science professor. By night, he is also a computer science professor, because he tends to work odd hours. At various other times (dusk? gloaming? teatime?) he writes a few words of fiction or the occasional song.

WILLOW CROFT

Willow Croft is a freelance writer who currently lives out on the prairie but dreams of a home by a tumultuous ocean. She's had short stories published in Mad Scientist Journal, Speculative 66, Sirens Call eZine, Rock N' Roll Horror Zine, and in a number of anthologies. When not writing, she cares for some (very lucky) rescued street cats. Come talk all things animals with her at her blog, *https://willowcroft.blog*.

MARY E. LOWD

Mary E. Lowd is a prolific science-fiction and furry writer in Oregon.
She's had nearly 200 stories and a dozen novels published, always with
more on the way. Her work has won numerous awards, and she's been
nominated for the Ursa Major Awards more than any other individual.
You can read more about the universe in "The Unshelled" in her novels,
Tri-Galactic Trek and Nexus Nine, published by FurPlanet. Learn more
at *www.marylowd.com* or read more stories at *www.deepskyanchor.com*.

K.C. SHAW

K.C. Shaw writes fantasy and furry stories as K.C. Shaw and hosts
Strange Animals Podcast as Kate Shaw. Find more of her fiction,
including her novel Skytown and related short story collection Skyway,
at *kcshaw.net*. She lives in East Tennessee with her lucky black cats,
Dracula and Poe.

HUSKYTEER

Alice "Huskyteer" Dryden's short stories have been published both in
and out of the furry fandom, and have won two Cóyotl Awards, two
Ursa Major Awards and one Leo Award. She edited The Furry
Megapack for Wildside Press.

She lives in south London, owns a motorbike and too many books, and
has a black belt in karate. She can bark well enough to confuse most
dogs, but has no idea what she's saying to them.

Twitter: @Huskyteer

huskyteer.co.uk

SU HADDRELL

Su Haddrell is a British writer living in a picturesque and peaceful area of Worcester that's been cleverly disguised as a noisy council estate. She has had stories published by Fox Spirit, Grimbold Books, Phrenic Press and Queen Of Swords Press. In addition to writing, she also enjoys drumming and organises the Lawless Comic Convention. She loves rum, her cats, her partner and movies where things explode within the first 14 seconds. You can find her on Twitter as @CherryBomb1618

DANIEL R. ROBICHAUD

Daniel R. Robichaud lives and writes in Humble, Texas. His work has appeared in *Sick Cruising, G is for Genies, H is for Hell, Infernal Clock: Inferno*, the Flame Tree Press Newsletter (May 2021), and *parABnormal* magazine. Forthcoming appearances include the *Haunts and Hellions, The Howling Dead,* and *Attack of the Killer* ____ anthologies. His fiction has been collected in *Hauntings & Happenstances: Autumn Stories* as well as the *Gathered Flowers, Stones, and Bones: Fabulist Tales,* both from Twice Told Tales Press. He writes weekly reviews of film and fiction at the Considering Stories (*https://consideringstories.wordpress.com/*) website. Keep up with him on Twitter @DarkTowhead.

FRANCES PAULI

Frances Pauli writes books about animals, hybrids, aliens, shifters, and occasionally ordinary humans. She tends to cross genre boundaries, but hovers around fantasy and science fiction with romantic tendencies.

She lives in Washington State with her family, a small menagerie, and far too many houseplants. You can find her newsletter, updates, free fiction and a bibliography at: *francepauli.com*

JUDE-MARIE GREEN

Jude-Marie Green has edited for Abyss&Apex, Noctem Aeternus, and 10Flash Quarterly. She attended Clarion West, is a member of Codex, and won the Speculative Literature Foundation's Older Writer's Grant. Her fiction has been published in Daily Science Fiction, The Colored Lens, and Electric Spec. She has a collection of short fiction, *Glorious Madness*. Her website is *judemarie.wordpress.com*

MARK SLAUTER

Mark currently lives in Virginia with his wife and two cats. Toward the end of his public service career, he published *The Diary Of A Novice Investor: The Bullet Train To Wealth Left When?* in 2017. He is currently writing short stories and creating digital art. "Like life, my art tends to come from random and chaotic processes." He is a member of the James River Writers group in Richmond, VA. He can be found online by searching for Mark Slauter.

S. PARK

S.Park began writing at the age of six, with an illustrated story about Care Bears, published in an eight page edition of one, bound with yarn. He has continued to write ever since, across various mediums and genres, creating everything from fluffy romance to blood-curdling horror, but his favorite genres are science fiction and fantasy. He likes to tell stories that draw on his real life experience as a queer and genderqueer person, telling everyday tales as seen through the "anything is possible" lens of fiction.

About the Artist

BELEOCI

Beleoci is a fulltime freelance furry artist that lives in the
Pacific Northwest with too many animals, and spends a lot of time
vacuuming fur. She typically draws furry, fantasy, scifi, and
tabletop art, which can be found on her
twitter: http://twitter.com/beleoci/

About the Editor

IAN MADISON KELLER

Ian Madison Keller is a fantasy writer currently living in Oregon. Originally from Utah, he moved up to the Pacific Northwest on a whim a decade ago and never plans on leaving. Ian has been writing since 2013 with nine novels and more than a dozen published short stories out so far. Ian has also written under the name Madison Keller before transitioning in 2019 to Ian.

While he used to be a Certified Public Accountant, these days Ian is focuse on writing on editing. He went back to school in 2018 to get a Certificate in Editing from UC Berkeley.

You can find him online at *http://madisonkeller.net* or on Twitter *@maddiekellerr*